BLACK ORCHID

Netherworld Books
Mirador Publishing
Mirador
Wearne Lane
Langport
Somerset
TA10 9HB

BLACK ORCHID

BY

RYAN IRVINE

www.facebook.com/blackorchidbook

Chapter 1

The world means nothing to me anymore.

I see but do I comprehend?

I have sunken back into a place beyond emotion, beyond judgement. That is where enlightenment truly resides, in a room void of judgement, not some shell shocked hippie dance, all of us prancing on our toes giving each other blessings and licking honey from the heavens. Without judgement, without emotion, without the ability to analyze right and wrong, good and evil, life just is.

Growing, breathing, contracting, evolving.

Here is where I sit, on a throne of silken threads dangling from the dark catacombs of my skull. A new psyche has risen, a new ego to watch over the shattered old one. I was a man, and now I am nothing, just a witness witnessing, no identity, no memories, no emotions, no judgement. No judgement.

I see but do I comprehend?

I do comprehend, but the bridge between the now and the past has been torched. I have lost all filters and I comprehend the world without sifting it through a colander of past experience. And the result? To sit and rot, to consume and grow? I don't know. I'm not sure, I look behind me and see only static. Loud, frantic, encompassing, debilitating. A crackling hissing wall that has toppled and buried me. And beneath the rubble I can hear the outside world, the machinations of man, the structures of time and distance, but why join in? Here is my purgatory, I have been sentenced and here I must remain.

The male nurse in front of me is a giant blob. He has unkempt, wild blonde hair that hangs down almost to his chin, square silver glasses that make his right eye look much bigger than the left, a loose fitting pale blue uniform and an expression that would suit an ageing grandmother more than a thirty something man. His hands are monstrous, fingers as fat as my wrist, with palms so smooth and spongy they make my ass twitch when he touches me. His lips are red and supple and when he mouths his words it looks as if he is sucking on a lollipop.

Marcus

So his name tag reads. Marcus the Giant Blob.

"Welcome, Mr. Doe." Marcus says politely, slipping his emollient fingers under my bicep.

"Let me help you to your new home."

We are in a hallway, over-sanitized, over-saturated. The walls are neutral, the lights fluorescent and the floor hard, acid-stained concrete. My eyes hurt. Marcus is guiding me past the front desk which is a buzzing hive of flailing limbs, frenzied words and cartoonish faces. The nurses, nurses-helpers, doctors, gatekeepers.

And the waves are a crashing, they're crashing, crashing.

Just beyond that is a common room wreathed in pleather couches and loveseats, infested with housecoat wearing loiterers. My eyes roam, looking for something or someone familiar, but I see only strangeness and strangers. A bearded man reading an upside down newspaper, a three hundred pound woman walking in circles stroking a plastic dandelion, poorly scrubbed urine stains on the achromatic area rug.

Where once there was nothing, only unity, an unbroken whole now there are many. A hundred little slivers, fissures in the shell over my eyes. The cloud of static that has been my home for so long has begun to settle and the world is coming back to me, piece by horrifying piece.

I look into the eyes of the living and see the accusations of the dead. I taste the breath leaving their lips, searing my nostrils, choking me with condemnation.

I am hell, I am hell, I am hell.

The smell of the hospital, bleach, unwashed bodies. The sound of my footsteps and distant lunatic whispers. The taste of my own dry, bacteria doused tongue. The feeling of the Giant's fingers and my own emaciated body.

Where am I? What the hell is happening???

The questions start to push their angry little heads through the fractures, demanding some god damn answers.

How did I get here? Why am I here??

They force their way into the antechamber of my soul, and there they die.

Cushhhhhhhh...

The thunder approaches and snuffs them out; it is over before it has begun. I cannot have any inquisitors in my purgatory. The past and the secrets there within, this identity, my memories, they must remain hidden. Some things are buried for a reason. But this automaton creature has learned a lesson.

The gates stay closed from now on.

I shut back down and let the giant lead me. The hallway is an endless chamber of placidity. We reach a room. A carbon copy of the dozen others we just passed but lacking that human touch. It's missing the bizarre little accessories people accumulate, even in a place like this. The walls are bare, the bed made, the curtains are tied back like a little girl's hair.

"Here we are." Marcus announces; his voice a syrupy confection.

I move like a zombie. Sit down on the flabby mattress. A clock beside the window counts down the seconds.

"Now, Mr. Doe..."

Words begin to pour out of Marcus the Giant Nurse's mouth, but I cannot hear him, I am somewhere far away.

The static has risen.

Chapter 2

Early morning in Fort Mckenzie and the town looks ashamed. The old brick buildings cower beneath the inquisitive eye of the sun like a brigade of horny old men caught leaving the dildo shop. The street signs and lights waver back and forth sloppily as if not fully recovered from the past night's debauchery and the sidewalks sag in embarrassment. Cars and their masters move in slow-motion, the air has a stale bitter taste. The few people walking around at this time of day take tentative, skittish steps as if their secrets might fall down their pant legs at any time, for the whole world to see.

There is only one person, or should I say one boy who seems unaffected. He is sitting on the curb beside me fully captivated by the antiquated comic book in his lap. I am a shitty guesser of age, but I would say he is somewhere between seven and eight. Short brown hair, freckles, pale skin.

"Cuz' his Dad's a cop." He continues saying. "He's an RCMP, he doesn't like dropping me off here, but he does it anyways. That's because he doesn't really like me, I know it, he would never say that, but I know it. And now I am just waiting."

Waiting, we're all just waiting.

I am waiting for Shane, the Youngblood. He slept at his "Auntie's" house last night. We are to meet here and then go into the Swancor office behind me and secure our financial futures. The office is open, but I prefer to sit outside and get a feel for this place.

Fort Mckenzie, my new home.

Hell on earth some people call it. A burgeoning abscess of humanity built on the hides of dead animals and perpetuated by the oceans of black viscous fluid being pumped in from the Athabasca oilsands. A magnet for the piteous, the innocent, the arrogant, the absurd, the asinine, the good, the bad, the ugly. All of us have congregated here, in this flat-footed place, to find our fortunes. Be it turning globs of tar-like bitumen into gold, humbly pumping gas or turning tricks in mouldy motel rooms. We are here, and we want our treasure.

But some of us either don't make it into the game or maybe can't handle the weight of a sack full of money on our backs. And the only path left is the one of least resistance, downwards.

I can see such a player now, ambling across the street like an angry marionette. His face is a manic distortion, ghoulish skin crumpled and weathered, eyes searching for a centre that no longer exists.

"Drugs." The Boy says, looking up from his comic. "He's on drugs."

I make a non-committal grunt. The tweaker hears us and turns. I look into his eyes and see only the faded memory of a human soul.

"My friend Kade says that all the druggies live in the old hotel on Bremley Street. He says they stay up all night doing drugs and fighting each other like in Fight Club. And that the ones who lose, get taken out to the oilsands and buried, and no one ever finds them."

I give the kid an appraising look. His face is emotionless as he speaks, trance-like.

"And he says they get these scabs from doing all their drugs because they think there is bugs on them, and they have to scratch them off, but there is no bugs, it's just in their imagination."

Meth scabs. I've heard of such things, tweakers get sores from meth coming out of their skin or from scratching hallucinations. I've even heard of some meth heads purposely getting them by holding their exhalations in their hands, so the chemicals crystallize faster and they can pick and eat them, to get high again. Reduce, reuse, recycle.

"And when they die in the fights." The Kid continues. "The scabs turn black and get big and if you eat them you get magic powers. You can become a superhero," he says, tapping his tattered comic.

Jesus, what a fucked up place. Drugs and drug culture have become so common here that they are now an ingredient in the kaleidoscopic imagination of children. Something as disturbed as eating meth scabs has now mutated into something bigger, more grandiose, mythological.

I look down at the book he is holding and see that it truly is an antique. The price tag in the corner advertises it for twenty cents. There is a picture of woman in a purple costume leaping off a building and a bunch of sinister looking men with guns.

"Black Orchid," I say, reading the title.

The boy gives me a sudden look of veneration.

"Yeah, that's what they should be called." He whispers. "Black Orchids."

I raise an eyebrow, confused.

"The scabs, the black scabs that give you super powers; they should be called Black Orchids."

As we stare at each other, I perplexed, and he fervid, the Youngblood, my old cohort jogs up behind us.

"Hey man," he says.

I turn, and he nods at the kid. His eyes are wild, and I'm guessing he had a long night at his "Auntie's" house, helping her get rid of all that extra cocaine she had laying around.

"Hey sorry guy, fucking took so long to get over here."

I stand up and brush the dust off my old blue jeans. I look back at the kid.

"Adios amigo," I say.

"Adios..," he says, staring into the distance. "Adios amigo."

Shane and I turn and walk into the Swancor office, leaving him alone with the morning greyness and his visions of black orchids.

We walk up to the counter and the Youngblood vomits up words in rapid succession.

"Hey man, yeah, we are supposed to be going up on to rig nine, my buddy Sizz, I mean Glen...Uhhhh... Thomas is the toolpush...And he like told me..."

The girl behind the counter stares at Shane with leaden

eyes letting him blather for a minute before interrupting with a bark.

"What are your names?"

"Shane, yeah, Youngblood," Shane says, jumping nervously as he answers.

"And you?"

"John," I say. "John Doe."

Usually that elicits some kind of response, but it doesn't even register with counter girl.

"Take a seat," she orders; typing into her computer.

We back away and sit down. Across from us is a giant poster of a clown-happy rig worker wearing spotless fire-retardant coveralls and a giant hardhat.

Responsible development for a brighter future!

Beside that is a picture of two native girls, painting the face on a totem pole blue.

Helping communities to see the possibilities!

Swancor. Just one of the many multinational oil companies digging for black gold up here in the great white north. Initially, when Shane told me about this job, I thought we would be working in the oilsands. Squeezing foul-smelling petroleum products from the rocks with our bare hands underneath a canopy of fire and radiant stars. It turns out, however, his friend "Sizz" is on an old fashioned drilling rig and if we get hired that is where we'll be going.

Either way, I won't bemoan leaving this town. There is an eeriness that permeates everything here, the buildings, the air, this office. They all seem to be impregnated with the same cold menace, as if everything and everyone were tied together by a throbbing artery of fatalism.

Counter-girl puts down her phone and squeals.

"You two!" Motioning us over.

"Yeah, there is an opening on rig nine, leasehand and one roughneck. Neither one of you guys have worked on a rig before?"

We both shake our heads.

"Okay, you long hair." She points to me. "You're roughnecking and you chatty Kathy." She eyes Shane. "You're leasehand."

The Youngblood is disappointed, roughnecks are a step above leasehands, and they make more money, but Shane is only five and a half feet tall and as skinny as the tweaker I saw outside. As first impressions go, he doesn't make a good one.

"You got all your tickets? Gear?"

We nod. Shane's buddy gave us the lowdown when we were back in Calgary.

Tickets: H2S, WHMIS, First Aid.

Gear: Fire retardant coveralls, Steel-toed rubber boots, Green Kings, Hardhat.

"Okay next hitch starts Wednesday night, be here at eight o'clock, do not be late."

We are sent on our way as a group of young newfies come in and assail the woman with a stream of incomprehensible questions. Outside the sun is trying to burn through the miasma without success. It is late fall and unseasonably warm, especially for up here. The deciduous trees are all bare and look humiliated because they stripped too soon. Hopefully it will continue like this for the rest of the winter, usual temperatures can get below minus thirty, and we'll be outside for all of it.

I see the comic book kid across the street walking around to the passenger side of a pastel red Toyota corolla. He disappears, I hear the door shut, and the driver looks my way. She is about to start driving, but freezes as our eyes meet. Unabashed recognition blankets her face, she *knows* me. And I know her. Not from here, not from this time, not from this life, from somewhere forgotten, somewhere buried. I can see her eyes glaze, even from across the street, and her lips start to tremble.

Shane says something but he is in the background, leagues away, somewhere in the forgotten peripheral. I see only her. The girl, with the brown hair, hazel eyes, freckles. Undoubtedly the little boy's mother.

She is from the past, my past, the missing past.

"Hey dude!" Shane calls loudly from the horizon.

My mind is whirling through different scenarios, sifting through memories, yet nothing emerges. I can't find her in the encyclopedia of retained experiences, she is from before, she is from the static.

I take a slow step off the pavement towards the car, and this wakes her from her stupor. She hits the gas and is away down the dusty road before I can come within calling distance. The Youngblood is behind me, questioning me.

"What's up dude?"

"Do you know that girl?" I ask him, still dazed.

"Uhhh, no guy, I don't think so. I didn't really see her. You alright? You look kind of fucked up."

"Uh huh," I say. "Uh huh."

Chapter 3

"And that was when she took my Mother's umbrella to the bowling alley! Margaret Archibald came down from her powder room and started crying and crying. 'Don't you piece together that lemonade tree in here!' But she wouldn't, ooohhh noooo, she wouldn't dare, not in front of the Bishop!"

The doddering woman beside me has been talking for hours now. Nonsensical words flow musically from her lips, through the air, into my ears and then back out, unused, unappreciated. I disregard them; let them slough off me like an unwanted uterine lining. I must, I am defenceless, unprepared to deal with conscious awareness. These shapes, these things, these people. How can one react to such tortuously tangled entities?

We are sitting at a large dining table, just the two of us. Marcus the Giant Blob fed me two hours ago and then left me here. Apparently I looked quite content and wanted to stay. Perhaps he thought the crazy woman with the oversized garden hat covered in plastic flowers, and I were engrossed in deep conversation. Honest mistake.

But really where else would I go? My days are spent in limbo, floating in a sea of oblivion. Sometimes I get close to the surface, like now, I can see silhouettes through the murk. Diffracted images, obscure shapes. Reminiscent of the ancient sea turtle, I rise just to the boundary of my subconscious and take a deep breath, and then I must retreat, this is not my place anymore. It is too harsh, too loud, too *real*.

Take for instance the boy on the floor. He is a misshapen thing, an insect-like piece of flesh, long thin limbs jutting crookedly from an oblong torso. His head is shaved and bobbles around violently as he moves, and when he does speak, which is sporadic, it is always an incredible shout of obscenities. Right now he is crouched in the doorway between the dining hall and the adjacent kitchenette. Blood from his fingers is smeared all over the lower hinges. He has the insatiable need and unbelievable ability to unscrew the bolts that hold the hinges in place with his fingernails. He has removed one fully and is working on his second.

This is the real world, the world of the senses.

Minutes pass by, maybe hours. The overcooked Grandmother beside me eventually ambles away, and I am left in relative silence. I sit, stare, breathe, witness. Then Marcus the Giant arrives with a stranger at his side. A woman, small in stature with long black hair, not unlike my own, worn loose around her shoulders. Black eyes, also not unlike my own, glisten beneath delicate silver glasses. She is wearing black pants and a black sweater that covers a blue, plaid button-up shirt. I can see flecks of moisture melting on the top of her head and a voice tells me it must be snowing outside.

"John," Marcus labializes. We're on a first name basis now.

"This is Doctor Lau."

I blink in recognition. She comes closer, and I can smell a bouquet of musky flowers emanating from her neck. As she bends down to speak to me, my eyes become transfixed on a teardrop shaped scar in the centre of her chest, just to the left of her laminated identity card.

"Hello, John," she says, articulating every syllable, as if she were a child counting money.

"My name is Doctor Lau, but you can call me Christine. I'm going to be your new facilitator."

If I cared to wonder, I would wonder what she was going to help me facilitate. Or is it *I* she plans to facilitate? Either way none of this really matters, her, Marcus, the gangly insect being picked up from his bloody business in the doorway. This is a show, and I am part of the audience not a participant. To prove my point, Marcus slips his elephantine arms underneath me and picks me up.

"We usually let them rest around this time for an hour before dinner," he says to Christine, who gives an all-knowing nod.

My world spins, my eyes roll like glazed doughnuts. I would never let a man do this to me in real life. I would smack his hands away from me. I would push back, I would break away, and if he tried it again as slippery-skinned Marcus the nurse, with his puffy red lips most assuredly would, I'd break his fucking nose! I'd knock him to the fucking floor and stomp on his fucking head. I would take these talons and rip out...

Cushhhhhhhhhhh...

No more. No more sound, no more light, no more thoughts. Back to the depths, where I am safe, safe from myself.

Marcus carries me to my room and lowers me down for nap time. I stare at the roof until sleep takes me and soon I am dreaming. It's the same dream I always have. Thunderous hooves stampeding all around. The smell of turned dirt and horseshit. An old man grimacing. Small fingers digging into weathered flesh, a nightmare collage of bone and cartilage and blood. A tiny voice calling from the shadows.

Laufen! Laufen!

Awake.

I lie in my hyper-accessorized hospital bed and let the nightmare drain down into the starchy sheets and mechanical arms. Soon I am back at neutral, stable, floating. This is where Dr. Lau, or should I say Christine finds me when she and Marcus enter my room. They both greet me warmly, and I see they are wearing different clothing. What happened to dinner? How much time *has* passed?

Marcus helps me sit up. I can walk today, so I follow them to, first my bathroom for a quick poopoo and peepee, and then down to the dining hall for breakfast. It is not usual for such an esteemed person such as Dr. Lau MD, FRCPC, to help me with my morning constitutional but her reasons are not solely recreational. She is studying me.

Every move you make, every breath you take.

As Marcus scoops up a spoonful of strawberry-banana yogurt and shovels it into my mouth, her little black eyes dig into my flesh. As my mandible moves up and down in the quintessential chewing motion, she creeps in close, sniffing, tasting the air for discrepancies, inaccuracies, deceptions?

Others have tried this approach. Doctors, nurses, cops, authority figures. They train their little microscopes on you, poke at you, prod you, take you in their divine, godlike hands and try to solve you. But when the days turn into weeks and weeks into months, they grow restless and eventually like a child fed up with its Rubik's cube, they toss you away.

Underneath the bed, out of sight, out of mind.

That is what Dr. Christine Lau is doing right now, analyzing me in the hope that soon she will be able to take her years of overpriced schooling and use them to save me from this dissolved state I am in. I stare blankly at her pinched little Asian face and wish her neither good luck, or ill will, and that is where the crux lies, in this apathetic indifference. That is why she will never find me because I don't care to be found, I am drifting in an ocean of detachment. Yet, she will still try, she has to, all things can be dissected, understood, categorized, even a human soul.

After I am finished consuming, Dr. Lau leads us out of the dining hall and down a corridor I have never been before. We make our way to an elevator that takes us up to a large cluttered room that smells of dust and neglect. Strange machines and props are set up in every available corner.

"Thank you Marcus, I can take him from here." Dr. Lau says and the hulking figure of Marcus minces away on tender feet.

Dr. Lau sits me down on a padded bench and pulls up a chair in front of me.

"Mr. Doe." She proclaims as she pulls a folder from her attaché case and opens it.

"John Doe. Real name unknown. Approximately twenty two years old. When you were taken by the police you had no identification, you were never registered in the fingerprint database as a child and had no prior arrests. The only thing you had on you besides your clothes was this."

She pulls a stained piece of fabric from her case. It looks to be an old handkerchief, but when she opens it up, two thin straps dangle from the sides.

Laufen! Laufen!

Dr. Lau holds the head kerchief in front of my face and gauges the reaction.

Formed shadows, ceaseless flames, a baby in her arms.

Apparently satisfied she puts it away.

"You were detained in Drumheller correctional for three months and then transferred to Ponolka because it was determined that you were not of sound mind. You spent eighteen months in Ponolka and last week were sent here. Your reports say that you have been diagnosed with post traumatic stress disorder, possible schizophrenia, and stupor. You have shown no signs of violence since the arresting offence, you have not spoken since detainment and you have shown no changes in behaviour up until very recently."

Dr. Lau stops reading and looks me in the eyes.

"What has changed, John?"

She puts down her papers and scratches the scar on her chest. Today her shirt is a little lower cut, and I can see the teardrop does not end but continues downward between her breasts in a straight line, resembling a glob of molasses.

"I've brought you here because I want to try some different, let's say alternative treatments compared to the ones you have been given. I believe the body and mind work not only in the framework of western psychology but also as a system of resonant bioenergy. I believe that within the human body, there are emotional and evolutionary hubs that receive information, assimilate sensory activity, store archetypal elements and release the potential for growth and involvement in the functioning world."

The brown teardrop dangles precariously in front of me. Will it fall? It's not the height that frightens but the landing below. Hard cement wrapped in battleship linoleum.

Broken Teardrops wooooo wooooooo...

Sounds like an eighties pop song.

"These hubs, these centres and how well they function define a person's behaviour. I also believe that sometimes one or more of these centres can get cut off from the rest, because of abuse or severe trauma, and the mind will suffer. Sometimes if the trauma is strong enough, the bioenergy can get violently pushed out of a centre because it is too painful to access that part of the experiential body and then it eventually becomes trapped somewhere else."

Back and forth it swings. Back and forth. Like the fake diamonds in an old chandelier. Back and forth.

"This can present itself in many ways, sometimes delusion, compulsive behaviour, even in minor things like jealousy or stress. What I am saying is that because of the things you have seen and experienced your mind has cut you off from certain places in your biocomputer, you are energetically disconnected."

A thread of saliva escapes from my mouth in search of greener pastures, I suck it back with a loud slurping noise. Dr. Christine Lau, in her impassioned state barely notices.

"And I think we can put those connections back. And since these energetic hubs exist on an emotional and somatic level we'll begin with some exercises that should bring your consciousness down to the more physical realm. Ready?"

I stare at her, expressionless. I am already fading back into the darkness.

Chapter 4

"They used to be called tar sands, but it's not actually tar, it just looks like it. They're actually a mixture of sand, clay and bitumen. A hundred and fifty thousand square kilometres, that's bigger than frigging England!"

The pilot's tinny voice reverberates through our insulated head phones. I look down at what he is describing and can believe his claim. The oil sands dominate the landscape below us in every direction, as far as the eye can see.

"There's two trillion barrels of oil buried down there, that's more than the rest of the world combined!" The pilot exclaims proudly, as if he had a hand in discovering it.

In fact, on the first flight that took us to camp, Shane told me his ancestors discovered the bitumen deposits and used them to waterproof their canoes, hundreds of years ago. Unlike that first trip, which was in the dead of night, this morning we have a clear view of the sprawling black and grey surface mines. Smears of flattened soil, canyon walls, huge pools of toxic water that from up here look like craters dot the surface everywhere. Reminds me of the moon.

The Youngblood leans over to me and laughs.

"Good place to bury a body!"

I have to agree.

When we flew out to camp two weeks ago, it was in a small prop plane but our triumphant return is in a helicopter.

"Every few months, a tonne of people fly out to Don Swan's place, so they need all the planes."

This is the brief explanation our boss, Glen "Sizz" Thomas, gave us as to why the new transport. And since we left camp, I've seen half a dozen small planes passing by en route to the fabled "Castle", Donald Swan's mansion hidden in the woods. In fact, I can still see one, deep in the distance.

"What do you think they're doing?" I say.

"Who?" Shane asks.

"All those people, flying out to the Castle."

"Fuck, I don't know man." Shane's face erupts into goofy grin. "Probably banging bitches and doing tonnes of blow! Haha."

Our token foreigner, Putu from Indonesia laughs with him.

"They're partying like I'm going to be partying tonight!"

The rest of the guys, the ones that aren't comatose, begin to chuckle and talk about the debauchery they are going to get into on their week off. I turn back to the plane as it flies into the rising sun.

We continue south, over the swollen dystopia until we reach the Swancor upgrader plant, where the mined bitumen is converted to synthetic crude oil. It is a mini city of smog-spewing columns and skeletal buildings. The Athabasca river runs beside it, and Olympic sized pools are locked in with berms. Tailings ponds they are called, the toxic by-products of separating the bitumen.

Most people don't know this, but the biggest dam in the world is here. A massive embankment, forty metres high and eighteen kilometres long, housing a giant tailings pond.

An ocean of foul-smelling sludge.

Not too many tourists racing north to cross that one off the bucket list. To prevent animals or birds from coming near, the eggheads at Swancor use a highly sophisticated system of fake falcons and air guns.

A couple of the guns go off as the chopper flies by and it feels like my compadres and I are going to 'nam. Or maybe just coming back from 'nam. The last two weeks weren't quite as hellish as war, but they were far from pleasant. Twelve hour shifts of picking pipe, running pipe, racking pipe, scrubbing, tripping out and making those fucking tongs bite! Good times.

We make it back to Fort Mckenzie before noon and head our separate ways. Shane drops me off at the rundown duplex I now call home, and we make plans to meet later. I waddle my way into the living room with my hockey bag full of rig gear and see four guys on the couch playing Xbox and smoking weed. They give me perfunctory nods and hey mans, which I return and continue past into my room, which is big enough to fit a child size futon, my rig bag and nothing else. I drop my gear, lie down and close my eyes.

I am more tired than I realized, and within seconds I am asleep. The dreams come, like they always do, even in the daytime they come. The faceless old man, the pounding of hooves. The sharp tang of animals. I hear the voice in the shadows and then I am there, in the darkness, holding the spectre. Its body is made of cold bone, reminding me of the towers at the upgrader plant. I am speaking frantically, but the words make no sense. I see the old man and his throat has been torn out. It must have been one of the animals. I shake the blackness, but the spectre is gone. I run for the barn door and the wilderness beyond.

Laufen! Laufen!

My eyes fly open, and I see that I am not alone. I left the door to my room open and standing just outside in the hallway is a skinny twenty-something girl in a Slayer sweater.

"You were talking in your sleep," she says.

My cheeks are slicked with sweat and my stomach aches.

"Oh yeah?"

"Yeah," her voice is warbly and petulant, and sounds strange coming from her grown up frame, like a talking blow up doll.

"It was weird, it sounded like German or something. Are you from Germany?"

"No."

"Do you speak German?"

"No."

"Well it sure sounded like it."

"Do you know what German sounds like?"

"Not really, just like some Rammstein music."

"Maybe that was it."

It turns out I like to sing German industrial metal in my sleep.

"That's weird."

The girl leaves my door frame, and I have to say, I am truly going to miss her.

I check the time, five fifteen. Shane is supposed to meet

me here at six. I get up and shower, letting the hot water scald my skin until it is raw.

Like Rawhide...

The nightmares always leave me jittery, like I need to run or fight. Or maybe it's being back in this town that is causing it. Anyway the shower helps and soon the anxiousness passes.

I put on a black shirt, jeans, leather boots, hoodie, vest. I have no money, our cheques won't be ready until we get back from the next hitch, but Shane says he knows a guy who can spot us. I go out to the living room, which has doubled in population since I left it and see Putu and the Youngblood waiting for me. Shane has a joint in his mouth and is half-yelling at a guy with a mohawk and massive beer belly.

"Johnny D!" he calls as I approach

"I went to high school with these guys."

It seems that Shane went to high school with everyone in this town.

I walk behind the couch to the kitchen island, which is a cornucopia of old pizza boxes, mouldy dishes, porn magazines and empty beer bottles full of cigarette butts and sit down on a barstool. The Xbox has been shut off, and a video of two guys beating the hell out of each other is streaming on the TV. The people on the couches stare intently and yell profanities at the two combatants. Shane gets pushed out of the way by the guy with the mohawk as one of the fighters is knocked to the ground.

"...Fucking stand up you pussy..!"

"...Matero can't do shit on the ground..!."

"...Take those fucking high kicks..."

"...Bitches..!"

"...He's fucked..!"

There seems to be no end to their opinions, and I wonder if the gladiators of ancient Rome had to put up with the inane comments of soft-knuckled spectators. Maybe not, maybe the crowds were more respectful because their lives were actually in mortal danger. But I doubt it. I look into the faces of the people around me, slobbering and swearing, and I think if there was a chance that one of the men on the screen might be killed, it would only increase their bloodlust.

I need to watch things die...

And their idiocy.

From a good safe distance...

The one in the blue shorts taps out, people groan and Shane makes his adieus.

We leave the jackals and hop into the Desperada, Putu in the back, Shane and I in the front. They want to get to the local titty bar as soon as possible, but Shane needs to get us our money first. We turn on to main street, and I can see the metamorphosis from daytime Fort Mckenzie into night time Fort Mckenzie in mid-transformation. The upstanding, respectable men and women that work in the banks and schools are dissolving with the dusk and being replaced by wolf-faced ballyrags, jaded strumpets and transient opportunists. The crisp air is turning thick and heavy, like the inside of a compost barrel, storefronts have become stark halloween masks and the back alleys are sprouting claws.

We pass a parked cop car, and I wonder what the police do with their time. Virtually every person out after dark could be arrested for something. There are underage kids running around knocking over fences and drinking bootlegged booze, coked up gear heads ripping up and down the streets, revving their engines, blubbery skanks giving blowjobs behind 7/11 for Oxycontin, the list goes on.

I can only imagine they must be sitting in their headquarters, plotting how to take down the Mexican cartels or the H.A. or something because if I were a cop I'd just walk up to one of the dozens of dealer or cook houses scattered around town, they are pretty easy to spot. Dozens of cars pulling up every day, sketchy dudes running across the lawn, the occasional garage sale of stolen shit, oil stains all over the street from idling jalopies. Not too difficult to find. But maybe that's the point, the barn is so full of shit no one wants to go in there in anymore. Just leave it to the animals.

Crossing the river, we make our way down to some outdated brown four-plexes known as Riverside, even though they sit blocks back from the river. There, we pull up to the most conspicuous building on the street, front door spray painted purple, piles of destroyed furniture strewn everywhere, three women apparently putting on a fashion show in the front yard, trying on different pieces of garbage. We stop on a multilayered fluid stain, and I wonder if the Desperada will shoot off a couple spurts, just to show the other cars it has been there.

"What are we doing here bro?" Putu asks from the back.

"Uhh, yeah, this is the dude who is going to hook us up with some flow," Shane answers, looking at me, his moustache twitching a little more nervously than usual.

Flared nostrils, heart rate up.

I look back at the hookups sketchy residence. Something feels wrong, or should I say excessively wrong.

"Who is this guy?" I ask.

"Uhh, just a dude I know, you know, from back in the day."

"What's the interest?"

"Uhh, nothing man, we just gotta pay him when we get back from the next hitch, you know? Don't worry guy, he's cool."

I am not worried, but he is.

I open the car door.

"Alright, let's go."

Shane's face lights up in revolt, he doesn't want me to come, but he says nothing and gets out.

We pass the fashion show unnoticed and head for the purple door. Shane knocks a few times and then someone bellows for within.

"Who is it?!"

"It's Shane dude."

Raised voices bickering. A dog barking.

Another voice rings out, this time a woman's.

"Who??!"

"It's Shane Youngblood!"

More bickering, someone sounds hysteric, something crashes to the floor and then the door swings open.

"Muthafucking Youngblood!"

The guy in front of us is tall and white, well built.

"Hey, RJ, how's it going man?" Shane asks.

21

RJ sees me, and the amiable mask falters.

"Who's this?"

"Ohh hey man, this is my buddy, Johnny. He works with me on the rigs."

Flinty blue eyes look me up and down. Discerning, assessing, categorizing.

"Johnny, eh." He eventually stretches out his arm. "RJ."

I shake his hand, and we go inside.

A half set of stairs takes us up to the living room slash swine-pen. I thought my place was a filthy hovel, but RJ's place is on another level. There is shit everywhere. Piles of garbage, old newspapers, car speakers, food containers, broken lamps, broken chairs, broken tables, stolen DVD players, stolen computers, stolen tires, cinder blocks, spools of electrical wire, overflowing litter boxes, clothes, dog shit. Sitting around a wooden kitchen table top that is propped up with a truck tire, there are three guys and one girl smoking rocks and loading gear. The table is a buffet of drugs and bio-hazardous material.

RJ plops down beside the girl, whose chest seems to be collapsing beneath the weight of her bulbous fake tits. They remind me of praying mantis eyes. She exhales a cloud of caustic smoke and then passes the glass pipe to RJ.

A twisty pipe they call it because of the way smokers twist it back and forth as they hit it with a lighter, just like RJ is doing right now. The three guys stare at us with untamed savagery and my Swara switches from Ida to Pingala, there is a definite possibility of violence here.

"So Youngblood what the fuck's happening?" RJ exhales and his girl reaches below her miniscule tanktop and starts fiddling with her exposed belly-button. She looks to be around six months pregnant.

"I haven't heard from ya in a coon's age, where ya been eh?"

We sit down on a couple of children's stools, the seats plastered with prancing Donald Ducks.

"Ohh you know, I was down in Calgary for a while there."

Shane's knee starts bouncing up and down.

"Right right, what were you doing down there?"

RJ puts down his pipe and picks up a giant antler-handled hunting knife and spins it in his palm. His lips creep back revealing stained brown teeth and receding gums. My heart rate increases.

"Uhh you know, doing some stuff for some people and working a bit..."

"Now you came back to make the BIG BUCKS!"

RJ shouts and his friends smirk. The hallway to the right has a small baby fence set up and an obese rottweiler runs up to it and starts barking.

"Shut up... Shut The Fuck Up, Tony!"

The dog relents but continues to stare at us through the diamond shaped holes of its prison wall.

The smell of feces and burnt plastic make me want to retch.

"Yeah..." Shane says anxiously. "I guess so, we're working for Swancor, rig nine."

"Sizz hook that up?"

"Yeah, he's toolpush now."

"No shit! I haven't seen that guy in years."

RJ's glossy eyes swirl unnaturally as if he just saw something fly under the back of his eyelids.

"I haven't seen you in years!" He yells, suddenly. "Fucking years and then he texts me out of the blue, looking for some cash."

His vacillating gaze settles on his buddies, who seem to grow grimmer by the second.

"Uhhh, hehe." Shane feigns laughter. "Yeah well, you know, we just don't get our cheques until –"

"Say I was wondering?" RJ interrupts. "Do you remember that fat fuck Griff?" He says, turning his sinister gaze back to the Youngblood. "Remember, your old buddy?"

Shane shrinks like a deflating tire.

This is what he was afraid of.

"Uhhh, yeah guy. I haven't..."

"Yeah your old buddy Griff, that fat tub of shit, you know what I heard about him??" RJ says, twisting the hunting knife in the air in front of him.

My nostrils flare needing more oxygen.

Ground down, legs engaged, focus on nothing, be aware of everything.

"A couple years ago, that fat fucking guy went out to my storage container, you know down the old dump road? And stole a bunch of my shit!"

Shane tries to look shocked but doesn't pull it off.

"Ohh yeah?? That's fucked dude... I didn't..."

"Yeah man!! That fat piece of shit broke into *my* fucking storage container and stole *my* fucking shit!!"

RJ is standing now, with the knife in his hands. His friends are on the edge of their seats, wolves ready to pounce.

"And you know what Terry Deacon told me?"

Shane stutters.

"Nnnnooo, man... I..."

"He told me that you were with him, YOU FUCKING HELPED HIM!!"

The knife is pointed at Shane now, and the old instincts kick in.

I leap from my Donald Duck stool, passing RJ'S blade before his drug-addled brain can register what is happening, slam my fist into his throat and grab the loosened knife. With a flick of the wrist, it's gone, through the air and down the hallway.

RJ's strength leaves him as he struggles to take in air. I pull him to the edge of the couch, past his girlfriend and throw him over the baby fence. He falls clumsily on to Tony the Rottweiler, and I turn back to the three friends who are now at their feet and fully mobile. The one closest to me steps on to the short table, breaking glass and scattering powder, and I punch him square in the kneecap.

A horrible snapping sound rings out and he begins to scream. The pregnant girl is also screaming, and Tony, who is now free from the burden of RJ is barking madly. The guy drops back, and before the other two can attack I jump forward and land my right knee under the chin of the next closest. He falls back but his buddy, a tall mongoloid grabs me with strong arms and pulls me in for a lovers squeeze. Before he can do anything else, I smash my forehead into his

24

nose, causing a spray of blood. I fall back to the ground and take a hold of his hair, pulling him down into my rising knee. Bone hits bone and then he drops unconscious onto a pile of newspapers peppered with cat shit.

Turning back around I see a rolling pin on the table and grab it. The first guy is still on the couch holding his knee and wailing. I crack him upside the head, knocking him out. The girlfriend is still screaming and decides to come at me with a blackened spoon. My left fist whips out before I can stop it and connects with her jaw. She falls down, everybody's down. Everybody but the dog. I step towards the fence, which Tony has almost demolished and bring the rolling pin down on his rabid head. There is a loud thump and then finally... Some silence.

Ahhhhh.

Calmness. Peace. Quietus.

Then the Youngblood has to wreck it.

"What the fuck guy!??"

I ignore him and step over Tony the now napping Rottweiler and walk down the hallway. Finding the hunting knife stuck in a doorframe, I pull it out and walk back to RJ's prostrated form. His eyes widen as I put the tip of the blade to his throat and whisper sweet nothings into his ear.

Like how if ever threatens Shane again, I will gut him. If he tries to find us and exact some stupid revenge, I will kill his girlfriend. If any of those idiots on the couch try to find us, I will kill them, then I will kill him and eat his dog.

RJ listens politely, nods when I ask him if he understands and remains on the floor when I get up. Shane, whose mouth has finally stopped moving, stares at me in disbelief.

"Let's go."

I say, walking past him and down the stairs. The purple door whizzes by and I see the three fashionistas are still playing dress up, completely unaware of the happenings inside. Walking around them I reach the car and hop into the passenger seat.

"Bro, these chicks are so totally messed up! They just had their tits hanging out!" Putu laughs from behind me; he too is oblivious to what just happened inside.

I pop open the glove box, push down some manuals and shove the knife in, Putu is so distracted by the girl's antics he doesn't notice. Shane has finally reached the yard and is speed-walking towards the car. When he gets in, the interior explodes with body odour.

"Holy fuck guy, like holy fuck!"

"Let's go," I tell him, in a voice that deflects all argument.

The Desperada roars to life and we are on the road, driving away.

"What happened?" Putu asks.

Instead of answering I stare at my old compadre, the Youngblood, the consummate simpleton as if to say.

Why the fuck did you ask that guy, that guy, of all people for money?

"I don't know dude, I don't know. I didn't think he knew about that shit with Griff, ya know? I... I fucked up man, I fucked up..."

***

Three days pass before I see Shane again. I spend most of my time walking the forests that lay a few blocks from my hostel of a home. There are a few assigned trails, but I get off them quickly, trying to find some solitude from the human world. I explore for hours, leaving at dawn and not returning until nightfall, when the air becomes crisp and burns the lungs.

I cultivated something in the hospital, something I didn't fully realize until now. A special awareness, built on the ashes of a cremated past, stacked brick by brick to form a monstrous edifice of austerity, and I can feel it being blemished, disfigured by this outside world. It seems to be a byproduct of humanity, this dissonance. And I barely noticed it was there until the beast was let loose for a few minutes and all the superfluous crap just fell away. In the heat of violence, all the sticky little cobwebs people leave on your brain burst into flame and you are left shorn and smooth.

But how to keep this state?

To participate is to lose our hold on divinity, only in the bosom of nature does it seems possible to keep the mind clean. Here, amongst the trees, away from the chattering

26

nonsense, this is where I feel the most stable. Breathing in the cold silence breath after breath.

Zero.

I am back at zero.

Well, almost, if the hospital was static zero we'll call this dynamic zero.

Zero Rolling.

***

One of the characteristics of the obtuse I truly admire is their ability to compartmentalize trauma. Three days ago Shane and I were in a knife fight at a drug dealer's house and today he is wearing his idiot grin like nothing happened.

...Yeah guy...

He reminds me of a retarded weasel or a dog with down syndrome. Something dumb but innately so, innocent and disturbingly likeable. Almost lovable.

We are on highway fifty three going west. A paper thin layer of snow covers the ground and the sky is an ugly bruise. Power poles look down upon us, sniffing at the interior of the car, smelling a witch's brew of sage, tobacco, kinnikinnick, bear root.

We are on a mission for Shane's "Auntie", whom I have found out is a former lover of his dead Father and from what my instincts tell me, Shane's current lover. The parcel of herbs and medicinal plants in the backseat is to be delivered to a reclusive medicine man by the name of Henry Yellowbird, who lives in the depths of the Stuwix Indian Reserve, Shane's birthplace. Known to most people as the "Biggest Shithole on the Planet."

White visitors are an extreme rarity out here. The only honkeys popping by are dope dealing bikers, who come to trade to bullets and blood with local gangbangers, paramedics and the horseless Royal Canadian Mounted Police. After the debacle at RJ's house of dog shit and good times, Shane thinks I am some kind of secretly trained government asskicker a la Jason Bourne and he is almost excited to take me somewhere famous for its violence. I don't share his enthusiasm. Some of the transients that frequent my living quarters have informed me of Shane's

27

past, and I wouldn't be surprised if there is a division of thugs waiting for our arrival.

Back in the 1960's oil reserves were found on the back forty of the Stuwix reserve and beginning in the seventies every bandmember, including minors, started receiving royalty cheques. Initially they were monthly payments that grew exponentially as the leases were developed, but Indian Affairs soon implemented a system of holding the money until children turned eighteen because women were pumping out ankle-biters like loaves of bread and spending their inheritance.

Now, a generation later, the kids are all grown up and for an eighteenth birthday present they get a bank deposit that can sometimes be up to a hundred thousand dollars. Shane was one of these genetic lotto winners. However, instead of taking his oil money and improving his stock portfolio, he was forced to pay back the drug dealers who'd been floating him for years. Combine that with a few impressive coke benders, trips to the casino, a new truck, which he wrote off within a month, and that leaves sweet fuck all.

Fast forward to now and I am curious if my intelligent, level-headed Indian friend might have left some debts or enemies lying around after he left? Something he may have forgotten about? Maybe someone like RJ from Fort Mckenzie??

"No, no guy. No worries," he assures me. "Most of the guys I was hanging with are gone man."

"Gone?" I ask. "Where?"

Surprisingly he becomes aloof, an emotion I have never seen him employ.

"Oh you know, just gone man."

"Yeah where?"

"Uhhhh, they just like shipped out."

His voice wavers and this makes me even more curious.

"Shipped out? What does that mean?"

"Uhhh, you know they shipped out man, it..."

He looks at me and his bizarre resolve breaks under my gaze.

"It's just what we call it. When people disappear, they got

28

shipped out."

"When people disappear?"

"Yeah man, sometimes if guys get into some bad shit or make too much noise they just disappear, I don't know, one day you just never see them again."

"So what, like killed or arrested?"

"I don't know man, nobody knows, nobody talks about it."

***

We pass a few cold and lonely homesteads with a few cold and lonely horses. Wisps of snow start falling and the divided highway retracts her spread legs. I can see a couple of old derricks beside the road in the distance, and when we get closer I realize they are fake and holding up a metal welcome sign.

STUWIX NATION

Birthplace of the Youngblood.

Just beyond the sign is an intersection, we turn north. Thankfully there are no bangers with guns waiting for Shane as we enter the heart of the reserve.

To the right and left are generic cookie cutter homes, just like in older city suburbs but they are strangely spaced a hundred metres from one another, making everything look too open. Some sit alone, missing the requisite trees and bushes, others are so popular they have an entourage of broken down cars, bicycles and other miscellany in their front yards. Further in the houses start get a little cozier with one another and a little more bedraggled. I count more than a couple riddled with bullet holes. Three have been burnt black. People however don't seem to exist here or more likely the cold has pushed them indoors.

Now that we are in the main town site the Youngblood starts rattling of resident's names and brief stories about them from his childhood.

"And that's Donny Samson's place, he once got caught wacking off in his truck, high on mushrooms..."

We pass by a gas station, lights on, vehicles at the pumps but no people. I look through the window of the restaurant next door and see no one. It's as if everyone has disappeared or is in hiding.

Or maybe waiting for us.

"...Yeah, fucking guy even had a condom on and everything, so he wouldn't jizz on his steering wheel..."

A deep paranoia fills my brain.

"...He was listening to Garth Brooks, like full bore..."

We pass by a dilapidated shack with a pair of frozen wretches in the driveway, and I am somehow reassured. They turn their heads and in their faces I see the wild ferine look so common around here. Sunken eyes, scraggly hair, early neurosis.

Junkies.

"What were they carrying?" I ask Shane.

The two tweakers were hauling plastic water jugs full of something distinctly yellow from their car.

"Awwww, it was probably piss man."

"Piss??"

"Yeah man, that's a cook shack. Guy who runs it is a real fucked up dude. He makes meth out of people's piss."

"What?"

"Yeah, I guess the chemicals or whatever come out of guys piss after they've smoked or shot up and so they keep it and trade it for more meth. I don't know man, I stay away from those dudes... There's my place!"

We have passed the heart of the town, and the houses are once again sparsely distributed. Shane points to a sad neglected powder blue box that has the windows and doors boarded up. Most of the curled brown shingles have blown off, and the painted shiplap siding is sloughing away. After his parents died, he and his sister moved in with his grandparents on the far side of town and this place was left to seed.

"Home sweet home," he says. "What a shithole."

The road twists around a creek, and tall spruce trees take over the landscape. We continue for another five minutes and turn on to a rutted dirt track that takes us down into a valley. As we descend deeper the trees become grizzled titans and their aura suffocating. The sky above seems like a distant memory. Shane reigns in the Desperada and straddles a

30

canyon of a rut, cutting through the fresh layer of snow and a house appears, seemingly out of thin air. Sharply pitched roof, stone chimney exhaling white smoke, wraparound deck decorated with hundred year old relics and oddments, exterior walls clad in timber, Henry Yellowbird's place looks like something from another time.

We park beside an old farm truck and a rheumy-eyed border collie comes out to greet us.

"Hey there, girl."

Shane pets the mutt's head and does a quick scan for the medicine man. Not seeing him, we each grab an armload of dried twigs and plants and walk around to the front of the house. There we see an elderly native man with long snowy-white hair coming out the front door. His face is clean shaven and lean. His eyes are a forest fire horizon, clouded yet warm. He is wearing jeans and a native designed vest over a wooly jacket. As we approach, his ancient mouth peels back into a molasses smile.

"Well, well. Shane Youngblood."

His voice is a resonant baritone. Slow and refined.

"Hey there, Henry. Brought ya some Christmas presents from Auntie Jo."

"That you did, that you did. Just drop 'em on the floor inside."

He opens the door and Shane steps inside, me following. I bob my head in greeting and Henry's smoke-filled eyes run across me, and I suddenly feel self-conscious, exposed even.

He's pulling me...

The presence of the old man is strong, earthy, grounded. I'm sure even the most insensitive dullard would notice something about him. They would probably say he looked wise or cool. They would quaff down his words and bow before his knowledge. But I know better. I've been trained. Psychic imbalance can be recognized and corrected if one is sensitive to such things. I sink my heels down, bend my knees, let his gaze run through me, let his hooks sink into my flesh. And then I release, I am nothing, I am smoke, there is nothing for him to hold on to and he reels in a ghost.

Welcome to zero. Welcome to the static.

Inside the house smells of cedar and burnt juniper, sage and fir boughs. We stomp the snow from our boots and drop the parcels on old wooden floorboards that run sidelong across the modest living room. Henry lets his old mutt in and goes to the kitchen, where a kettle is singing.

"You boys want tea or cider?"

Shane looks at me and rolls his eyes.

"How about some whiskey?" he quips.

Henry gives him a hard look.

"Cider it is."

We take off our jackets, the black wood burner in the corner is blazing, and the place is stifling hot. A homemade driftwood table sits against a wall in the kitchen, and we take a seat. Henry's house is simple, adorned with more memories than decorations. It is surprisingly well kept for a bachelor pad, clean counter tops; swept floors, organized couch pillows, even some fresh flowers in a vase. I wonder if he has someone come out to take care of things for him, there's a definite *woman-ness.*

Henry puts two steaming cups in front of us and sits down. His eyes once again scan across me, but this time there is no pressure. He only looks.

"So how's it going out here?" Shane asks. "You getting ready for winter?"

"Ohh, there ain't too much to get ready. Your Auntie Jo's been keeping me pretty well stocked. How are things at that oil company?"

Henry's question is hard and direct.

"Uhhh. Pretty good." Shane looks slightly abashed. "Yeah I'm doing real good Henry, real good. Staying away from, you know all that bad shit and yeah just laying low. Working hard, working real hard. Gonna do a few more shifts and get a new truck. You know?"

"Mhmmm." Henry takes a sip of his drink and stares at Shane through a cloud of steam.

"You just remember where you came from, Shane Youngblood. This is the land of our ancestors and those oil companies don't care about none of that. You need to remember the face of your mother and father. New trucks and all that other stuff can help you but they won't help this community."

Shane introverts and nods. Then Henry's tone softens.

"But I'm glad to see you doing so well son. Auntie Jo says you been doing real good."

Shane brightens and launches into a story about Putu being late for a shift and how to get him out of bed Sizz threw a bucket of dirty ditch snow on him. I am listening silently when something behind Henry catches my eye.

A small silhouette.

A picture. A reflection of a picture.

Two people, the archetypal Mother and Son.

The light outside has changed and the window reflects a portrait on the side of the fridge that is hidden from where I am sitting. Like a pair of vagabond ghosts, I see the comic book kid and his Mother. Involuntarily my breath quickens and my heart starts hammering in my ears.

Laufen! Laufen!!

Henry notices the change in my composure and follows my gaze. He sees the reflection and I wonder if he moved the picture out of sight on purpose. Perhaps taking the reflection as an omen or rethinking his decision he walks to the fridge and brings the picture over. Holding it out to me he says.

"Maggie and Jake."

She is wearing a restrained smile and tired eyes. He is younger then when I last saw him and smiling brightly.

"Who are they?" I ask.

Henry looks at Shane when he speaks.

"When you were gone down south, I broke my hip. Fell down the steps at Coop's store there and I needed a nurse for while, until I could walk again. The hospital sent out Maggie. Real nice girl."

Shane looks at the picture but the girl's plain features don't hold his attention for long. Henry passes me the framed photograph and sits back down. I try to seem only vaguely interested but my features betray me.

Who are you?

I could question Henry.

33

He won't tell you anything.

The old man doesn't trust me; either that or he knows something I don't.

Shane slurps down the rest of his cider; I haven't even touched mine yet, and slams the cup down on the table.

"Well Henry, we should probably get going, eh."

Henry doesn't take his eyes off of me.

"Oh yeah? You got some important business do ya?"

The wind comes in low and strong and the house shudders.

The old collie lets out a long mewling sound.

Give the picture back, centre yourself, breathe normally.

I force myself to give the photograph back to Henry and meet his inquisitors gaze. His face is all-knowing and I am overcome with helpless fury.

"Yeah just gotta get ready for the next hitch. Going back out tomorrow, it's pretty cool they fly us out on a private jet. Haha. James Bond style."

Shane gets up and I follow. We grab our jackets and head back out to the cold. The wind is pushing its way through the trees and causing a stir amongst the sleeping snowflakes. One of Henry's hanging knicknacks is spinning like a top. A blur of white and red. Then as I really focus on it, the ornament abruptly stops. I see one side briefly, a bird with a large beak and white feathers. Then the other side, an eagle bathed in blood halts in mid-flight and stares down at me.

"Red power," Henry intones.

I look at him questioningly.

"The condor represents the white power, the feminine, peaceful side of nature. The eagle represents the red power, the male, hostile side of nature. Both are necessary in life. They travel together and while one flies, the other rests."

The red eagle glides smoothly in front of me as if we were magnetized. The wind is raging and the ornament should be reeling.

I look at the old medicine man, and his eyes bleed crimson smoke.

"Hmmmm."

Is all he says and then the door closes.

Chapter 5

Dr. Lau has my tongue in one hand, my cock and balls in the other.

"The Taoists," she says. "Believe there is a meridian line at the front of the body that connects Muladhara Chakra to the upper egos. The current of manifestation. It begins at the perineum and ends at the tip of the tongue."

I am lying on a padded table in the fetal position, wearing only a medical gown, my junk pulled between my legs in what the kids call a fruit basket and my tongue stretched from my skull with a pair of plastic tongs.

"When the tip of the tongue is placed at the roof of the mouth behind the teeth this completes a circuit. A psychic energy circuit between the current of liberation that runs up the spine and the current of manifestation that runs down. This is called the macrocosmic orbit."

Christine's hand is protected from my bacteria laden ball sack by a latex glove.

"Many people believe that there is only one channel that connect the lesser egos with upper, the Sushumna that runs up through the chakras of the spine but this is not true and when dealing with psychic blocks forcing more energy up can worsen the problem. In cases such as yours, we must direct the Pranic currents downwards away from the blockages in Ajna and Sahasrara Chakra and back into the more gross form of consciousness. One way to do this is by stimulating the manifesting channel on a physical level as we are doing now."

The latex grip tightens and my privates are pulled alarmingly far from the rest of my body.

"Now I want you to take your breath, breathe in, up through the nostrils, into the brain, down the spine to your genitals and up the front of the body, clearing any blockages along the way and then out the mouth. Feel as if your exhalations are coming out the very tip of your tongue."

Christine's face is flushed with exertion, her mouth quivering. Perhaps she sees herself a goddess, bestowed with divine healing powers.

Through the crushing of thy ball sack, I shall cure thee!

The stretching lingers, she is holding her breath. Then she relaxes and my current of manifestation relaxes with her.

"We will do this a few times more," she says in a long exhalation. "Remember take in your Prana, bring it into your brain through Ajna Chakra, let it purify your thoughts and then carry your consciousness down your spine to Muladhara Chakra, let it linger here a moment, let it bestow your lesser egos with the gift of divine awareness and then release it back up into the universe. Breathe in."

The breath comes in, and the genitalia go out. Unbelievably they go even farther this time. I wonder if all this Pranic stimulating will leave me with eighty year old man balls, dangling between my kneecaps, all saggy and sad looking.

I try to follow Christine's instructions. Trailing the Prana, from my brain to balls and back. I feel almost obliged to, she has been picking away at the barren shell of my being with the tenacity of a worker ant. Day after day she comes, plucks me from my reverie and brings me up to her little macabre studio to perform bizarre, sometimes torturous practices.

I don't know where she learned these so-called exercises, but I do know they mostly involve my ass or balls or more correctly the space in between, my so-called root Chakra, Muladhara. The four-petaled lotus that holds a yellow square, representing the earth element and within the square an upside down triangle, the symbol of Shakti, the wife of Shiva the vessel of liberation and coiled within her the red serpent Kundalini, lying dormant until the Sushumna is opened and supporting them all is an elephant with seven trunks and blah, blah, blah. I don't know what any of that shit means but I have to admit it has kept me present. The days have become clearer, with a definite beginning and end. I can even recall what happened the day before and the day before that.

"Now just relax for a moment here, John."

I am catatonic, where would I go?

"I want you to focus on any changes you feel. Notice the

flow of energy through your body; try to bring your consciousness down into this reality."

I lay on my side feeling nothing, staring at nothing. Christine gets up, goes to a sink nearby and cleans my saliva from her tongs. The room around us is still cluttered with outdated exercise and physiotherapy machines, but they have been pushed back, organized and the layers of dust removed. Christine comes back and sits down, the teardrop scar dangling on her chest. She watches me in silence as I watch her. The teardrop glares at me, daring me to meet its gaze. I do, and time slips by.

Seconds pass, then minutes.

My eyes start to blur, slowly an image appears.

A memory.

A woman reporting the news.

"Five young men were found dead this morning. Presumed murdered. The men, aged eighteen to twenty one, were found in a park in the Radisson Heights area by a postal worker early this morning. Another man, possibly a minor was also found on the scene. Details are unclear, but eyewitnesses say the man was covered in blood and sitting near the victims. He appeared to be unharmed and was taken into custody by the police."

The camera blinks.

"I was walking to work and saw a bunch of cop cars and ambulances so I came over and there were bodies in the field with sheets on them. The police were talking to a postman and this kid, he was probably seventeen or eighteen, but it didn't look like he could talk and by the way he was dressed he was probably homeless. There's lots of homeless kids sleeping in the park this summer ...Yeah, yeah his whole face was covered in blood and...

Back to the news reporter.

"It is unknown if the man was involved in the killings, but police will say that the five men were victims of extreme violence, one man reportedly having his head twisted all the way around..."

These are things I should not remember. These are the things I have buried.

My hand moves, on its own accord. It reaches out to the fading images, to the scar on Dr. Christine Lau's chest. She doesn't move, she sits as still as a statue, barely breathing. My fingers find her skin, and she trembles with excitement.

"Yesss..." she whispers and in her bespectacled eyes I see triumph.

***

Later that night as I sleep, the walls close in. Recent events fill my mind, breaking down barriers, stamping their veracity, refusing to leave.

Where is my ocean of solitude? My floating barge of quietus?

It would appear the good doctor is making more headway than I realized. It is becoming impossible to leave this reality.

"Five young men, found dead, presumed murdered."

A teenage face, red hair turned grey in the moonlight.

"Victims of extreme violence."

A black birthmark.

Screaming for their lives.

"Covered in blood."

Twisted steel.

He threw the bottle.

"One man reportedly having his head twisted all the way around."

Cartilage, bone.

They thought it would be so funny, something they could laugh about later.

Now they are all gone, white sheets in a field. Pale ghosts harassing me in my dreams.

Why am I here? Why have I not risen?

The ghosts gather before me and cling to my limbs. I am bound to the present. It is time.

***

I awaken to the infantile face of Marcus the Giant.

"Good morning, John," he says too enthusiastically, his breath settling upon my face like a cloud of steamed semen.

He picks me up into a sitting position, and I feel genuine outrage.

38

Something feels different.

Something is different. My eyes or my hands or my feet or maybe all of it. My whole being feels different.

Marcus goes to grab me, but I drop to the floor on my own. The linoleum is cold on my bare skin, the black and white pattern literally popping with sharpness. I go to the toilet and amazingly my testicles don't unravel like taffy into the water, they hang comfortably as the sound of urine hits porcelain. My nose hairs twitch at the smell of my own feces. These are things I am not usually so *involved* in. Normally, I am awash in music that only I can hear, a soothing drone. Now I notice everything. The television down the hall, the voice of the doddering old woman, a speed-rap of fucks from the gangly insect.

And not only that I can feel things. The hair on my arms, the itchiness of my beard, the dryness of my throat, *the descending current of manifestation.*

As I eat breakfast the feelings intensify. I relish in the smell of oranges, the taste of powdered eggs and bacon, the sharp edge of a straw across my lips and the creaminess of milk on my teeth. My body quakes as the door to my senses unlocks. The static has become a distant buzz, and I wonder why I have hid for so long.

A rolling black thunderhead.

Run motherfucker, run from what you did to us.

Five bloodied faces.

I try to recede, but there is no escape.

I am becoming present.

***

Dr. Christine Lau is wearing a white blouse and mischievous smile. Her perfume rises above her, olfactory angel wings, as she hovers in front of me. The gossamer frame of her glasses twinkle and Marcus's more rigid ones twinkle back as if they have some little secret between them. Breakfast ends and we head down the hallway to the elevator. When the door opens, and we step into the rehabilitation room, Marcus the Giant Blob does not stay in the elevator as he usually does but exits with us.

Where are you going?

Dr. Lau sits me at my usual spot, as Marcus tiptoes over to a closet and starts rummaging through the contents.

"So, John, yesterday I think we may have had a breakthrough. I am sensing a major change in your awareness level and with a little more coaxing..."

She puts her small delicate hands over mine.

"...I think we can bring you back to the real world."

Marcus pulls all manner of junk from the closet. Dumbells, steel cables, flat blocks of yellow foam, wooden half-cylinders, chairs with the seats removed.

"I believe that the physical component of your being is at a place where it is ready to receive an influx of psychic energy. The root Chakra is the anchor that keeps the mind from losing itself in disassociation, like yours has. It is the centre for survival, the need to fight or take flight and its demon is the demon of fear. Fear for survival can cause a person to run and hide, just as a mind can be caused to run and hide from fears of past experiences. But fear is also a very important ally; it is the drive that keeps us alive when threatened. When put into a life or death situation, the root Chakra pulls the conscious down into the here and now and makes it erupt with the power needed for self-preservation."

Apparently finding what he was looking for, Marcus emerges from the closet with a small aquarium. He looks to Dr. Lau, she gives him a, *that will do*, bat of her eyelashes, and he proceeds to fill the glass box with water at the sink. As the water runs, Christine reaches into her attache case and pulls out a long cigar-looking stick with chinese writing on it.

"This is a moxibustion stick, John, it is made of mugwort, and when lit it burns at a temperature that comes very close to human chi. I am going to use it to direct your trapped energy downward."

With the flick of a lighter, the moxibustion is soon burning, its thick grey smoke filling the air and sticking to my pores. Dr. Lau moves behind me, pulls my hair away from my shoulders and holds the hot ember at the top of my spine. Within moments a ball of warmth envelopes my neck and slowly spiderwebs across my skull. The sound of the running water from the sink melds with the sensation.

"Think back to a time when you felt that you were fully expressing yourself, that your voice was truly being heard, your creative identity was in control."

My mind is caked in sludge, moving at a snail's pace. The heat spreads and in a matter of moments, I start to see something.

Hands etched in dirt, a braid of hemp.

A necklace that I made under the tutelage of gypsy girl that was on her way to Vancouver. You should come with me, she said.

I was living on the streets, collecting bottles.

The heat descends as Christine moves her magic stick to the middle of my back.

"Now, John. Try to remember a time when your heart filled with love, until it was about to burst."

The gypsy girl and her strands of twine coil into sand and are swept away. My mind turns its gaze down to the charred remains of my gutted heart and hesitantly pokes at the ruins.

There are pieces there, smoldering pictures of the people I once loved.

But they are beyond Dr. Christine Lau's ability to resurrect. They are from a childhood long forgotten.

Laufen! Laufen!

Christine moves her stick lower. Veins of succulent fire encompass my torso.

"Now," she whispers softly into my ear. "Envision a moment of triumph, of power. Let this feeling fill every corner of your being. Let it consume you."

My internal gaze descends with the heat and ever so slowly another picture forms.

No! I don't want to see it!

Five young men appear, boys really, not much different than myself. They are dead, spread in a circle, their bodies twisted into unnatural shapes, and I am at their centre. The blackness of the eclipse, horrible and jubilant.

A fleeting moment.

The triumph did not last though, it burned like a comet, and when it was gone I was left alone in a place of horror.

Run motherfucker run.

I smell burning hair as Christine moves the moxibustion lower, to the very base of my spine.

"From here we will activate the two bottom chakras, first Svadhisthana, the Chakra associated with sensation and motion and sexuality. It is the element of water. Once the survival needs are met, the next thing that humans seek out is pleasure. I want you to explore your body, find a place of sensation, something pleasurable, the touch of a lover, the taste of something delicious, something gratifying."

It is here where my introspective journey ends. The depths of my body and so the depths of my emotions are not a place I want to visit, let alone relish. As if sensing this, Dr. Lau, my trusted physician reaches her free hand underneath the front of my robe and begins to trace tantric phrases upon my inner thigh. This is not the touch of a healer.

It is of a woman, an undoer.

Her perfume becomes an intoxicant as she speaks into my ear, her lips so close they brush my skin.

"Guilt is the demon of Svadhisthana, John. Guilt polarizes us, pulls us from our senses. Guilt from actions passed, immobilize the flow of energy in our body, preventing the currents from above to reach their manifested counterparts below."

Rounded fingernails slide across my leg in ever widening circles. The glowing ember at my back burns an angry red. Dr. Lau moves her fingers further beneath my robe.

Marcus the giant nurse fills his aquarium.

"Now I want you to bring your consciousness all the way down, release your emotional identity and embrace your primal identity. Come back to your infancy, to the very base of the collective unconscious, where there is only the world of the senses. Connect to your surroundings, listen to your instincts."

As she says this, her hand burrows beneath my testicles as though it were searching for a good place to hibernate for the winter. Her bare skin is dry and cool against my own.

No latex glove today dear doctor?

Marcus shuts off the tap and picks up the water-heavy aquarium, sitting it on his immense belly. Christine motions him to place it on the empty spot beside me. He does, and she pulls her hand from beneath my robe and extinguishes her moxa stick in a cup of rice. Her black almond-shaped eyes lock with mine.

"Now I want you to trust us, John. We are about to invoke your survival instincts, and I want you to try and harness any of the descending energy and use it."

She stands me up and turns me, so I am facing the pool of water. Marcus is at my side, and in my peripheral I can see that the gelatinous bastard is grinning.

"One minute?" he asks Dr. Lau.

"To begin with," she answers.

Marcus wraps a giant paw around my neck, his marshmallow fingers squishing into my flesh. Christine is behind me, her hands just above my exposed ass crack.

"Now," she says, and Marcus tightens his grip and pushes down.

Then I am drowning.

A shock of cold tap water envelopes my head as he thrusts me into the aquarium. Bubbles and ripples scatter before me and I half expect a singing crab to appear.

...Under The Sea...

Pressure builds in my chest and head. My eyes close and in the darkness an amorphous nebula approaches. Purples and reds and oranges sail towards me.

Pulled back up, warm recycled air fills my lungs.

"Don't run away, John!" Dr. Lau orders, prying my eyes open. "Fight. Fight or you will die!"

I am sent back under. Longer this time. My eyes begin to close but Dr. Lau won't let me slip away, she grabs my baby maker and starts to tug at it furiously. Long seconds pass and I am pulled back once again. Oxygen comes in and with it, the realization that the overseer of my mental rehabilitation, is thoroughly insane.

"Fight, John!" she hisses. "Fight for your fucking life!"

Through a cascade of hair, I see Marcus. Marcus with his dry skin and gluttonous eyes.

I bet this shit just rubs your buddha, eh buddy?!

He smiles as if hearing my thoughts and throws me back

43

into the aquarium. Water fills my ears and fury fills my soul.

Fuck You!

Dr. Lau's fondling has taken effect; the arousal just angers me more. I feel like a slave-prostitute, alive only for the amusement of degenerates.

Fuck You Too!

The seconds pass and I start to tremble. Rage mixed with the liquid fire of self-preservation set off a string of detonations, sending my limbs in all directions. Marcus struggles but continues to maintain a death grip on my neck.

I want to live! I need to live!

And it happens, the release. I realize it immediately. As if my head were a buzzing hive, suddenly drained of all it inhabitants, thousands of electrified currents make contact. My nervous system becomes a storm-cloud unleashed.

I am *present.*

My legs press down for traction as my bony fists smash out the sides of the aquarium. Dr. Lau releases a lamb-like bleat and jumps back as water and glass hit the floor. In a moment of shock, Marcus momentarily loosens the grip on my neck.

It is more than enough time for me to spin in position and knock his arm away with my elbow. He slips in the water to his knees, stripping me of my medical gown in the process and then I am on him, kicking and punching and biting and screaming. His soft skin ripples as my fists reach him and turn him into a soggy mass. His glasses fly from his face with a kick, and he is left wobbling. I am naked and roaring to the gods in Valhalla. My erect member is at a height with his face and staring at him as though it were another fist, preparing to knock his fucking lights out.

...Prick...

A needle is jabbed into my right ass cheek.

Dr. Lau from behind.

I turn to see her watching me warily, syringe in hand.

Sneaky Bitch.

My vision begins to cloud as I step towards her. She backs away. My legs give out beneath me. Sweet oblivion.

Chapter 6

"Have you seen them?! Have you fucking seen them?!"
I think back.

I don't think I have seen anyone, not since I left Shane and Putu at the bar.

"They've been following me man, fucking watching me man. They usually don't take women, but they know I know too much. I know where they take them!"

"Take who?" I ask politely.

"Fucking everybody man. Skinny Pete, Cobb, Wilson...Buck! Fucking everybody. They come in the night, saying they just want to talk to you, and whatever, but then you disappear. All of 'em man, shipped out, just like that!"

"Shipped out?" I say.

I remember the Youngblood using the same phrase on the reserve.

"What do you mean, shipped out?"

"Shipped out, shipped out, shipped out! They fucking grab you and your gone! Gone!"

"Who?"

The frantic woman comes in close. There's a black hole where her teeth should be and she stinks of vomit.

"Fucking Don Swan man," she whispers. "Don Swan."

Don Swan, the billionaire oil baron. Owner of Swancor, my employer.

"Don Swan took your friends?"

I heard Bill Gates collects meteorites; maybe Don Swan collects meth heads.

"Not him, his people baby, the fucking police man, they take them out to the castl..."

The shadow of a human in front of me stops speaking and cocks her head as if she heard something. Together we listen to the sounds of downtown Fort Mckenzie, cars humming, people in the distance, snow crunching beneath our feet. Then, like she was never there, the woman is gone. Around the corner in seconds, gone man, shipped out. I am left alone in the blackness of night, and slowly, I continue walking home.

**

The next day I am back on Rig nine.

"Kraker. Remember that guy??"

Putu's mouth is a mash of gravy, potatoes and roast beef.

"Jesus, of course. How do you forget a guy like that?"

Mark the Flatlander tears a chicken leg in half and starts wolfing it down. Driblets of grease run down his chin in sparkly rivulets.

"Why? What do you mean?" Reggie our new greenhorn chimes in.

"Well let's see." Mark answers academically.

"The guy was like eight feet tall or something, huge like ripped, no fat at all, shaved head and had these crazy tribal tattoos all over his face."

Putu concurs.

"Crazy man. Crazy. Like all around his eyes in these big swirls. Back home we have this style Batik, it was kind of like that."

The Flatlander nods and a greasy drop falls off of his chin and lands on a slab of meaty lasagna. Say what you want about the oil patch, long shitty hours, monotonous labour, exposure to freezing weather, questionable company, the food is god damn fantastic.

"Yeah and he hardly ever talked. Just like, Johnnie D here. Just kind of stared at you, with those fucked up tattoos, like he was gonna kill you."

"I seen him twist off a lug nut with his bare hands," Putu says, and surprisingly nobody contests this.

"Yeah man. We used to say if you got a flat on a lease road just call up Kraker. He was the only guy who could change a tire without a jack or a tire iron. Haha."

Putu laughs and Mark chuckles with him.

"What happened to him?" Reggie asks and their faces turn grey.

Strangely so does Shane's, even though he didn't know the man. It seems to be an unwritten law around here that you don't ask about the past.

"Ahhh who knows man," Mark mumbles and looks to the clock.

"He get skidded?" the Greenhorn persists.

Shipped out maybe?

"Not sure, not too sure, that was years ago..." Mark sucks back the rest of his Ocean Spray juice box and gets up.

"Well pitter patter, let's get at 'er, eh?"

The five of us get up as if we are going for a prostate exam. Once on the rig floor we split up into our assigned positions. It is night and winter is in full bloom. The thermostat says minus twenty eight, but when the wind picks up it feels even colder. My face is a frozen contusion; fingers brittle stalactites ready to break at any moment. This is when Doctor Lau's training really helps. I can sink back and let my body do the work while *I* witness from afar.

The rig floor is an opium den flipped inside out, palisade walls made of steam surround us, half a dozen lights encase us in a deceptively warm amber glow, girders and beams and railings stick out at inconceivable angles, preventing our escape. And before us, the derrick, the great obelisk rises high, almost to the stars and lounging at its apex is a frost-bitten Indonesian wondering why he left the warmth of his homeland.

For the cash my man! For the cash!

Shane is beside me as we dance back and forth, unscrewing long phallic pieces of steel with the help of futuristic mechanical arms. Reggie is close by, helping us and receiving tutelage from Mark the Flatlander. We are pulling the pipe out of the hole and racking 'er back. The geologist has declared that the bit needs to be checked. We are only a few hundred meters in the ground, and there are superstitious murmurs amongst the crew. Something isn't right, and everybody can feel it. We pull up a strand of pipe from the wellbore and Shane, the consummate simpleton is singing to himself, oblivious to everyone else's uneasiness.

"*Hmmmm Hmmmm Hmmmm*"

We break the connection and send the pipe into the pipetub.

"*It burns...burns...burns...*"

Another strand gets pulled out of the hole, and I hear something up top, a heavy gurgling sound.

"The ring of fire..."

My ears start to burn. The breath in my lungs won't come out. Something is wrong.

"The ring of FIRE!"

The world goes black. A column of mud, a foot thick comes rushing up through the rotary table like a geyser. Rock and debris follow and within a heartbeat, the floor bushings; two hundred pound metal cylinders, shoot straight up, smashing into the frame of the derrick, causing deadly havoc. The sound of crashing metal and gushing drilling fluid is deafening, yet I still hear Mark screaming.

"MOVE! GET THE FUCK OUT OF HERE!"

I look over to see him chaining down the brake handle and grabbing Reggie. As they head for the stairs, a rock the size of a pumpkin bounces of a girder and hits the Youngblood in the shoulder. He flips backwards. I jump to my right, dodging a barrage of more rocks and roll to where he is lying in a muddy heap.

It is so cold that the drilling fluid is already starting to freeze on the rig floor, and my feet struggle to find purchase as I lift Shane up. His mouth opens, and it looks as if he is howling, but I hear nothing except the maelstrom beside us. Something hits my calf and we both go back down. Gritting my teeth, I push, launching us forward until we are at the stairs. We near tumble the fifteen feet to the ground and then I remember.

Putu!

He's at the top of the derrick on the monkey board. Just as I turn to look back, a rock smashes an electric light, the spark ignites the escaping gases and night turns to day. A column of flame rises from the depths and runs up the derrick. Even from down on the ground I can feel the exquisite heat. The sound is like nothing I have ever experienced, it makes me think of a rocket being fired or a space liftoff. Above the inferno I see him.

Putu!

High up on the rig mast, there is a platform where the

derrickhand works called the monkeyboard. While working, he wears a seat belt like contraption called a fall arrestor that locks up if there is any sudden movement, and a safety harness that is attached to a railing in case he falls. In the event of an emergency, like right fucking now, he is trained to unclip the lanyard and fall arrestor, climb aboard a fun little device we call an easy rider, essentially a T-shaped bar attached to a cable and slide down to freedom. Easy.

Easy to do on a sunny afternoon in summer when the birds are singing but a little more difficult when the sky is raining stones, and you are dangling upside down from a rig on fire as Putu is now. Either he was knocked over the railing by the explosion or tried to escape the flames and fell, the little Indonesian is now hanging limp in his harness with his fall arrestor locked up. Trapped.

Whump!

I yank Shane close to me as an anvil of a stone hits the ground, just missing him.

His eyes are dazed, and his face contorted with pain.

"Can you make it to the muster point?!" I yell.

He stares at the burning derrick, tendrils of red and yellow blazoning his skin and I yell again, repeating myself. This time he hears me and gives me a slow nod.

"GO!" I shout, pushing him away from the rig.

He starts to jog haphazardly through sheets of falling gravel, holding his left shoulder and I turn back to the rig floor. Once there, I drop my head, using my hardhat as a shield and drive forward into the heat, piercing the outer rim of the blaze. Rocks and gravel have become perpetual shrapnel, and they bounce off of everything with terrifying violence. Every window and light has been shattered.

The fire senses my intrusion and wraps its deadly tentacles around me in an attempt to snuff me out, but I push through to the far side of the derrick. Then I am jumping, bouncing off of girders and other steel protrusions until I am on top of a corrugated shack we call the Doghouse, where the higher ups turn the mighty wheels of oil production. From there I get a better look at Putu. The Indonesian is as limp as a corpse hanging from the gallows, swaying back and forth with branches of fire coming within an arms length of him.

He's going to be cooked alive.

Above him is the easy rider cable that runs down to the manifold shack on the ground. The middle of the cable is directly in front of me about twelve feet away from the edge of the Doghouse. I toss my hardhat and tighten my gloves. Eagle, Condor, Red, White. Whatever, there's no time to pray. The world is a blur, horrible screeches of metal collapsing, I am moving. The roof is a shit-smeared bog, and I slip like a drunkard on ice. But the final step, the most important one supports my weight and then I am soaring.

...Flying through the sky, so fancy free...

For an instant, I can see the dark forest past the lease. So calm, so uninvolved. Then the cable is glancing off my eyebrow and scraping across my ear with excruciating viscosity. White hot pain rips across my face. I scramble to grab the cable, but it is dripping with drilling fluid and I start slipping down the line. My hands hold long enough to get a leg up and around and then I clamp down. I stop moving, and after a quick breath I get the other leg on and am able to inch my way up the line. After a few seconds, I get a pattern down and am able to pick up the pace.

Hand over hand... Condense.   Hand over hand... Condense.

In the distance I hear my crewmates shouting, barely audible beneath the roar of the fire. Pebbles pelt my face and arms, my hamstrings cry out in pain. All of it surrounds me in crystal clarity, but nothing can steal my concentration, or I will make a mistake, a muscle will tremble, a hand will slip, and all these theatrics will be for nothing.

Finally, I reach the top of the rig mast. Looking down, I yell at the lolling form of Putu, but there is no response. I go a little further and drop my feet on to the outside of the monkeyboard. The fire is still raging, but luckily the wind is blowing the flames away from us. I bend down, hooking one arm through the railing and reach out to Putu's leg.

"WAKE UP MOTHERFUCKER!" I holler, but he's out cold.

Or Dead.

Then it is time. I momentarily withdraw, sucking in a hot breath in preparation, this will be my last sprint, there will be nothing left after this.

Not even zero, less than zero.

I wrap my leg around the railing and lower myself down. A rock hits the monkeyboard floor with a loud *Ping*, sending a shiver down my spine.

Stay focused. There is only the goal. Only the destination.

I grab at Putu's mud soaked coveralls and pull with what is left of my strength. He is a runt of a man, but the mashed potatoes have fattened his belly.

A loud creak from below.

Could the rig fall?

The wind relents and the flames come towards us licking the bottom of my boots.

The muscles in my back strain to the point of tearing and my voice is raw from screaming. The filthy sack of brown meat has become my anathema. I almost hope the little Indonesian is dead, so I don't have to deal with his fucking shit anymore. I pull again, roaring in fury and finally the fat little prick is back up on the monkeyboard. I place him on the ledge and keep a hand on him, making sure he doesn't fall again and catch my breath.

For an instant, my eyes wander, and I truly see the height at which we are sitting. The derrick is a double, and we are probably over a hundred feet off of the ground. Fear starts to clench my heart, so I turn to Putu and check that he is still breathing. He is, his face however has become a child's nightmare. Under the mask of caked on mud, I see swirls of blood coming from a gash on his forehead and his obviously broken nose. His right eye has retreated beneath a mound of swollen flesh, and a piece of his nostril is dangling like a fishing lure.

HEAT!

Flames on our backs and flesh burning. I smell an acridness and realize my hair is on fire. Slapping at the back of my neck with my greenkings I decide it is time to move on. I pull Putu to his feet, and I hear something familiar.

"...Hgullphhh..."

The little fucker is awake.

Well semi-conscious at least. Enough to straighten his legs a little.

I unhitch his fall arrestor and hold him steady with one arm. Reaching up with the other I grab the T-bar shaped seat of the easy rider and pull it towards us.

"Alright Putu, let's do this."

I lock the hand brake and lift him up on to the bar so that he drapes over it with his legs and arms dangling. It is a precarious position, to say the least, but I see no other way. I swing a leg over, facing Putu and sit down. My balls are crushed by my own weight, and I wonder insanely if I ever have children, will they come out mushy?

Something hits the cable above us, and it releases a psychedelic *Thwkor* sound. We start bouncing up and down as if we were just a couple of friends on a merry-go-round. I press myself tight against the vertical bar and hold on to Putu with a death grip. The bouncing continues and my entire body trembles with exertion. Down at the manifold shack I can make out the excited shapes of my crew-mates.

Hello Friends! Catch us if we fall, would ya?

The cable is still moving, but I can't wait any longer. The wind has changed direction, bringing the flames towards us, and unless my addled brain is imagining things, there must be more gas escaping because the column has thickened and is rising double the height of the derrick. Reaching up to the hand brake I slowly start to lower us. The easy rider slides a good forty feet and then stops, and my heart almost stops with it. We are sixty feet above ground and the only thing to catch us if we fall is a stack of heavy drilling pipe.

Looking up I see the problem. Mud has caked the braided cable and froze, causing the sliding mechanism to jam. Up top it wasn't a problem because of the heat of the fire, but I can see the next six feet are afflicted. Despair rears its ugly head.

If only...

A figure comes running towards us dodging falling rocks. It is Mark the Flatlander, the Driller, the farmboy from Saskabush. He is holding something big and metallic.

"JOHNNY! CATCH!" He shouts, tossing up the tool.

My eyes are still open, synapses are still firing. The stick of metal floats up, and when it is close enough I snatch it from the air. It is a large crescent wrench.

Balancing on the easy rider I start to smash at the frozen mud, causing large chunks and flakes to go flying. Soon, enough is gone that we can start moving again. A couple feet and the process needs to be repeated. It is taxing work, and I am nearly at the end of my reserves mentally and physically. Pebbles fly through the air in shotgun waves, and I imagine myself as a medic in a warzone trying to save a fallen soldier. I swing the wrench again and again, holding Putu with one hand and myself with my thighs and finally the last of the drilling fluid is gone, and we are once again moving down the line.

Twenty five feet...

The easy rider is rolling smoothly.

Twenty...

Putu is mewling like a dog, but at least he isn't moving. I am so spent that I am barely holding him anymore.

Fifteen...

The ground is approaching, and I have the strange sensation I am looking through binoculars. The right side of my head has become an amplifier for my pulse, every heartbeat brings dull pain.

Ten...Nine...Eight...

There is a full on posse waiting for us down on the lease. Mark, Reggie, Sizz, Jerry, the geologist, the engineer, some directional guys, a couple of truck drivers and thank ya sweet Jesus a medic.

Four...Three...Two...

A crowd of hands reach up to catch Putu. They pull him down, lay him on a stretcher and start running. Stone fragments are still falling, and it seems the only safe place is all the way off of the lease. Jerry and Mark come to my aid, but I don't need their help. I start to climb down from my metal steed and *...Whoa!...* My legs buckle beneath me. The good Samaritans grab me and help me to my feet. Mark puts my right arm around his shoulder and Jerry takes my left, and

I have to say I am thankful, without them I would be crawling out of here.

Moving as a unit we make a hasty retreat to the outlying lease road. My right calf throbs with every step and the muscles in my back have begun to seize. We reach the muster point, and finally I can let go, it is over. Putu is being loaded into a truck, Shane must already be gone. We made it.

I look back at the burning derrick, the great obelisk built in the name of Mammon, spewing yellow carnage and false meteors. Is this what Sodom looked like? Have we sinned against the earth? Is this God's punishment?

I don't believe in God but could I be seeing the handiwork of someone else's?

Perhaps.

There.

If I stare hard enough, I can see it. The breast of an eagle hidden in the folds of the blaze. It's fearless head, sharpened beak. Wings rising up to the heavens, tips smoldering.

Red Power.

***

Cuts, bruises, scrapes, a stone the size of a marble embedded three inches into my calf, first degree burns on my back, three black fingernails soon to fall off, a sprained ankle, twisted knee, fractured shin, torn right ear that thankfully was sown back on and some burnt hair.

And the doctors tell me I am the lucky one.

The taste and touch of Mountview Hospital in Fort Mckenzie reminds me of a bad lay. It feels as if we are going through the motions and she knows I just want to finish my business and hit the dusty trail. Luckily the doctor only made me stay the one night, and I can leave today whenever I please, but I feel obligated to pay Putu and the Youngblood a visit.

The right leg took the brunt of the punishment but thankfully it doesn't need a cast. Still, putting on pants is going to a bit of a tribulation for the next while. This proves true as I struggle to pull up my jeans and put on my boots. Once up, I grab the cane Mark brought by and left me. It's a bull's cock that's been stretched and hardened. It was his

Grandfather's but he said I could keep it, as a gift for my bravery.

A few of the boys came in and saw me this morning, looking dog tired. Sizz, Jerry, the truck drivers who helped carry Putu, Mark and his dick cane. They told me that both Putu and Shane were doing good, well as good as can be expected. Shane ended up having emergency surgery because the impact of the rock started a heart valve problem. He also had to have surgery on his shoulder, which I imagine, must have been like gluing back together a shattered vase. Putu had a broken nose, cracked cheek bone, fractured jaw, a couple missing teeth, a concussion but no permanent brain damage.

"Hopefully." Mark was pessimistic. "You never know with that shit."

The two truck drivers hung back, and I noticed an awkwardness pervading from the others as well during the visit. At the best of times, I seem to emanate an aura that keeps people distant, but it appears to have taken a different shade. They gave the expected compliments. They asked the expected questions. But deep in the crevices of their eyes there were other things they wanted to say. Only Reggie the Greenhorn had the uncouthness to put words to his thoughts.

"That was crazy man."

Mhmmm hmmm, it was.

"I never seen someone move like that."

Neither have I.

"I mean like it was crazy. You were a blur. How did you do that? Were you like in the military? Do you have some kind of training or something?"

I don't know, I can't remember.

"It was like watching a movie being fast forwarded."

That's not what it feels like. It feels like everything goes into slow-motion, half-time, but I am still moving normally.

When Reggie was finished talking, and my silence became too uncomfortable the guys made their abrupt farewells.

***

My hand rests on the dick cane and I take a few steps,

feeling like a geriatric runaway. I ask the nurse where my friend's rooms are, and she points down the hall. I begin to walk briskly, purposely causing a riot of pain.

Buck up, buck the fuck up.

They say that people who have spent a lot of time in hospitals as children hate going back as adults.

Just like eating broccoli and buttfucking. If you were forced to do it as a child, you won't enjoy it as an adult!

I can't say I hate hospitals. I just feel nothing when I am in them now. No emergence of repressed emotions, no claustrophobia. No subjectivity. No connection to the institutions of the past. It feels like a place I have outgrown. A giant diaper full of shit. Thanks to my dear Doctor Christine Lau I can use the toilet of civilized society like a big boy now. Just like the rest of you.

Mountview is a busy place. Waiting rooms are full of disheartened faces, hallways jammed with nomadic patients and hard-heeled nurses and doctors. Angry voices, abrasive voices, sad, pleading, bored voices.

A boy of about thirteen sits in a wheel chair, his eyes gushing tears, his face pulled back into a joker's grimace.

Pain.

What is the absence of pain?

Pleasure? That just leads to boredom.

Is that what we strive for, the absolution of one in the arms of another? When you have been to a place of neutrality, a place that lacks duality you see the necessity of opposites. It is what we are here for. Only this finite existence can give us the hatchet to cut something eternal into little temporal pieces. There we can smell the stench of a lover's breath in one instant and the deliciousness of their sweat in the next. That is the key to pain. Understanding that it is both perpetual and impermanent.

I stop, bending down to tell the kid in the wheel chair this, but he's already behind me, rolling away, hopefully to find his peace and maybe some understanding.

Walking on, leg and back and ear squalling, I start to check room numbers.

...314 ...315...

Down the hall, I see a face known yet unknown. Long auburn hair, freckled skin. My pulse quickens, my injuries start to throb. A lump catches in my throat.

Maggie.

The girl from the picture. The girl from the car. The girl from the static.

Her back is turned to me. She is walking away, past a Pepsi cooler she disappears.

I don't know what to do. She is my phantom, my ghost of Christmas past. There is no such thing as coincidence, I came to this specific shithole town for a reason and she is a part of it. The first fifteen years of my life are missing, a vast gaping hole that not even Christine Lau could illuminate. My childhood, my family, my real name, all of it gone. But what can I say to this woman? She looked at me with such trepidation that day on the street.

What if I did something? Like before the arrest?

It doesn't matter; I have to speak to her. Ask her how she knows me, what she knows about me.

I move as fast as my injuries will allow. Pinballing through the meandering crowd, causing a few raised eyebrows in the process, I turn down another hallway that leads to the main entrance. I catch a brief glimpse of flowing hair and a brown jacket through the glass doors.

Shit!

I waited too long. I chase after the phantom girl, but I know it is too late. The hallway is long and the people thick. I get to the exit, but I don't see her. Leaving the hospital, I stare out at the frozen bodies of the cars in the parking lot. The air is cold, and my breath lingers, giant flakes of snow are falling. In the distance, pulling on to the street, tires spinning on the ice I see a faded red Toyota corolla.

White on red.

Red on white.

***

Rig nine burned all through the night and eventually collapsed into a heap of tangled metal, crushing a couple shacks and a water truck. It was decided that the blowout was no one's fault, just a rare case of trapped gas at an unusually shallow depth. The entire crew were given paid leave and because of our injuries, Putu, Shane and I were put on workman's compensation until further recompense is decided upon. They both stayed in the hospital for a while longer but have been released today and are ready to spend some of that free money and celebrate the miracle of life by getting ripped at the ripper's.

***

"You know why this place is called Mary Jane's?" Shane yells at me, over the din of eighties hair metal and jubilant VLT's.

We are sitting at a booth with Putu, Mark, Jerry, Sizz and a few other guys I don't know. The table is full of drinks, and on the raised stage a bored stripper is rolling on the floor in what I assume are supposed to be provocative poses.

"Because the owner's wife used to be a stripper..."

We've only been here for an hour, and Shane is spitting his words.

"...And her stage name was Mary Jane Rotten Crotch!"

Sizz, who as Toolpush oversees the three crews that work Rig nine, usually keeps a respective distance from the rest of us, but tonight he has removed his hard hat, so to speak, and is drinking like a fish and more chummy than I have ever seen him.

"Shut the fuck up, Youngblood!" he hollers at Shane. "He named it after his ex-wife because of her rotten snatch! Speaking of nicknames, you guys wanna know what we used to call this guy back in high school? Huh? Chief Stumbling Buffalo. Haha. That was his name in high school because we were playing baseball, and he goes to catch a flyball and wham, trips on his own fucking feet and hits the ground."

Everyone starts laughing, and Shane turns purple.

"You weren't even there guy!" he replies as the music dies, making his sharp voice even more grating.

"The fucking gym teacher called him that! Chief Stumbling Buffalo!" Sizz counters, causing another fit of drunken laughter.

The stripper gathers her things and exits the stage. A bouncer wearing a collared shirt and tie comes up with a

58

wide broom and starts sweeping up her change. In Alberta, it is pretty customary for an exotic dancer to hunker down after stripping for three songs, spread her legs, slap a Toonie or a Loonie on to her vagina and let guys throw coins at it. If you knock it off you get a lovely keepsake, most likely a poster or a keychain or a fridge magnet, and if you are lucky you might just get an autograph. The coins have to be worth at least a dollar, try throwing a quarter or a nickel and you'll be politely escorted to the back alley and have the shit pounded out of you.

Drinks are downed, and another round is delivered.

An excited voice from the DJ booth resounds overhead.

"Alright Fellas...Give a warm Mary Jane's welcome to Portia De Sossi!!"

The guys start pounding the table and the keeners on sniffer's row unleash a torrent of applause. A loud whoop escapes from Putu's cracked lips. The swelling around his eye has gone down, but his many stitches, flattened nose and blood filled eye still prompts many stares. His gratitude was a deluge, more than I could ever want, he said he was going to write a letter to the Governor General and tell them I should get a medal or a ribbon or a plaque or something. I told him to just make me one himself.

Shane is beside him and looking rough but not quite as battered. His left arm is in a sling, a few scratches mar his cheek, but the majority of his injuries are hidden. His shoulder will take months if not years to recover. The surgery on his left ventricle was a success, but the doctor told him he needs to quit one of his favourite past-times; dabbling in the Columbia disco dust.

Fuck guy...

The lights turn low and a familiar children's song starts playing through the speakers. Quizzical expressions fill the table and the raucousness pauses. A six foot tall Winnie the Pooh prances up the steps and on to the stage, his giant head sporting a serial killer smile. He waddles around the stage, pretending to chase bees away from his honey pot, fuzzy arms waving.

Doooo da dooo da doooo...

After the invisible harriers have left him in peace, he dips his hand into the pot and smears imaginary honey all over his face.

Winnie The Pooh...

Apparently full, he puts down his pot.

Winnie The Pooh...

The song ends and he looks up as if seeing the crowd for the first time. Suddenly bashful he drops his head, and his hands go to his chest. The bar is silent; I look to the DJ booth and see a bearded long-hair grinning like a demon. Then the music starts up again, booming heavy metal, so loud the air quakes. The Pooh's head snaps back with enough force to take it right off, revealing long bleached blonde hair, a smirking face, sparkly lips and thick blue eyeshadow. His chest tears open and instead off teddy bear innards, giant silicone boobs come tumbling out. Soon Winnie the Pooh is gone and a porn star goddess has risen in his place. The crowd heralds the transformation and cheers erupt.

Holy Fuck Guy!

***

The night continues like a hurricane. We move from bar to bar, invading, laughing, offending, arguing, conquering. The boys drink as if the war just ended and they made it home alive. They drink until they are disproportionate caricatures of themselves. They drink until the world is singing with them. They drink until the nightmares of fire and terror are lost in a swirl of merriment.

Somewhere along the way we picked up stragglers, loose looking women attracted to the dollar bills flying out of my compadres' wallets, friends of friends, drunken acquaintances and other delinquents like ourselves. Eventually, there are over a dozen of us walking the streets of some forgotten corner of the city. It is unseasonably warm, barely below freezing and some of the women are wearing skirts with only thin stockings to protect their pale skin.

It's all about the fashion.

The air is clear, and the sky above is alive with stars. An almost full moon presides over the night kingdom and I start to think of all the planes I saw flying around today. Three months ago it was the same, a small fleet of private jets arriving and then zipping back out, going to the Castle, Don Swan's mysterious mansion at the ends of the earth. It was the same with the moon also, almost full.

Don Swan man!

The frenetic tweaker comes back to me in vivid detail.

Fucking Don Swan!

Every three months, before the full moon, the eagles take flight.

We walk and walk with no apparent destination. Whoever our leader is, they must have left their compass back at one of the watering holes.

Shane is beside me, his good arm around a buxom girl with dazzling green eyes set in a young smiling face. The only reason I haven't gone home yet is because I want to make sure he gets through the night without falling on his head or getting beat up. He is blathering, people are crooning, others are pontificating and finally someone takes the reins of this operation. One of the tag-alongs, a young gangsta with a puffy jacket and sideways hat.

"Yo, follow me people I know where a crazy party be happening!"

The mob takes little notice of the kid's words, but when the puffy silver jacket crosses the street and goes down a set of stairs to an underground parkade, they follow.

"Where the fuck are we going?" Sizz asks behind me, his eyes rolling around the stairwell in search of another drink.

No one responds. Everyone is lost in deep meaningful conversations.

"Yeah guy!" Shane hollers at the girl beside him.

"Can you believe that shit? Guy was totally spun, in the bed next to mine, jerking for ten hours the nurse told me. There was a curtain in between, so I didn't see his dick or nothing, but I could hear all this like grunting and shit..."

Somehow the girl helps him down the stairs and also manages to dodge the spray of saliva that follows his every word. We reach the parkade and surprisingly it is full of cars. Nice cars. Really nice cars. Escalades, Landrovers, Porsches, long black Limos. A wave of oohs and ahhs emits from the group and puffy jacket man does a spin with his arms out as if to say *what...I told you.* Immigrant drivers with little black ties gape at us from behind the steering wheels of some of the vehicles.

What are you guys doing here?

They silently ask, putting down their cell phones and magazines, and I wonder the same about them. Past the cars at the other end of the underground garage, there are five well-dressed bouncer types guarding a remarkably average looking elevator door. They see the mob approaching and speedily form up into a steroid infused wall. One mouths unheard words into his collar, probably calling for backup of some sort.

What is this place?

My curiosity if fully piqued.

We reach the five muscled suits and unfurl. The Armani-wearing giants stare down at us with undisguised revulsion, their chests swelled like emboldened matadors. Puffy jacket struts up to the leader and says.

"Yo man, what's happening?"

The leader, a neck-less bulldog replies with a voice so penetrating and full of rage, it must have been tempered on an anvil.

"Get...The Fuck...Out Of Here!"

"Whoa man...!"

Puffy jacket steps back into the safety of our ranks before continuing.

"Yo man, we just heard there's a party up in this place and wanted to join in on the festivities. You know what I'm saying?"

The bulldog takes a step forward, the veins in his neck bulging.

"It's a private party; now get the *fuck* out of here!"

Fifteen people stand before the bouncers, most of them hard working, hard partying, heavily intoxicated men and even though I'm sure in the sober world none of them would give a shit what a bouncer said to a goofy kid with a fake gold necklace and sideways NY hat, but right now they take it very personally.

A chorus of insults rises from the mouths of the group.

"...Fuck you!..."

"...Fucking prissy looking faggots..."

"...Go suck your buddy's dick..."

"...Roid Monkeys..."

Everyone is yelling out curses, even the chubby angel-face under Shane's arm.

Testosterone rises and the crowd is about to surge forward but the pimply bulldog unbuttons his jacket and reaches for a holstered pistol. His amigos do the same and now we are at gunpoint, and the insults cease. Everyone stumbles back and freezes. Angel-face cries out, two guys in the back start running, one trips and smashes his face on the concrete.

For me, time slows down. Wheels turn, trajectories are calculated.

The sound of an engine roaring.

Pulling up from the right, a pearl white Rolls Royce extended limousine pushes its nose into our ranks, forcing the group back. Mark the Flatlander and a tall blonde with poor posture are nearly hit, but the car has an opulence force field around it that repels us blue-collar serfs.

The backside passenger door opens, and at the same moment a ding rings out behind the bouncers and six more well-tailored goliaths arrive. Five of them join the bulldog as he surreptitiously puts his weapon away. The other one walks over to the Limo and extends his hand to a dazzling Thai woman wearing a crimson ball gown and high heels. Following her is another Asian ravisher, this one wearing a sparkling green gown and a diamond-studded necklace, then a long-limbed African with bouncing curls.

The women walk behind the partition of bouncers towards the elevator door and stop, looking extraordinarily out of place in such an insipid locale. They have the practised arrogance of the constantly desired and not one of them seems to have noticed the motley group of ragtags staring at them. Next out of the car is an older man with thick black hair and a regal face. He was probably a ladykiller in his prime, but too much meat and wine have made his eyes sag and jowls have formed beneath his chin. His manner is of one who sees no man as his equal only servants and inferior adversaries.

Someone close by sucks in a breath.

"Don Swan," they whisper.

Don Swan?

The oil baron struts over to his entourage, giving us an annoyed cursory glance. His green eyes twinkle with anger and his tanned face pulls back into a gentleman's snarl. He looks to his enforcers, and a wordless message is conveyed.

Get rid of this trash.

The last person out of the limousine is a monster. A mountain of a man, bigger than I have ever seen or thought could exist.

How did he fit in the car?

His iron-hard face is painted with elaborate tattoos, and I know who he is before three voices around me utter.

Kraker.

He turns to us with death in his eyes, his gaze lingering on the faces he must recognize as if to say.

Leave...Leave Now...I am not the man you knew...

The limousine door shuts, he turns, taking huge strides and joins his master. They disappear behind stainless steel doors as the elevator closes.

Chapter 7

My body is an emaciated shell. My once youthful muscles have shrivelled with dormancy, my skin has forgotten the face of the sun and looks to be cut from tallow. Inside my sapless chassis, torpid organs and tissues go about the business of living with all the virility of a family of sloths.

How did this happen? How could I let myself become like this? What drove me to abandon my body and let it wither?

Murder...

Hmmmm. Oh yes.

My new nurse arrives to take away my potty tray. He is large, not as big as Marcus but more stout than fat. His face is dark brown and stern, and his shaved head ripples when he looks down and checks my leather restraining straps. He is not afraid of me, although he is wary. I'm sure he was well informed of the attack on Marcus the Giant Marshmallow before being assigned to me, and he is more than diligent with his checks and protocols.

Without saying a word, he goes about his business and exits the room. I am in a new ward of the hospital now. My room has no windows and only the most rudimentary furnishings. I am confined to my bed with four thick brown leather straps that look enormous on my bony ankles and wrists. Two days I have been tied up here, as if I were Hannibal Lecter and could strike out at anyone who comes too close and bite their face off.

Just don't try to drown me and I won't eat your liver. I promise.

For the last couple years, I could have been tied up like this and not given two shits. I was happily lost in the cradle of catatonia, and now that I have been given the gift of awareness again all I want to do is move, walk, run, jump, read, eat, anything. And I can't. All I have is the blank, monochrome roof to look at, and my thoughts to keep me company. It's strange that the next thing to afflict a newly cured crazy person would be boredom, but it is true. I think if by some immaculate intervention, all the patients in the mental wards of the world were suddenly healed, within hours they would relapse just because of the tedium of this existence.

However I have my distractions. Not the least of which is my trusted physician, my recent baptizer and sometimes dominatrix Dr. Christine Lau. Whose flowing ribbons of perfume precede her as she steps into my room. Today she is wearing a grey sweater that folds over her petite frame in a series of triangles. Her pointed nose sits academically on round black nostrils, and her lips are tinted a warm peach colour. As she grabs a chair, her gold watch catches the ugly neon lights from above and somehow transmutes them into angelic rays. Sitting down, she pulls her little notebook out and looks at me with one of her unreadable expressions. I could be a dog she is about to pet or a frog she is preparing to dissect.

"Hello, John. How are you today?" her voice is somehow both clipped and singsong.

"Bored," I grumble, my voice gruff from under use.

"Bored," she replies with trained sympathy. "Well I am sorry for that, but we need to keep you restrained until we are one hundred percent sure you won't attack anyone again. Marcus was quite badly injured."

My eyes narrow.

"Well, as long as no one tries to drown me in a fishbowl, I won't attack anybody."

Dr. Lau nods and begins to scribble in her notebook, as if I just reminded her she needs to pick up shampoo before she goes home tonight.

"I apologize if you we caused you fear, John, but we needed to take a forceful approach to your rehabilitation, and look at the results, we have made huge steps in your recovery."

We lock eyes, and I can see where the weakness lies in Dr. Christine Lau. Pride, vanity, conceit. She solved a puzzle that no one else could and now she takes that success and soaks in it until it crumples her smooth hazel skin.

"Now would you mind if we continued where we left off yesterday?"

She waits patiently for a reply and when I don't give one she continues.

"Okay we are going to close our eyes. I want you to focus on the breath coming in and the breath coming out."

Christine closes her eyes. I watch her chest heave as she takes in breath. My gaze goes up to the curves of her neck and jaw.

"Follow the breath coming in down through the throat, all the way to the Hara and watch as it comes back up. Don't try to change the breath or judge the breath, just let it come into you naturally and let it leave you naturally."

I close my eyes, attempting to quell the fire in my veins. I listen to Christine's voice and pretend that it is someone else's, the Angel perhaps or the Mother, some archetypal woman who can guide me without the taint of seduction.

"Now we are going to add a mantra to our breath, John. With every inhalation, I want you to silently say, So, and then with the exhalation, Hum.

"Soooo...Hummm...Soooo...Hummm."

Christine's words become my thoughts and after a few minutes the outside world begins to fade further and further away. Soon there is only the breath. Nothing else. My body attunes itself; my convoluted thoughts become bubbles rising from a boiling pond.

Sooo...Hummmm...Sooooo...Hummmm...

The water settles and stills. Christine's voice comes to me as through a tunnel.

"According to the sage Patanjali, the stages of liberation are pratyahara, dharana, dhyana and samadhi, full immersion. Today we will attempt to sustain the first three. First pratyahara, the disassociation of consciousness from the outside world, then dharana, concentration on an object and then dhyana, sustained meditation."

My concentration falters as I listen but then Christine picks up the mantra once again.

Soooo...Hummmm...Sooooooo...Hummmmm...

Air comes in through the open cave of my nose and

descends through the core of my being.

Soooooooo

My belly, my hara, my dantien fills and then the breath rises back up.

Hummmmm

This continues until time immemorial.

"What are your first memories of childhood, John?"

The black miasma in front of me swirls into something recognizable.

"Fear," I say.

"Fear from what, John?"

"The old man."

"What is the old man doing, John?"

"I...he is watching, yelling."

"What is he saying, John?"

"I don't know, his...his words are backwards..."

"Do you know who he is?"

"He is the *Krieger!*"

"What is a Krieg –"

"– she is there as well, but he can't see her!"

"Who is she, John?"

"The girl, the girl with the baby."

"Where are you, John? Can you describe what is around you?"

"I am in a wood building...a barn. It is cold, I can see my breath."

"What is happen –"

"– no more talking! They are coming!"

"Who's coming, John?"

"The animals!"

"What animals, John?"

"AAAAAAAAHHHHHH!!"

"Wake up, John! Wake up, it is alright."

I awake to the sound of my own voice screaming.

Dr. Lau is at my side, her smooth palms upon my sweaty cheeks and forehead.

"It's okay, John, you are safe now."

My throat closes and I am left with the thudding of my heart in my ears.

"What happened?" I ask when the panic subsides.

"You were telling me of a past where someone was hurting you." Dr. Lau is still holding my face as if it were a fragile piece of china.

"A past? Like when I was a kid?"

"Perhaps." Christine's voice takes on that self-important tone that all vain intellectuals adopt when talking to an inferior.

"But from what you have told me and what I have learned from studying your sleep patterns."

My sleep patterns?

"I believe you may be experiencing a side effect from the excess of energy in your sixth chakra. You appear to be remembering a past before this life."

"A past before this life?" I repeat, just to make sure I heard my physician properly.

"Yes," she says, releasing my face and walking back to her chair in swift, methodical movements.

"I'm sure you don't know this but sometimes when you are sleeping you speak in a foreign language. I have recorded you on various occasions and done some research. You have spoken many words in Biblical German, which was spoken in southern Germany between the fourteen and sixteen hundreds and also Carinthian German, which was spoken in the eighteen hundreds in modern day Austria."

"What does any of that mean?" I ask, not really believing her.

"Well I think that you are remembering experiences from your incarnations before this one. Past life experiences. Because of the trauma to your lower egos, your upper chakras have opened and you are receiving psychic input that most people cannot."

I stare at Christine's googly eyes and find myself amazed by her quackery.

How is that you can run around vomiting up such fucking nonsense and I am the one in the nuthouse?

"What about my childhood? Why can't I remember anything?"

Her pen begins to scribble again.

"What *do* you remember, John?"

My mouth pulls back into a grimace; she knows this story, we went through it yesterday.

"I remember living downtown on the streets, collecting bottles and picking dumpsters."

"When was this, John?"

Scribble, scribble, scribble.

"I don't know a few years ago, when I fourteen of fifteen maybe."

"How did you get there? Do you remember anything of your family?"

"I don't know. It's like I was born there, no family, no friends, just there. I told you this."

She gives me a manufactured smile.

"I know John, but perhaps there was something we missed."

We...We...there is no We, there is only You and I.

"I was living down by the river, sleeping under a tarp most nights. In the winter I would go down to the Mustard Seed sometimes but usually I just stuck to my own."

"And the park in Radisson Heights, do you remember going there?"

"Yes."

"Do you remember the attack?"

"Yes."

"Can you describe what happened to me?"

"They attacked first!"

"I know, John..."

"They came at me when I was sleeping!"

Christine's thin black eyebrows furrow in understanding.

"I know, John, I know, I have seen the video."

"Video?" I say and it comes back to me.

The cameraman.

"What's on the video?" I ask.

"The entire attack, John. Now..."

"Show it to me." I interrupt.

"I don't think that is a very good idea, John."

My torso rises and the restraints dig into my skin.

"Show it to me."

Christine's authoritarian facade cracks and for a second I see the mask beneath. It is pale and weak and quivering, waiting for someone like me to wrap a collar around it.

"I don't think..."

"Show it to me."

We glare at each other. She reads my face and sees the unwillingness to give in.

If you don't give me what I want, you will never get access to my thoughts again.

And that is all that Christine Lau wants, especially now that I, her little science experiment have begun to bear fruit.

Her head rises the most minute of degrees and sinks down, her hair shifting like silk.

Okay, I'll show you.

Chapter 8

The forest is as still as a graveyard. Nothing moves, nothing breathes. The bloodless hand of winter has settled upon the naked land and coaxed it to sleep with oaths of protection or perhaps more likely, gentle asphyxiation.

The snow is almost thigh deep, and I am exhausted. My breath comes out in giant balls of steam. My pack swings clumsily as my tired legs stumble through the drifts. Around me are the graven torsos of a thousand hibernating trees, scantily clad in pink and purple rays from the setting sun. Darkness is coming quick and I have to make camp, but I want to find somewhere a little more sheltered. Not far ahead, there is an old Grandmother black spruce fallen on her side, exposing a chin high root ball. Good place to throw down a tent.

I trudge over to a flat spot lying in the shadow of the tree, release my pack and start pulling out the contents. With my last pay cheque, I purchased an expensive, ultralight four season tent, a miniscule camping stove, a headlamp, some space-age clothing and a down sleeping bag. The tent is up in minutes and soon I am inside making a bag of freeze-dried lasagne, listening to the thrum of the flame and the nothingness outside.

Not long after the blowout on Rig nine, I went in for an X-ray of my leg at the doctor's request. The results showed that I have a tiny piece of stone still embedded in the back of my shin bone, and there may be some osseous tissue floating around. Because of the angle or the depth or the doctor's ineptitude, whatever the reason I would have to see a specialist and have it removed before I could go back to work. The waiting list for said specialist was at least two months. Two months paid vacation.

Vacation in the asshole of the world.

Because my leg felt fine and my other injuries were healing briskly and also because I despise where I live, I began extending my hikes into the woods, starting with short overnight trips that now have gone on for nearly two weeks. This one has been the longest so far, thirteen days and nights, wandering alone in the brush and muskeg in the depths of winter. With their season ending before new year's, not even the hunters are out. I am truly alone.

The Boreal extends from the Yukon all the way to Labrador, a last gasp of emerald brilliance before the great wasteland of the Tundra begins. In the brusque months of summer it teams with life, chirping birds, bloodthirsty flies, mosquitoes, deer, elk, moose, caribou, small predators, coyotes, foxes, wolverines. The nomadic grizzly and black bears, rabbits and hares, whooping cranes, giant timber wolves and further north, even roaming herds of buffalo.

But now it feels empty. Most of the inhabitants have fled town in search of warmer pastures or locked themselves in little dens where they can sleep and dream of a time when the air didn't try to murder them. That's not to say it truly is empty, on my marches I have crossed paths with white-tail and mule deer and dodged their frozen nuggets of shit, seen the odd rabbit camouflaged in white, heard the chorus of birdsong when the sun comes out and unnervingly at night listened to the howls of roving wolves and coyotes.

The night comes early and stays late. The moon and stars and sometimes the vast shimmering ribbons of the Aurora Borealis have become my close companions. As I step out of my tent, I see all three gazing down at me, watching me devour the one meal I eat a day. One more bagged lasagna and I will be completely out of food, one more night, and I will have to go back to civilization, back to the noise, the dissonance of man.

The food is gone, all too quickly, and I am left hungry but soporifically so. I stand, breathing, listening, watching the hypnotic sway of the treetops in the wind. Small distractions swim my way, little mysteries, questions about the past, strange coincidences but I let them go by, they are not allowed here, this is a place of intuition not intellect, feeling not thinking. My hand strays to the old bonnet I keep in my pocket, but I pull it away.

Keep your focus here, in this moment.

The minutes pass. The treetops sway, the forest sleeps.

Soon I am too tired and cold to stay outside anymore, and I retreat to the relative warmth of my overpriced tent and slippery sleeping bag.

Sleep comes here with more ease and acceptance than anywhere I can remember. My nightmares have been extradited, and in their place a warm, calm void has been erected.

Tonight, however, the paradisal vacuum must have sprung a leak. The barren screen cracks and bleeds. I am the prisoner of a hundred terrible images, the old man and his soulless eyes, the crying girl in the darkness, the burning derrick engulfed in flame, thin sheets of burnt skin peeling off of my own back, Putu's battered face. Maggie, her pale Son telling my about black orchids, the gaping maw of the tweaker, Don Swan, Kraker's twisted tattoos, Henry Yellowbird's lapidarian profile. All of it swirling like a cyclone until I can take no more and must run back to consciousness.

Rise.

A strange flapping sound near my feet is the first thing I notice. Then the angry whips of cold lashing my face. Flipping on my headlamp I see the cause.

The tent has been slashed.

Ragged strips have been torn into the thick poly-urethane wall, leaving a six inch hole. I hop quickly out of the sleeping bag and grab the large antler-handled hunting knife from my sack. RJ's knife. Outside I hear snow crunching under padded feet, cautious movements. Then more footsteps further to my left and a slow sullen growl, too cryptic to be a coyote's.

Wolves.

I turn the headlamp off and spin around. With two quick slashes, I cut another hole behind me and roll out of the tent. Because of the temperature I sleep fully clothed but not with my boots on and my stocking feet sink into the dry wetness as I stand up. To my right is the wall of frozen dirt and roots, to my left three sets of razor-sharp teeth. Timber-wolves, two white and one charcoal black, the size of Tibetan Mastiffs.

These are bison-killers, powerful enough to take down a full grown bull buffalo or moose. As my eyes adjust, I see the black one must be the Alpha. He is in the lead, the other two trailing him like ghosts. I inch my way backward, steadying my breath, preparing for the attack. All three of them, six sets of glowing eyes, are trained on me, my perceived weak points.

When wolves are chasing big game like Elk or Bison, they bite chunks of flesh from the animal's soft perineum region, causing massive blood loss. Usually three good chomps and their prey can no longer fend off the rest of the attack.

An ache runs through my shrunken testes as I envision this. That has to be the worst way to die, having your ass and balls torn apart by a pack of wolves. But this trio won't go for the soft tissue of my nether regions; to them my whole body is soft tissue, weakened by evolution and central heating.

The black leader is snapping and growling, the fur of his back spiked like porcupine quills. On his flanks, the acolytes are strangely quiet and reserved as if content to watch for now. My breath becomes as still as a sleeping baby's. Perception expands and snaps back inside out. The giant black Alpha leaps forward, his jaw loosened and ready to clamp down on my throat. The hunting knife is moving, I am moving, it thrusts out tip first as my legs propel my torso right. My face comes within millimeters of being consumed, then I am on my knees, my right arm extended, the blade of RJ's knife buried hilt deep in the neck of the wolf, whose twitching body lays sprawled on the snow.

I quickly retract the blade, noticing a tear in my jacket above my forearm and a dull pain beneath. Swivelling I prepare for the other two, the ashen twins, but they have not moved. In fact, they appear to be molded in place, two identical statues, silently watching, *witnessing*.

Perhaps I had it wrong, maybe they are the leaders here, the King and Queen, Osiris and Isis, brother and sister. And the steaming black heap was their enforcer, maybe their only son, their Horus.

The three of us stare at each other for what seems like an eternity, my eyes darting between their calm imperial faces and indecipherable carmine eyes.

Red in white.

Beside me, blood from the dead wolf's neck has begun to pool and sink into the melting snow.

White in red.

The moment passes, as it must and the white ghosts turn from the murder scene and nervelessly slip into the folds of the forest. The corpse beside me has stopped quivering and I am once again left alone, but the silence no longer fills me with peace, it fills me with something sickening and tragic. My heart breaks under the weight of my own existence. Life is a game I have never understood, and it fills me with disgust and rage. I look to my fallen opponent and see myself.

That will be me one day.

But not today.

Despair above all other emotions can be the most damaging. It is not the heat of love or betrayal, but the insufferable frigidity that follows and, therefore, it must be purged as quickly as possible, lest we lose the will to stand up, to put on our boots, to continue existing.

On a surge of instinct, I decide I will take the dead wolf with me. Day is still hours away, but the idea of sleeping seems laughable. I pull apart my ruined tent and build a make-shift stretcher for the wolf's body. If it were a deer I killed I would eviscerate the body right now so the meat didn't contaminate, but I don't want to eat this kill. I don't know what I want to do with it, I just feel compelled to take it with me. So I roll it on to the litter, grab my gear and start the long journey back to reality.

***

"Jesus Fucking Christ guy, is that a wolf?"

The Youngblood's eyes are as wide and round as a cartoon characters.

Using my new cell phone I gave him a call when I reached the forest's edge. An hour later he arrived in his freshly purchased extended cab Ford F-250 with five inch lift kit and chrome bumper. The machine is so big, Shane looks like an infant when jumps down from the driver's seat. Now he can finally call himself a true Albertan.

"You know where we can take this?" I ask him as he comes closer, gaping at the hulking creature.

"Fuck man. I don't know, what do you want to do with it? Like stuff it or something?"

"No, no. I just didn't want to leave it in the forest to rot."

Shane scratches his wiry moustache.

"Well I know Henry uses wolf bones and shit for medicine sometimes, he'd probably take it."

Henry Yellowbird, good I wanted a reason to see him again.

"Alright then," I say, pulling down the tailgate.

"So like what the fuck happened here?"

"Here give me a hand." I motion to the back legs which are facing the road while I walk around to the forepaws.

"Did you shoot this thing or something?"

"Alright, one, two...Lift!" With a solid heave, we get the beast off the ground.

"Holy crap guy, this thing is heavy!"

A few awkward steps later we are at the tailgate, and I am sure the Youngblood is regretting buying such a stupidly high truck. One more heave and the wolf is in the box. Shane pushes up the tailgate and looks to me, pain on his face.

His shoulder!

How could I have forgotten?

"You alright?" I ask, feeling like an ass. Shane is one of those rare kinds of humans who would do pretty much anything you asked him, even if he killed himself in the process.

"Oh yeah man, no problem," he says, but his face tells a different story.

Really looking at him for a moment, I see something else on his face, something beneath the pain. A thin film of shame and distress, unease.

It's a look I've seen a lot of in this town.

You better get a handle on those drugs my friend, before they get a handle on you.

As if reading my thoughts, he slinks from my gaze and climbs up into his idling behemoth.

"Alright guy, let's motor."

***

Henry Yellowbird's tanned face looks to be made of carved stone. Long, graven lines stretch across his skin as if he'd been whittled by a river for a thousand years. His every wrinkle seems to hide a story. And when you think you have counted them all, the folded pages of the medicine man's past, he moves or changes expression and a dozen more appear from nowhere.

"Wolf eh?" He says to no one in particular.

We are behind Shane's parked monstrosity, looking at the dead canine. The rheumy eyed collie is at my feet, trying to see with its nose what its eyes can no longer distinguish.

Death.

That is what you smell old boy.

"Yeah, yeah. Johnnie, took him down in the forest up north," Shane replies excitedly.

"Hmmmm..."

Henry murmurs, as though he were not in the least bit surprised. He moves closer to the tailgate and puts a respectful hand on the wolf's head. His strong hands pull open its mouth to reveal the deadly razors inside, set in blue-black gums. After a quick examination, he flips open the animal's eyelids, unveiling dead black on black eyes and for a frightening instant I see my reflection in their depths.

Remember brother, the soul of the fallen lingers on the blade of the victor.

Then it is gone.

Apparently finished his inspection, Henry releases his grip and the dead eye's fury is extinguished.

"Shane, in the back of the barn there's a wheel barrow, would you mind grabbing it for us, Son?"

The Youngblood turns and saunters off down the stone path past the driveway. Henry and I are left alone. His smoke-filled gaze turns to me as he says.

"This is a noble creature. Very strong, very powerful, very

78

ancient. I've never known anyone to get close enough to kill one with a knife before."

Henry waits for me to respond and when I do not he says.

"My ancestors believed that when a man separates a creature's soul from its body, the body goes back to the land, to the Great Grandmothers and Grandfathers, but the soul needs more time. The soul is denser than the flesh, you see, and it takes longer to unwind, and breakdown, it is different when an animal dies of old age, its soul is ready to disperse like a plant gone to seed, but when it has been separated early the soul sticks around for a while and sometimes..."

Henry licks his cracked lips.

"...If there is one nearby who is similar in nature, the soul will bind itself to the soul of another."

I've heard superstitions before, but the way the old man tells it I could almost believe. He leans in close and whispers conspiratorially.

"The soul of the fallen lingers on the blade of the victor."

Shane arrives with the wheel barrow and I feel a state of madness approaching.

Didn't I just think that?

"So what do you think Henry?" Shane huffs. "Can you use some of this thing?"

Henry turns and his long white hair trails behind him.

"Oh yeah, yeah, I think so little brother. There's a lot of medicine to be found in the body of a wolf. The liver can get rid of migraines and edema, the teeth can be worn to ward off evil spirits, the tongue can cure epilepsy. And even the hipbone can be ground down and used to treat addiction."

These last words make Shane uneasy, and he shifts on his feet. It seems the old man truly doesn't miss much. I pull the beast towards me and lower it down on to the wheel barrow. Henry decides he'll hang the carcass in the barn; there he'll perform a ceremony to send its soul onward.

If it's not inside me already.

And then set about removing the usable organs and bones and tissues.

As I lift the wooden handles and start following him down to the barn, Shane's cell phone rings. He stays at the truck as

79

Henry and I descend the snow-laden path, the old collie following and sniffing.

We reach the faded shiplap barn and go inside. The smell of stale hay and dust sucks the moisture from my nose, and for some reason it seems colder in here than it does outside. There is a stainless steel table in the corner and that is where Henry asks me to drop the carcass. I reach underneath the furry black torso, and suddenly my mind's eye fills with a vision of the two white ghosts. Isis and Osiris, who watched their only Son die.

Once the wolf is on the table, Henry puts a hand on my shoulder in an unexpected show of emotion.

"I heard what you did for Shane and those boys on the rig," he says. "How you saved them. Shane told me if it wasn't for you, he and the Asian boy wouldn't have made it out alive. I want to thank you; Shane has always been like a grandson to me, especially after his parents died."

The medicine man looks at me with an expectant smile, waiting for some sign of recognition, some word or look, but my guard does not want to drop. Something about this man puts me in the defensive, yet I know if I am to make any headway I need to give in, even just a little.

"You're welcome," I say slowly, mechanically.

Loosen, like the reed in the wind.

Henry's fissured face brightens. It seems those two words or perhaps the actions that preceded them have changed the old man's opinion of me.

"John." He begins and for some bizarre reason the sound of my name coming from his lips fills my heart with warmth. And for some even more bizarre reason that little spark of warmth makes me angry.

"What do you remember from your past?"

What do I remember from my past?

A lost mouse runs over my boot, and my ears start to burn. The stale air of the barn clogs in the back of my throat.

"What do you mean?" I croak.

"Your childhood, do you remember it?"

Childhood.

The air grows thicker, and my hand involuntarily reaches

for the bonnet I keep in my pocket. The wolf's lips pull back into a toothy smirk.

"No, I don't."

There's no point in lying.

"Do you remember Maggie?"

My ribcage is a stampede of thundering hooves. The wolf begins to laugh.

"No...But I recognize her from..."

...The face in the shadows...

"...Somewhere."

"She told me about you, how she saw you on the street. She remembers you from a long time ago, when you were both children."

The thunder increases, my ears are on fire. It feels as if I am back on the burning derrick.

"She does?"

"She does."

"What did she tell you?"

The old man shifts his weight backwards.

"I think." He replies softly. "I think it would be better if she told you herself."

My muscles stiffen and for an instant I am beating the answers out of the old man.

"Tomorrow, if you come again, you two can meet and speak."

The black Alpha grins at me through his death-head.

Cleave the meat from my chest. Never let me sleep, never let me rest.

I nod.

Tomorrow.

***

"I read a story about you."

The girl in the Slayer shirt is back at my doorway.

Remember, always close the door!

"Yeah. It said you saved two guys on a Swancor rig."

Don Fucking Swan Man.

"It said that the rig was on fire, and you saved an Indian guy and some guy from Polynesia or somewhere."

Past the trilling notes of the girls' voice, I hear the

familiar sounds of men yelling at the TV. UFC Night.

"Was it scary?" she asks.

The girl is leaning on the doorframe, her grey stretchy pants outlining firm shapely legs. She is barefoot, her toes painted a garish red. Her brown hair is streaked with blonde and her blank, but attractive face is painted up with too much lipstick and mascara.

I've been waiting for you.

Even a thimbleful of fame can make a face as ugly as mine appear suddenly fuckable.

"I don't remember," I say, continuing to fold my freshly cleaned clothes. As I snap a pair of jeans, the old polka-dot rag, the bonnet falls on to the bed and the day's events come flashing back.

Tomorrow. Maggie.

"What's that?" The girl asks, her head swooping forward, mannequin eyes glistening.

"Nothing."

And the piece of fabric is gone, back in my pocket.

"You don't remember if it was scary?" She asks, petulant lips all a quiver.

"No," I say. "I don't remember."

In the living room, the cacophony rises to unbearable heights.

Fuck this! Fuck that!

Idiots yelling just to hear their own voices. The silence of the forest seems a lifetime ago.

The girl is rambling, finger twirling her streaked hair.

Something about this one time. Something about being afraid. Something about not having a boyfriend anymore.

My meager pile of clothes is folded. My head is full of crap.

This is reality, this is humanity.

Dissonance.

I decide to go out for a walk even though it is getting close to midnight and I am utterly worn out. I brush past the girl with the tight stretchy pants. She asks where I am going, her breath a bouquet of fake raspberries, and in my tired state I am tempted to stay but I continue on, mumbling something about needing some air. The energy in the living room is livid and asphyxiation purple. Florescent television light bounces off a dozen rabid faces. I throw on my jacket unnoticed; head downstairs and out the door. The night welcomes me back with a frigid embrace and I am already regretting not grabbing my vest. Ce la vie. Onward and outward.

If I turn right on to the street out front, I will eventually make my way downtown. I turn left. The thought of downtown Fort Mckenzie at midnight on a Saturday makes me want to retch. I walk to the end of the cul-de-sac and turn down a narrow footpath. Once through I find another set of twenty year old duplexes, same as on my street. A few are lit up, but most are cloaked in darkness.

Watching, witnessing.

I move briskly trying to build some heat in my legs. The clear night sky above retains no warmth, the stars too far away and the sun on the other side of the world. Is it bright and sunny in China? I wonder. Then I wonder, not for the first time. What the fuck am I doing here?

The cash my man.

The cash has been gotten. I have enough money in the bank to start a new life somewhere where the average person's life doesn't revolve around the size of their truck, their wallet or their girlfriend's tits.

The answers my man, the answers.

The answers. Maybe I'm not supposed to know the answers. Maybe I am just better off burying the past forever and jumping on a bus outta this shithole. Maybe I can find a place that will put my faith back into humanity. Maybe I'll go to BC and find me a hippie commune, start smoking weed and growing carrots. Live in a teepee with some hairy bushwoman picking mushrooms and wiping my ass with a crystal.

Maybe.

Maybe after tomorrow.

All of a sudden I am lost. Too many twists and turns and I am walking the back alley of some pretty seedy looking houses, more than a few wearing plywood bandages. The air is painfully still, and only the barking of a distant dog cuts the quietness. From around the next turn, I hear movement, voices, feet slipping on ice, a cry of pain. I trot forward to see what is happening, and before I make it to the corner two wide-eyed derelicts appear and almost run into me. The scraggly duo, one man and one oddly familiar woman come to a skidding halt as they see me. Their pockmarked faces, white-washed in fear tremble like aspens.

"You!" the woman says, and I suddenly remember her.

The tweaker from the street.

Don Fucking Swan Man.

The man's giant pupils dance between us. Past the sound of their heaving breathes, I hear the screech of tires and the man starts running.

"Let's go, Misty!" he yells as he passes me.

"C'mon man!" Misty the Tweaker cries, taking my hand and then we are off, running down the blind alleyway.

We race to the end, take a left, run another hundred metres and then cut through a snow-filled backyard, somehow ending up in another back alley.

Where are the fronts of these houses?

The crazy junkies are running for their lives, and I am running for hell of it. It reminds me of an old joke about swimming.

Sometimes you do it for fun, and sometimes you do it, so you don't die.

The ramshackle houses give way to a new development. Half finished buildings in various degrees of completion stand in a row. The man slips in his mismatched cowboy boots and falls into a pile of coiled weeping tile. Writhing frantically, as if he were an Amazonian native caught in the clutches of an anaconda he works his way out, as Misty runs to his aid. A smile cracks my lips as I watch their tribulations. This is the most fun I have had in a while.

I should hang out with these freaky drug addicts more often.

The mismatched cowboy, who I think is called Russ, gets to his feet, and we are running again. Eventually we reach their destination, an inconspicuous two-storey, and Russ helps Misty through an open window into a gravel basement. Once she is through, I grab Russ by the forearms and let him down.

"Thanks man," he whispers, looking into my face and seeing an ally.

Once he is down, I hop the eight feet to the gravel floor. Surprisingly, there are two more people in the basement. Two men, one tall and rail-thin, the other spouting a wild mane of hair. They run over, obviously familiar with Misty and Russ. Frantic whispers abound. The four meth-heads hushed speech is so fast I feel as if I am watching a ping-pong game.

"...You lose 'em? Where's Cholo?"

"...Fucking Higgins man!...It was him!"

"...Back at Neighbours..."

"...Gone man, gone man..."

"...They were looking for you Misty!..."

"...Busted right through the door..."

"...A black van...Two of them..."

The dark basement fills with light and the talking ceases. A large vehicle is outside, and I hear the slamming of doors. The four ghoulish faces shrink with untold fear. Misty looks at me and puts a tobacco stained finger to her lips.

Shhhhhh.

Oxygen is galloping through my bloodstream. Who could be out there? What has these idiots so afraid? Other junkies they stole from? Bikers they owe money to? Maybe it's RJ and his friends? It seems the town's state of hostility has infected me. All I want to do is fight, purge, destroy. The evening's previous lethargy is gone in a whirlwind of primal energy.

More lights appear as another vehicle arrives at the front of the building, shining through two glassless window holes. The tweakers huddle together and the pungent scent of shit tickles my frozen nose.

Jesus, they are afraid.

Two more doors closing, two more sets of footsteps. The colourless beams of flashlights appear, swinging back and forth. I feel as if I am in a Nazi concentration camp. The tweakers shiver until it seems they will shatter. But I am not afraid, not even nervous anymore. My heart rate is falling fast, my Swara switching from Pingala back to Ida. Drug dealers and rival junkies don't carry flashlights, especially long black Maglite flashlights. Only the...

"Police!"

...Do.

"This is the police, we know you are in there."

The meth-head to my left, the tall scarecrow, starts to babble feverishly.

"Oh man, oh god, oh fuck, fucking fuck shit man..."

The other three take up the chant, glancing back and forth from the lights at the front of the house to the ones in the back. The voice from the front, leather-tough and authoritarian barks out a command to the officers at the back of the house.

"Stay put, watch the windows."

All exits are covered.

Trapped.

But I don't understand the panic. The four musketeers are literally about to explode with terror. What could they possibly have done to cause such a fear of retribution? Murder? Robbery? Rape? They look about as dangerous as a warren of rabbits, but drugs make people do crazy shit. Maybe they kidnapped some kids and started a dead baby puppet show?

The RC's have entered the building. The subfloor rattles with boot fall and the joists sprinkle fairy dust into the yellow air. The only way down is a set of floating stairs that hang a few inches above the gravel. The stairs are facing away from us, the yet to be built landing obstructed from view. The footsteps continue, dust dances in the headlights. They reach the top of the stairs.

Misty grabs me with feral strength.

"You gotta help us man, you gotta man!"

I give her a sympathetic look. There's nothing I can do, whatever crime they committed I'm not the one who is going to save them.

Call your lawyer.

In fact, I might have to call one myself just for being caught with these wackadoos.

"It's them man, it's Higgins!"

"They are going to take us man, we ain't never coming back!"

The searching flashlights have reached downstairs. The tall scarecrow loses his nerve and runs to one of the lower window frames. After a couple tries, he is up and through. The lights in the backyard swivel, two voices call out. Then he is falling, something has hit him in the back.

Taser.

Two people run over.

As this happens, two more dark figures arrive in the basement, their features indistinguishable behind the blaze of their flashlights. My eyes narrow. A slow comforting voice resonates from the shadow on the left.

"You know why we are here, just come along peacefully."

The scarecrow outside lets out a groan as the backyard cops come to pick him up. I think of the flying monkeys in the Wizard of Oz.

The cops draw nearer. Misty's fingernails dig into my flesh.

A pile of scrap wood is nearby; stupidly Russ begins to move towards it, his entire skeleton shaking. A hiss of compressed air comes from one of the approaching shadows. Two tiny electrically charged harpoons fly through the air.

Could I catch them?

Suppressing the urge, I watch as the electrodes hit Russ in the throat. Misty cries out, leaping towards him. Another set of metal darts fly by catching her in the chest. Now, only crazy hair and I are still standing. The wraith-like figures approach, their weapons trained on us.

"Put up your hands!" The one on the left says in a smooth voice.

We do. And reality sets back in.

What if they hold me past tomorrow?? What about Maggie?

They come closer and their faces become visible. The one on the right is your typical asshole cop. Buzzed head, self-righteous expression, cauliflower ears from his wrestling days back in college where he would put on tights and grind away those homo-erotic tendencies. The one on the left, the radio voice, is a black man with flared nostrils. A gap in his front teeth reveals a bright red Bolshevik tongue, twisting like a serpent in a cage. His eyes are exuberant.

I just love tasering these Meth-heads, he he he.

A name tag on his chest announces. Higgins. Officer Higgins. Constable Higgins of The Royal Canadian Mounted Police.

His twinkling pupils lock with mine and for a brief second I can see what lies beneath.

Poison.

Then I am in handcuffs. The cowardly lion is in handcuffs, so is the Tinman and Dorothy.

Hot, sour breath is on my neck as cauliflower ears grunts.

"And who are you pretty boy?"

The other two RC's show and the four of them drag us upstairs. I let myself be taken, even though every inch of me wants to revolt. There's no other option at this point. Better to wait, maybe a better opportunity to escape will present itself.

Escape. I should have done that a long time ago, when I had the chance but I didn't think the tweaker's fears were valid. What could the police do? Throw me in a cell, ask some questions, realize I am not part of this drug-addled posse and let me go. But now I know, these are not chubby donut eaters, here to serve and protect, these are hunters and we the fallen prey.

***

More than an hour has passed since being thrown in a black unmarked van with Russ and Misty. Scarecrow and crazy hair were taken in another black van, with no windows or police markings whatsoever. If we were going to the police station we would have been there a long time ago. A part of me thinks I should have just stayed home and gotten better acquainted with raspberry lip gloss girl but another part is fully intrigued, awake, alive, waiting to see what will happen next.

Another hour passes. The interior of the vehicle is pitch black and the only sounds are the tires on pavement and the heavy breathes from the other two prisoners. Misty's haggard voice is repeating over and over.

"...shipped out man...fghhh...we're shipped out..."

Russ seems to be asleep.

We pull to a stop. Muffled voices.

The opening of a gate?

The van is moving again, another twenty minutes. We take a few turns and the van tilts forward as if driving into an underground parking garage. A loud thump emits from the ground as Russ falls off of his seat. A few more minutes, we stop and stale florescent light spills in as the doors part. Two figures approach.

Isis? Osiris?

Strong hands reach out and put a cloth bag over my head, sinking me back into darkness. I am pulled out of the van, Misty and Russ following. I hear the approach of the two other tweakers; the cowardly lion is crying and making awful honking noises. Something hard hits me in the kidney as I am prodded forward. Rage begins to surface.

A few more steps and we are in an elevator. Bodies press in tight, chests heave with heavy exhalations. Russ is imploring the cops to please let us go but they remain silent. I picture them behind us, simpering faces flush with excitement.

I've never ridden in an elevator blindfolded before. The feeling of descent is much more noticeable. If I were to guess, I would say we were flying down to the centre of the earth, maybe to the pits of hell. Crazy hair honks a little too loudly and gets a knock from one of the cops. This just intensifies his squalling.

"Shut the fuck up!"

Ding!

We have reached our destination. The hand around my biceps tightens and I am thrust forward once again. Boots echo on hard flooring. After ten feet we stop, a new voice rings out, a woman's.

"Mr. Higgins," she says in greeting.

"Ms. Hutchinson," he responds.

"Gentlemen. What have we here? New recruits?"

"I guess you could call them that." Higgins laughs.

"Have they all had background checks done?"

"All of them except this one." A hand goes into my pocket and my wallet is taken.

"Thank you. Alright I'll look into this and...Is that a woman?"

"Yeah, we had..."

"Please!" Misty interrupts. "Please man, please man, let us go, we didn't do nothing!"

Her words become muffled as something is pushed into her mouth.

"We should have ball-gagged these fucks," Cauliflower ears says.

Higgins continues.

"We had to take her in, she witnessed another pick up a few weeks back and got away. We've been looking for her ever since. Can you use her anywhere? Maybe in one of the executive suites?" He laughs and then she is laughing. The other cops start laughing. The shit in Scarecrow's underwear is laughing.

"Yeah, right," Ms. Hutchinson says, when the chuckles have subsided. "No we'll figure something out, maybe with the Bestiarius. Just put her in number four, the others can be taken to number six. Two new combatants just arrived from Russia yesterday and Mr. Kraker."

Kraker?

"Wants to see them in action before the games."

"Tonight?"

"This morning."

"Yeah, yeah."

"Yes, now that we have some extras."

"Well, we might as well stick around for a bit boys."

The other cops murmur their approval.

"Go right ahead Mr. Higgins; just get them penned up quick, so I can get started on this check."

"Yes maam," Higgins says and we start to move again.

***

The holding cell is a dimly lit stainless steel box, big enough to hold twenty men. The walls are twelve feet high with recessed lights, impossible to reach. The floor is black and made of some kind of epoxy, hard as iron. The only things breaking the monotony are two prison toilets and a half a dozen drains set in the floor.

An easy room to hose down.

I settle against a smooth, cold wall and try centre myself. In the gloom, the tweakers are pacing, lost in various states of anxiety. Russ comes to me and begins telling me the details of what Misty told him about the last raid.

"They took Cobb and my buddy Buck, a fucking hell-cock if there ever was one."

Beneath his chin is a distended lesion, long as an eyebrow, dancing hypnotically as he speaks.

"Misty told me they got 'em at the Regent, the hotel on Bremley Street."

The voice of the comic book kid, Maggie's son Jake, comes back to me.

"My friend Kade says that all the druggies live in the old hotel on Bremley street. They stay up all night doing drugs and fighting each other like in Fight Club. And that the ones who lose, get taken out to the oilsands and buried, and no one ever finds them."

"She told me she hid beneath a bench in one of the old booths in the restaurant."

The lesion squirms like a worm under a child's thumb.

"And he says they get these scabs from doing all their drugs, because they think there is bugs on them. And when they die in the fights. The scabs turn black and get big and if you eat them you get magic powers. You can become a superhero."

Russ and his mismatched cowboy boots continue to speak. The giant meth-scab dances provocatively.

If you died right now, would that thing turn black?

Black Orchid. The scabs, the black scabs, they should be called Black Orchids.

The tweakers race to a corner as the door of our holding pen opens. Six men file in wearing dark uniforms and carrying vicious looking metal rods. Surprisingly, Russ doesn't scurry away. He holds his ground and says.

"Where's Misty? Where's my friend?"

The leader comes forward; close enough for his face to become visible. Beneath a slick of greasy hair and acne ridden skin, his eyes throb like hemorrhoids.

I know you, the bouncer from the parking garage.

"Those two," he points to Russ and me.

The five henchmen come and grab us and haul us outside. I get a brief glimpse of the scarecrow, his confused mouth stuck somewhere between trepidation and relief. Russ spits curses as I look in wonder at the hallway we are being dragged through. Above us are giant obsidian archways, twenty five feet high, cut from giant blocks of granite. Walls adorned with plant-shaped lanterns made from brushed copper illuminate our path with languid, orphic light. Beside them, carved in immaculate detail are long pale bas-relief sculptures depicting all manner of depravity. Man fighting beast. Man fighting man. Fat cherubs gazing down upon a rolling orgy of sex, murder and cannibalism.

We reach a circular landing, its magnificence potentiated by a massive copper dome that sings our every footstep. From here we turn right and the floor becomes soft and invisibly black.

Sand?

The lights die away and only a checkered shadow is visible in the distance. As we approach I recognize its shape, it looks to be a portcullis, the giant iron gate at the entrance of a castle. Beyond it is a white brilliance. The angry bulldog yells out a command and the gate starts to lift. The guards yank us to a stop and take off our handcuffs. Once free, they toss us forward and the bulldog growls.

"Good luck."

Russ's head is in front of me, a black ball bobbing in an ocean of luminance. We pass under the portcullis and my pupils start to shrink, shapes become visible.

Two shapes.

Human shapes, moving towards us.

Two men with murder in their eyes.

Chapter 9

Turn down the lights. Grab the popcorn, take your seats. The show is about to begin.

Dr. Lau places the laptop down on the padded bench, in the exact spot where only days before she tried to drown me. The shattered aquarium and its entrails have been swept away, and there is no evidence of any prior shenanigans.

I am sitting in a plastic chair, unrestrained. Christine declared, after yesterdays interview that I was no longer a threat to the security of the hospital personnel. I'm sure the rest of the staff weren't quite of the same opinion, since I turned Nurse Marcus's face into mincemeat, but I'm sure they would be a little more sympathetic if they knew the circumstances.

Christine fiddles with the computer until a blurred, frozen countenance fills the screen. She turns to me, and her face resembles a reluctant school teachers.

"Are you sure you want to see this, John?" she asks, her lips pressed tight into a thin line.

I answer without thinking.

"Yes."

"You are in a fragile state, reliving those violent moments could trigger a regression to your previous stupor."

My gaze is glued to the screen.

I am already reliving those violent moments.

She moves in front of me and gives me a look of concern. It is the first real, genuine expression of worry I have seen on her little Asian face since I have met her.

Are you certain?

I look up at her, my cheeks flush with fire.

"I need to see it."

She moves aside and clicks on the play button. The outside world fades to black and the computer screen wraps around me like a blanket.

I watch as the smeared face comes to life. It is the

cameraman, he has the camera turned round on himself and the electronic light makes his pale skin shine. His chin juts forward and nearly takes up the whole screen.

"M to Tha C!" he announces.

"M to Tha C, with my homie Alpha B!"

Another face enters the screen. It is the kid with the red sweater, a bottle of malt beer in his hand. His eyes tighten as if he were a supermodel as he repeats.

"Alpha B!"

The camera spins around and focuses on someone else.

"With Mugsy!"

Mugsy does his best Gangsta impression and belts out a baritone, Oh Yeah. His arms swing like poplar twigs, and I wonder his parents call him? Scott maybe, or Darren or fucking Melhouse. Whatever it is, it's not Mugsy.

Beside him is a wiry Vietnamese thug, with venom in his eyes.

"And my boy E Lan."

E Lan folds his finger into some kind of gang sign as another Asian enters the screen and does the same.

"And Muthafucking Taks!"

Taks is almost identical to E Lan, except his eyebrows are pierced with silver barbells. Behind them, the landscape is urban and dark. The light of the streetlamps fan the pavement with amber rays, it looks to be midsummer.

The camera spins back to M to Tha C.

"This is a Bottle Topz production, we's like to call taking out the trash!"

He puts the camera down, and the five thugs gather in a line, posing. Alpha B holds up his forty like it were his standard.

Bottle Topz!

M to Tha C lopes back to the camera, and the platoon marches down the alleyway. In less than a minute, they reach a small park. The air is silent except for the cameraman's heavy breathing and the excited whispers of the thugs in front of him. They gather beside the jungle gym and point to something nearby. The camera turns and I see myself, lying in a dark heap on a wooden bench.

The camera turns back, and I see the scared, laughing faces of the Bottle Topz crew. Only the tall Vietnamese kid, E Lan, looks to be unafraid. For an instant, I am looking into his face as if it were right in front of me, right here, right now.

Dead. They're all dead.

I am watching corpses.

The posse quickly irons out the details of their attack and Mugsy, all one hundred and thirty pounds of him takes a half dozen steps forward and yells.

"Wake up Muthafucka!"

This is where my memories begin.

A loud noise, people nearby.

As I sit up, Alpha B races forward and tosses his empty beer bottle. It smashes into my forehead with a sickening thump.

Stars! A Constellation of Stars!

They brandish their weapons, whooping and whistling. E Lan swings his baseball bat. The impact sends me sprawling onto the ground.

"Yeah you fucking dumpster digger! Huh, Huh! What the fuck you say? You do you! I'll do me muthafucka! You do you!"

Taks is next, lifting a steel pipe over his head and bringing it down hard on my back. My unconscious form makes no sound. Laughing hysterically, he jumps to the side as Alpha B steps forward and kicks me square in the face.

Andromeda... Pegasus.

The posse turn to each other, laughing and clapping each other on the shoulders.

"Yo yo yo, muthafucking Bottle Topz." Mugsy says into the camera, waving his bat with a flourish.

"This is how we be, this is how we do, we takes out the trash, you know what I am saying!"

"Mugsy! Mugsy!" his friends holler.

He steps over to me and looks down in disgust. I am in a heap; face down, an old faded black raincoat wrapped around my thin frame. My hair is long and scraggly, a dead raven clinging to my skull. I am a homeless teenager, sad and pitiful looking.

95

Mugsy arcs his leg back and kicks me in the ribs. Nothing, I don't move.

The night sky turns to black. Andromeda and Pegasus fade.

He kicks again and again. His smooth, baby face giggling with every impact.

On the ground and the pain is extreme. Glass in my lungs.

Mugsy steps back as M to Tha C runs up and punts me in the back for good measure. The camera jiggles happily. The others encircle and finally the levee breaks, all five of them begin to stomp and dance as if I were on fire.

Aaaaaaagghhhhhh! The pain turns to rage!

A high pitched wail, so unnatural and ear-splitting it causes everyone to jump back, fills the air. When it stops, the group looks to one another, not sure of what to do next.

"What the fuck man?!" M to Tha C says from behind the camera.

Mugsy steps forward and lifts his bat in a poke.

Die Motherfucker! Die Motherfucker! Die!

I spin from my position, with such speed, the camera catches only a blur. The bat disappears from Mugsy's hand, and I sink my teeth into his cheek. He screams and tries to pull away, the skin of his face peeling like a banana. The others drop their weapons and reach to pull him free, but my grip is firm, my centre of gravity low. My left hand pulls back and shoots forward with so much force it pierces the flesh of his neck. I do it again until his Adams apple is in my hand and blood is filling my mouth. His eyes bulge, and his tongue tries to leap from his gullet.

The rest of the Bottle Topz gang pull again, and I let Mugsy go. Taks and Alpha B fall on to their asses and horror fills their faces as they see the pulsing wound in the boys's throat. E Lan is not so squeamish and goes on the offensive. He reaches into his pocket for something, a blade perhaps, but I am already on him, biting and clawing. A piece of Mugsy's larynx is still in my hand, so I shove it into the Vietnamese kid's mouth as he calls out for help. A piece of rebar comes flying, but I see it and roll on to my side, taking E Lan with me. The rusty metal clips the back of his head, knocking him unconscious. We roll again, and I jump to my feet.

M to Tha C is screaming.

"Get him, get him!"

He is still holding the camera, perhaps believing that if he keeps things two dimensional he'll remain safe. Alpha B has the rebar in his hands and is preparing for another strike. Taks is beside him looking terrified. Alpha B swings, I sidestep it easily and yank the metal from his hands. Continuing in a spiral, I bring the rebar down in a slashing motion that hits him in the temple, causing a spray of red that matches his shirt. He drops to the ground, and I sink into a low stance.

My face is a morbid display. Streaks of blood fan above my eyebrows. The tattered raincoat hangs down to my heels, turning me into a caped villain. My eyes reflect a soul gone fanatic.

Both Taks and M to Tha C lose the scant remains of their nerve and decide to run. The camera falls to the ground and lands facing the battle scene with the prostrated Alpha B at the forefront and E Lan visible beyond him. I disappear in pursuit, and only the horrible sounds of the two last survivors being butchered can be heard.

The camera shows none of this, but in my mind's eye I witness it all. Taks was next, a piece of rebar run through his spine. M to Tha C nearly got away, but I took out his knees with the bat and clubbed him to death.

Dr. Christine Lau cannot see this happening, but I'm sure she saw pictures of the bloody remains. Shortly after the cries of pain stop, I am back on the computer screen walking with an unbalanced simian gait, Taks baseball bat dangling at my side. I walk over to the rumpled body of E Lan and begin to wood chop. I swing at least twenty times, bringing the bat down on the dead boy's skull until I am heaving with exertion. Christine gets up to turn the video off, but I stop her, my hand clamping down on her wrist like a vice. She glares at me with alarm, and I release.

"Please," I say apologetically. "I need to see this."

This is where it all began to disappear.

She relents and sits back down. On the screen, I have moved from E Lan to the misguided young man known as Alpha B. Chills run up my spine as I watch myself raise the cylinder of wood and bring it down again and again and again. This carnage is closer to the camera and far more disturbing because of it. Pieces of bone and brains explode from the boys head with every strike and cover my body in gore.

And the waves are a crashing, crashing, crashing.

This is when the blackout started. When my soul began the retreat from body, borne by abhorrence and revulsion.

The hammering continues, for seconds and then minutes. Eventually I can barely lift the bat and there are tears running down my face, slicing through the blood in alabaster rivulets. I am on my knees, the bat rolls out of my hands on to the flattened earth. My tormented face turns to the night sky above, my skin as slack and neutral as a mannequin's. My eyes glaze and then I am gone.

The static has risen.

Chapter 10

Robert Higgins was a man with a content heart. Life was good. He had a dutiful wife, Belinda, whose skin was still smooth and stomach tight, even at the age of forty two. He had two intelligent, well-mannered and obedient children, Chastity and Kade, who looked upon their Father with the perfect ratio of awe and fear. He had a two story walk-out with triple E windows and granite counter-tops in the affluent neighbourhood of Robson Heights. He had a 1964 Mustang, that had never seen a drop of rain or fleck of snow. He had not one but two mistresses, a couple of young Cambodian girls, whose real names were unknown to him, but he liked to call Betty and Veronica. For a forty something cop living in northern Buttfuck Alberta, he had it all.

There was an empire here in Fort Mckenzie. The Empire of Swan. Don Swan was the Kaiser, the Caesar, the Khan, the overlord and ruler of all that was in the wastelands of the north. He controlled the police, the elected officials, the ignorant sheep that worked and lived, the land and the riches buried beneath. He was a member of the world's richest and most elite. He was a mighty king and Robert Higgins was fortunate enough to be a General in his army.

And he was grateful. He followed every order given to him by the great lord Swan with zealous determination. He stewarded Fort Mckenzie and the outlying regions as if it were his own personal garden, watering the seeds of sin, watching as the junkies and the peddlers and other scum grew until it seemed they could not be stopped. Until their bodies bent, like stalks of wheat, overburdened by their depravity. Then, as though he were the scythe of God, he reaped what had been sown, cutting down the morally weak, the losers, the dregs of society and bringing them to his master, the mighty Don Swan. He was a Baron, a games-keeper, and he loved what he did.

When his family and friends looked at him, they saw a

man of honour and integrity, a hero. They saw a man of the law, a servant of the people, there to serve and protect. Of course, only a handful of people knew what he and his subordinates at the Fort Mckenzie police force actually did in the depths of the night, but this bothered Robert Higgins not at all. He *was* a man of honour and integrity, he *was* a hero. He suited up every day and faced the evils of the world. And the job he did for Don Swan was just an extension of that. He looked upon the sad sacks that inhabited his city's back alleys and street corners as nothing more than walking corpses, suicide victims still twitching. They were garbage, people on a downward spiral that they themselves chose, no matter what the therapists or fucking narcotics anonymous pamphlets said. And since their lives were forfeit anyways, why not put them to some use.

That's what he did; put those zombies to some use.

Stepping into the viewing booth, Higgins was handed a scotch from his subordinate Constable Drake.

Aaaaah. Johnnie Blue.

His Favorite.

Taking a sip, he saw the massive form of Kraker entering the booth next to his. The monster was dressed in a black jacket and matching pants, cut from enough cloth to make two normal sized suits. Flanking him, were three crude looking Russian gangster types.

The sellers.

Human traffickers.

The four men sat down and the Russians cajoled Kraker with stories of their fighters' prowess. The giant listened silently and locked eyes with Higgins. The two were not friends by any definition of the word, but there was a mutual acceptance, they both were in the service of a great man and their cause was one and the same. Yet, Higgins was wary of Swan's pet lion. He knew that if ever he betrayed or displeased Swan, it would be the tattooed colossus he would have to answer to and Kraker would hunt him down without mercy.

And the fucker would enjoy it too.

They were in one of the many underground practice

arenas, this one particularly small. A black sand circle, one hundred meters in diameter was in front of them, entombed in a marble and granite amphitheatre. The roof above was a smooth cold pale shell that glowed with eerie luminescence. Torches lined the ten foot high wall that separated the lustrous ground from the viewing boxes and added to the smoky, palatine ambiance. Higgins and his subordinates were seated together in a Persian themed booth, mantled with lush pillows and cushions. A low table, cut from an exotic hardwood sat between the four men, its surface cluttered with bronze cups and stone ashtrays for their cigars.

Higgins didn't quite understand Swan's fascination with the ancient past. His compulsion to spend ludicrous amounts of money; building what he saw as modern reproductions of the greatest spectacles in history. However, as he sipped his hundred dollar scotch and pulled on his fifty dollar stogie, the Policeman appreciated it. Because of his service to the great lord Swan, Higgins had a life he never dreamed possible. Enough money to give his children a future they deserved, an outlet for his special talents and a backstage pass to the mystery. There was a secret world that only a select few were privy to and he was a key player, a baron, a general. He not only saw behind the curtain but got to fuck the showgirls and pick the stars.

Life was good.

And as he sat back and revelled in the perfection that surrounded him, the show started to get underway.

There were four entrances into the arena, two to Higgins left, and two to the right. In the Grand Arena, where the games were held every three months on the full moon, there were twelve entrances, each leading to some cavernous corner of Swan's underground city and its stadium seating could hold a thousand people. A thousand of the most affluent and rich people in the world.

Both portcullises to the left were raised and from within two large vicious looking Russian brawlers came strutting out, wearing only grimaces and tattered prison issue pants. They were big men, with giant arms and barrels for chests. One had an assortment of poorly drawn tattoos and a missing ear, the other was the victim of a terrible burn that left him with a scar that covered most of his back and torso. As they approached, their eyes drawn tight while their pupils adjusted to the light, one of the Russians beside Kraker stood up and yelled down at them in Russian. The words were brief, but their meaning easily interpreted.

Kill Mutts Kill.

Another voice rang out from somewhere distant and Higgins recognized its owner, Fallon, the pitbull that ran Swan's in house security detail. He shouted again and the iron portcullis on the upper right began to disappear into its recession. Stumbling into the black sand arena were two of the meth-heads he had brought in earlier. The one was your typical Fort Mckenzie loser, dishevelled, scabby, wearing a stained jean jacket and what appeared to be one black cowboy boot and one powder blue cowboy boot. Higgins remembered the spray of saliva he had unleashed when Constable Drake hit him with the taser.

Dumb Fuck.

The man next to him was younger, probably in his early to mid twenties. His hair was almost to his shoulders, straight and black. His face was sharp and sunken, wrapped in a pointed beard that contrasted with his corpse pale skin. His eyes were big and black and gave him a mordant appearance. Unlike the junkie next to him, he didn't appear to be afraid at all. There was a strange air of confidence that surrounded him as he entered the arena and scanned his surroundings.

Must still be high.

In the booths, all eyes were now on the arena floor. The two Russian combatants wasted little time and went straight for the newcomers. The older tweaker spun frantically, his white hair floating above him like a dead jellyfish as he searched for somewhere to run and hide. He tried to escape the way they had come, but the iron portcullis had been dropped, and the smooth walls of the arena were unscalable, there was no escape. He looked to the tattooed murderer coming towards him and put his hands out in surrender. Higgins swore under his breath. This would be no show at all.

The other Russian, the one with the burn marks on his back, had his sights trained on the black haired vulture and was now within striking distance of him. Higgins watched as the kid, standing like a statue, whispering to himself, suddenly sprang forward.

Here we go!

The next few seconds were a blur. It was as if Higgins brain couldn't quite decipher what his eyes were showing him. The kid with the long hair disappeared and in his place was a smeared patch of reality. This smear, this whirlwind surrounded the two Russians and distorted them as well and before anyone had time to blink the Russians were lying face down in the sand, their throats torn out

Never had Higgins heard a silence like the one that followed. All around him, stone cold shock.

What the fuck just happened?

Soon the spell ended and the traffickers were on their feet cursing and yelling. First at the young man, then at Kraker. Kraker ignored them and turned his attention to the floor, where the top right portcullis was quickly being hauled up. Six security guards, including the pimple ridden Fallon ran into the arena with machine guns pointed at the bloody victor.

Higgins and the rest of his posse were now standing, their police instincts making them need to be a part of the action. Without weapons, however or any idea of what needed to be done, they could only watch impotently.

The black haired ninja put up his arms in surrender as the security guards closed in on him and put him in chains. Higgins looked back to the two dead bodies, bleeding out into the sand and wondered.

Who are you?

Chapter 11

I am thrown into a cell, chained to a wall and beaten. The six guards gather in a circle around me, swinging their batons in quick furious motions. After the first impact, I drop to the floor, protecting my face and skull from the worst of the barrage.

Just in case I ever get serious about that modelling career.

The beating takes less than a minute, more of a display of dominance than anything else and the six hulking figures unchain me from the wall, exit the room and lock the barred door behind them. The walls of my cell are thinly spaced vertical bars, and I can see through into my neighbour's room and watch as the guards march down the hallway and out another door, this one solid steel. I appear to be in one massive room, cut up into cramped prison cells.

As I sit up and spit the blood from my mouth, I taste something much more offensive in the air. Unwashed bodies, sweat, shit, urine, mold. I take a look around and see movements in the shadows. There are prisoners all around me, and now that the watchmen have left, they are rising from their hiding places and pressing their hollow faces against the bars of their rooms, trying to get a look at the new arrival. I see men so ferine they resemble wasted canines more than humans.

I'm back in the nuthouse.

The prisoner in the cell next to mine begins to bark like a dog and pull at the bars that separate us. Blood surfaces as he crashes his skull into the metal cylinders.

Woof Woof, to you too Motherfucker.

His voice echoes off the brick walls, gathering momentum, and within seconds the rest of the imprisoned ensemble begin to join him in a barnyard cacophony that makes my skull rattle.

If I wasn't insane before, I will be soon.

As the din continues, I take a second to assess the damage done by the guard's batons. A few sore spots, chipped tooth. All in all, I think I came out pretty good; I have undoubtedly taken worse beatings. Looking down I see the blood from the two men in the coliseum on my hands, now pink-black in the gloom.

Monsters.

The memory of their deaths is fragrantly fresh, and I push it away.

Should have just stayed home and watched UFC on the tele.

Instead, I am in the UFC, except in Don Swan's version there appear to be no rules.

The barking madman has finally stopped and is content to just stare at me. A crimson spiderweb of blood has crept across his forehead and is now dripping from his eyebrows and the tip of his nose. I try to ignore him and look around. The lights above are barely on, and the place is submerged in a dank twilight. Outside, I am sure it must be morning. The birds are probably chirping, the air around Fort Mckenzie full of the scents of oil production, gas and sulphur. I almost miss it.

Should have just stayed home.

Or better, I should have stayed in the forest and forsaken this screwed up human world. The rest of the prisoners have lost interest and retreated back to their hovels. I move from the floor up onto my bed. It is made of solid concrete and is missing the foam that once covered it. The bruises on my back cry out as I lay on them, so I shift on to my side. The night's previous excitement has left me exhausted and even though I try to keep my eyes open, sleep takes me in seconds.

Goodnight everybody, sweet dreams with sugar.

My dreams are a chaotic mash up of reality and fantasy, frequently interrupted by the intermittent screams and squalls of my new neighbours. At some point, I'm not sure if I am awake or sleeping, a cantillated voice reaches out in provocation.

"Speaking in tongues, in tongues, in tongues he speaks,

speaking in tongues as he dreams. He He He. Little flower do you hear me, do you hear me little flower?"

I press my hands over my ears.

"Yes, yes you hear me don't you little flower, I can see into your mind, I can see into your mind. You speak in tongues you know, a hundred words, a thousand words, but I know what they mean, the words you speak. He He He. This is a place of beasts, of wild beasts, but I have ears, ears like a cat, eaten by a cat, I can hear the words you speak. They are the words of the bearded men, the old men, unfriendly men to people they don't know. They live alone, fuck their women alone, eat their potatoes alone. Is that you little flower, are you one of the bearded men? Hmm?"

My dreaming eyes open. I can see the speaker, sitting cross legged, through the metal bars, behind him an aura of ghoulish green flame.

"Yes, yes of course you are, or that is to say you were, now you are one of us, but is it prophecy you speak? Hmm? Is it prophecy? He He He. If you are the prophet, what do you see, what do you see, what is your prophecy? Hmm? He He He."

Who are you?

"Me, who am I? Who am I? Who are you little sister-fucking flower? He He He. I am Raphael. I am Michael. I am Gabriel. I am the three fold flame. I live among the beasts and drink the blood and silence the wicked hearts. And the crowd cheers my name, the new Romans, these Caligulas, they cheer my name, I am god to them, I am Icarus, but I will never drown, I will never drown. He He He. You! You, little flower, little sister-fucking, potato-eating flower you will drown, die in the games like the rest of them but I have faced a lion, I have killed tigers little flower, they took my flesh and gave me godhead. I am god to them, and they cheer my name."

The Games?

"Hmmmm, Hummmm, little flower. Speaking in tongues as he sleeps, speaking in Teutonic tongues. We are the games, we are the games! He He He. They come to watch us live or die, the Romans come to watch us live and to watch us die. The mighty Caesar and his citizens of grey, they spit, and they drink and they fuck, they fuck as we die, as you die, I am forever, the panther has made me a god, I am the archangel, the threefold flame. He He He. You potato-eater, little flower, the panther will shred you to pieces."

The sitting spectre rocks forward and comes on to all fours, posing like a feline. He is filthy and horribly scarred. Running sideways across his face are a series of thick lines that resemble claw marks. His left eye is missing, and so are his ears, torn from his skull with savage imprecision. His one remaining pupil finds me through a cloud of curdled milk.

"Speaking in tongues he speaks, speaking in tongues. Speaking in tongues he speaks, speaking in tongues while he sleeps."

The human cat stomps around in a circle until the shadows take him. My eyes close and I don't know if am going back to sleep or about to wake.

Days pass, at least I think they pass. There is no time in this place, no clocks, no watches, no cellphones, no sunrises, no moonsets. The only noticeable change is when a guard enters and gives us our daily meal, a large but tasteless gruel of boiled rice, wasted vegetables and grey meat. Accompanying our food and water are a palmful of tiny clear crystals. Crystal meth I am guessing or crack. Whatever it is, the prisoners gobble them up before they hit the ground. Being the only non-junkie undoubtedly has its benefits here, I save my ration and trade with my neighbours for extra food, most of them barely eat anyways.

These are the longest hours of my life, far worse than anything I can remember. The sights and sounds of the prison are so vehement and chilling I find myself sitting with my body facing the brick wall most of the time, keeping the lunatics behind me. I attempt meditation, sitting or standing for hours and hours. I repeat Christine's mantras in my head, I stare at the old rag I keep in my pocket, I follow my breath, I sense the Prana in my cells. Sometimes it works sometimes it doesn't. The noise of the others rises like a living thing, a monstrous sea creature that comes from the depths and overcomes the world, crashing and writhing.

My closest neighbours are generally the loudest culprits. The barking dog spends most of his time watching me and groping himself. Occasionally, usually after his dinner of splintered diamonds, he smashes his body and face into the bars that separate us in an attempt to reach and possibly eat me.

The other one, the chew toy to my right is an irrepressible fountain of nonsense. One minute he is the Greek god Ares, spearing all those who oppose the will of his father Zeus, the next he is a gentle Bodhisattva, postponing his own nirvana so he can help the rest of us ignorant mules attain liberation. Between the two of them, I am unwinding, the strings of my sanity slipping with every passing second.

More days go by and the choler increases. I try to think back to the last full moon I saw, the last time I saw planes filling the skies, inexplicably going north to Don Swan's mansion.

Every three months, the eagles take flight.

Soon, it must be soon.

In my dreams, I see Shane and Putu and the rest of the guys from the rigs. I see Christine and Henry, Maggie and her Son Jake. I see the past, I see questions unanswered. Mysteries I will probably never solve now. My old nightmares have faded away, my nightmares happen now while I am awake. They are around me at all times, screaming and shrieking, smearing their chests with shit and semen.

I am lost, I am lost, I am lost.

Not even the static can find me anymore.

Then it arrives, the day of the games. Somehow my philosophizing neighbour knows before the guards arrive to take us. He is frenzied with excitement, literally frothing at the mouth.

"Wake up little flower! Wake up! Time to die, time to die!"

I put the stained rag back into my pocket as the guards come and put us into chains. At their helm is the neck-less bulldog with the pubescent skin and bulging eyes. He grabs at my chains with unrestrained ire as he and the rest of the guards lead us out of the prison cell that has been home for what must be weeks now. I count thirteen men, thirteen dishevelled, crazed men whose stink must match my own. We trudge down a massive hallway and the lights above, although they are still dim, make my eyes water. In front of me, the barking dog is pulling against his restraints and trying to keep his deranged gaze locked with mine. Eventually, the guards grow weary of this and yank him to a complete stop and begin to beat him mercilessly. The thump of their batons on his flesh echoes as we pass.

We turn a corner and the architecture changes from drab brickwork and cobbled floors to brilliant arches and black sand. The corridor continues for what seems like miles and then I begin to hear something. Something immense. We turn another corner and the noise thickens, reminding me of a rolling train. There is a portcullis ahead, the same height as the other one I remember but much wider. The guards lead us to its mouth, and the noise becomes recognizable.

People. Hundreds, maybe thousands of people.

Through the holes in the portcullis, I see a massive open arena surrounded by stands full of shouting people.

The Games.

The guards seat us and the maimed Archangel begins to sing.

"Stout bodied omnivores... Slink their way across the floor...For scraps...Of pinstripe pants!"

My atrophied mind is racing, trying to assimilate what is happening. I force myself to take in ten long controlled breaths through my mouth.

Soooooo Hummmmmm...

Out through the nose.

Sooooooo Hummmmm...

The bulldog is in front, his pimple ridden face daring me to do something stupid while his companions release my constraints. Soon all of us are unchained and Michael or Gabriel or Raphael, whatever his name is still singing.

"Strap me down...To the tracks...Unleash the sun upon my back...Until I'm forged like Rawhide!"

He regards me like a swooning groupie and his volume increases.

"Rawhide...Rawhide...Rawhiiiiiiiiiiddddeeee!!!!"

The portcullis lets out an anguished squeak as it begins its ascent. The men are on their feet and so am I. The guards are behind us, prepared to prod us forward into the coliseum if necessary. But they don't need to, the prisoners are under the gate as soon as physically possible, pushing and clawing at one another, and I can guess why. Twenty feet into the coliseum, there are six straight edge swords stuck in the sand, as if they were graveyard crosses.

Thirteen men, six swords.

I enter the fray, pushed by primal necessity, but I am too late, the mass of men is impenetrable. The portcullis is now fully open, and the six quickest are racing towards the swords. Beyond them is a stadium of cheering people. My eyes widen in shock, my body momentarily frozen with sensory overload. Instinct, however, quickly brings me back to the task at hand.

Get a fucking weapon!

The prisoners are driven by fear, but they are weak with malnutrition. I leap past the slower half of the group in seconds and start to gain on the other six. I see the Archangel ahead of me, his mutilated skull bouncing like a ball of malformed wax. He is the first one to grab a sword and pull it from the ground. Blade in hand, he continues running into the centre of the arena, spinning and screaming in triumph. His thoughts are written upon his contorted face.

I AM THE THREEFOLD FLAME! I AM A GOD!

The next prisoner tries to grab two swords but he is quickly overcome. A melee breaks out and one weapon is left unattended. I am beside a native man, whose chest is heaving with exertion as he runs. For a second we are neck and neck, our wills reaching for the same thing, our destinies entwined. Both our hands reach forward, reaching steel and then we are rolling in the sand, a blade between us. He bites at my face, but I pull back and bash my forehead into his nose. He falls back unconscious, blood streaming, and I wrench the sword from his grip but now something is on top of me, heavy and sweating. Fingernails, fine as razors slash at the skin of my back.

WOOF! WOOF! WOOF!

The barking dog. I thought the guards had beaten him to death back in the hallway.

Apparently alive, the lunatic wraps his legs around me, and his voice becomes a muffled growl as he bites into the flesh of my shoulder. A howl escapes my lips and I bring the hilt of the sword down upon his temple with a backwards swing. His grip falters and I push away, rolling on the soft sand. Another man approaches and is about to attack, but I bounce to my feet and point the tip of the blade at his chest. He backpedals as the barking dog gallops forward in a kamikaze assault. Without thinking, I sidestep left and swing the metal blade in a descending arc, severing his arm at the elbow. The freshly separated limb drops to the ground, and the wounded dog looks at it dumbfounded. His eyes fill with tears as blood spurts from the stump and his gaze turns to me, heartbroken.

Why? Why man? Why would you do that?

Sorry amigo. Can't have you raping me in front of all these people; that would not be cool.

He drops to his knees defeated and I spin around, taking in my surroundings. The men have divided, the ones lucky enough to have weapons have loosely gathered to my left, the others to my right, glaring at us hungrily. I step back a few feet, putting some distance between myself and the others on both sides. I see the Archangel, still in the centre of the Arena shouting and waving his sword.

"Bring them! Bring them upon me!" He yells and the crowd roars in reply.

The audience is not what I expected. I see men in polished tuxedos and Arabian robes, women wearing their finest ballroom gowns and glittering jewels. All of them on their feet, spitting and swearing. I turn and look behind me, seeing an especially ornate booth supported by carved marble pillars. Seated within I see the patriarch of this gallery, the high priest himself.

Swan.

He is wearing a modern tuxedo and bow tie, and his face is held high, looking both regal and patricianly pompous. Beside him is his tattooed bodyguard Kraker. Flanking them are some more suits, guards, women, and higher ups and also the black cop who brought me here.

Higgins.

For some reason, he is wearing the full RCMP ceremonial uniform, known as the Red Serge, complete with red tunic, dark blue banana pants, riding boots and wide brimmed stetson. He reminds me of Dudley Do Right, the dipshit hero from the Rocky and Bullwinkle show.

I turn my attention back to the situation before me. The prisoners have spread themselves out further, and no one has taken up arms against anyone else.

What are they waiting for?

I thought that was the point of this game; get the weapon first so you can kill your opponents.

Maybe I was mistaken?

As this thought enters my head, six of the opposing portcullises open with dramatic simultaneity. I look deep into the gaping holes but see only emptiness. The air shivers with silence. The grip of the sword, hard and smooth, feels alien in my palm.

The stunned native man I fought for the weapon wakes, and sits up. I get a better look at him in the light of the arena and see that he is badly scarred. Fat angry red lines crisscross his back. I look at all the men, most have long cicatrices on their bodies, and I realize why we are here.

Bestiarius.

Suddenly there is movement; huge feline shapes erupt from the darkness with frightful speed.

Lions!

Or some crossbred version of lions, ranging in color from stark white to pitch black. The beasts are immense, long and lean, their faces cowled with shaggy manes. Inside their mouths, razor sharp teeth protrude in search of flesh. The men without weapons move back against the rounded arena wall, searching for an impossible corner as the others prepare for the onslaught. Only the Archangel stands his ground, in fact, he runs to meet the beasts head on, his sword held high. A tawny creature with a black mane greets him as the five other lions thunder across the floor of black sand towards the rest of us.

The barking dog attracts the next lion, the stump of his arm still bleeding as he stares up into its calico maw. It kills him with a swipe from its paw, his stunned face never to woof again, and continues forward. My former enemy, the scarred native moves behind me in the hopes that I can provide him some security. The lions reach us, and the mayhem truly begins.

The calico coloured beast finds us first, the blood of my cellmate still fresh on its claws. It comes like a beautiful nightmare, eyes a violet star-burst, fur a piebald mixture of crimson and saffron and ochre. It comes seeking an easy kill, but I am trained, I have the quickness. It rushes forward with its fangs bared and I scream in response, baring my own. It fills the sky, eclipsing the amphitheatre and the crowd watching from their seats. It descends, about to crush me under its vastness.

But I am trained, I have the quickness.

The world slows down, and I am moving. The lion arrives, but I am gone. The sword in my hand lashes out and sinks into tensed muscles and constricted tendons. I hear a roar so loud it curls my beard. Claws are thrown, teeth snap, but I am too fast, too quick. The blade slashes out again and again, finding flesh every time until there is blood running down the hilt. Within minutes, the beast is on its side, alive but hollering to the skies, pleading for death.

My head swivels searching for other immediate threats. Of the six lions, four still remain. Of the thirteen men, five are dead. The native fled when the lion came and I see him now with two others, fighting off a mythical looking animal, with zebra-like stripes. Past them, the Archangel seems to be holding his own in the centre of the arena. To my left I see a prisoner facing a lion alone, with a freshly killed prisoner at his feet and I run to his aid.

The prisoner, a comically frightened looking figure, is pressed tight against the arena wall, and the lion is only feet away. Above him, the crowd of people are cheering and throwing champagne down upon him, and I am filled with the sudden urge to toss my sword into their heaving mass. I come upon the lion as it is raising its killing blow. My sword finds its left flank, and it turns on me enraged. The skeleton flees to the right, and I am left alone to fight the beast. I raise my sword, and the carnage continues as though I were in a dream.

The lion is killed, and another takes its place. There are now two lions left, the one before me and another, surrounded by the surviving four men. My muscles shake with fatigue as I brace for the attack.

This lion is the strangest yet I have seen. Its mane is fire-engine red, and its face is painted to resemble a panda bears. It is smaller than the others but faster. We dance in circles, feinting and clashing until I pull the beast in close and thrust my weapon into its exposed chest. The tip hits bone and can't press through. I let go of the handle and roll to safety as the brute comes crashing down. The sword is still stuck in its chest as it coils to face me. There is a brief pause as we both assess each others condition. In my peripheral, I see that the four other men, including the Archangel and the native, have defeated the other lion and are now watching as I face off against the last lion alone.

Thanks for the help Fellas!

I skirt the lion's perimeter until I am near a dead prisoner, who still has a sword locked in his hands. The lion moves closer, as if reading my intent. My breath locks in my chest, my Prana surges and then I am diving. I reach the corpse and yank the sword from his grip. The lion, with its paradoxically gentle looking face, rears up on to its hind legs and is about to strike. I slash at its two front paws, severing them both and sending them flying. The lion collapses on to the ground, its incomplete limbs slipping in the sand and my original sword, still stuck in its chest thrusts up into its body and through its heart. A soft gurgle escapes from the lions lips and it is dead.

The crowd is on its feet cheering and repulsively, my ego rises with their adulation.

I am a God!

Row upon row of spectators clap their hands and chant madly.

Bestiarius! Bestiarius! Bestiarius!

Even the illustrious Don Swan is on his feet, putting his hands together in portentous applause. So are the rest of his entourage, his overdressed affiliates and play mates, only the giant Kraker stands unmoved by the spectacle.

I turn in place, reeling with adrenaline. I raise my sword and the crowd cheers even louder.

Be careful man, this is a drug just like any other.

But I don't want to hear it. I am drunk with glorification. It is something I have never experienced, applause for my actions, praise for my hidden talents.

This is why I am alive!

But not all agree. The maimed philosopher, the Archangel Micheal, Raphael, Gabriel. The threefold flame sees the crowd heaping attention upon me, and in his face I recognize murderous displeasure. He surreptitiously begins to slink towards me, a sword dangling at his side and a grimace on his lips. We lock eyes.

Don't do this, not if you want to live. I don't want to fight you.

My intentions however mean nothing. This is *his* arena, this is *his* crowd, *his* glory. And I have dared to take that away from him. As he nears, his body coiled in a fighting stance, I hear the words under his breath.

"There was a time, there was a time little flower, little sister-fucking flower. There was a time..."

The crowd notices his approach and silence suddenly chokes the air. They see the drama, they recognize the characters. The ageing veteran no longer the people's favourite, the brazen upstart, hungry to steal his laurels. It would be cliche if it didn't involve my life.

The Archangel sidesteps closer, dumbly trying to conceal his weapon with his body as if I haven't figured out what he plans to do. His whispers remain soft until he drives forward swinging and then he is shrieking.

"There was a time before this hell, when the little strings

on my silver bells, were bonafide, rawhide...
RAWHIIIIIDDDDEEEE!!!!"

He swings hard and fast, but clumsily, and I see where his blade will arrive days before it does. I jump left as he runs his sword into the ground. A look of shock blanches his ruined face. He looks to me as if to say.

That was it; you should be dead, what happened?

With my left hand, I make a fist and smash it down into his jaw.

"No, no, little flower. Not yet!" I say and in my voice I hear something new.

Malice.

He rises back up; swinging, but his blade finds only air. I spin around him like a top, deflecting when I need to but mostly just toying with the demented man. He is no match for me and soon he is wheezing and just hucking his weapon around. The crowd is fully engaged.

I have them. I have them all in the palm of my hand.

It's as if my opponent's narcissistic disease is being transfused in to me with every passing glance of steel. And then I do as I know I must.

If I want to keep them all in my pocket, you have to die, dear little angel. You have to die.

The philosopher, the Archangel with his missing ears and mutilated face slouches before me, his one good eye glowering in its pool of cream. I thrust my blade into his stomach and his chest and his throat. I hack at his head and his arms and his shoulders. I kill not because I need to but because I feel compelled to.

For the crowd...

When he is dead, I drop my weapon and raise my face to the winds of providence. I feel the tightness of the skin on my skeleton, the fire in my Hara. I pull back my lips and howl until my breath runs dry.

I am a monster.

***

Later, when I am back behind the portcullis sitting in chains, I bear witness to the full scope of The Games. Don Swan's great and secret show is an evening long presentation of violence and murder. After the three surviving *Bestiarii* and myself exit the arena, the stage is set for another showcase, this one full of galloping chariots and armoured combatants. Men die, the rubberneckers cheer and sadly my diseased heart wishes those cheers were for me and me alone.

After this, a giant stage is lowered to the floor, and the place goes black. Music is pumped into the coliseum, and a vibrant display of acrobatics begins. Women, wearing only glittery body paint, glissade across the stage and fold themselves into unimaginable and provocative shapes. The show ends in a pornographic free for all that would have made the tyrant Nero blush.

Once this reaches its gushing conclusion, the stage is removed, and the people in the stands straighten their ties and pull up their zippers. The arena, drenched in twilight once again, seethes with anticipation as ambiguous shadows move large round shapes on to the sand from an open portcullis. Minutes pass and then the air begins to shake with the sounds of booming tribal drums. Two spotlights erupt from the high ceiling and create identical circles on the arena floor, at the opposing ends. The first man steps out, and the audience chants.

"HURON! HURON! HURON!"

The man is aptly named. He is dark-skinned, wearing only a breech cloth and deer-skin leggings. His head is shaved except for a long braided mohawk that reaches down to the centre of his back. Across his eyes and chest are bands of black paint, giving him a menacing appearance. In his hands are two weapons, a short dagger and a long wooden war club that has a vicious looking ball on the end. He pounds his legs into the ground and shakes his weapons. He calls back to the crowd, revealing long yellow teeth that have been ground down to points.

The man at the opposing end, his adversary enters the stage and the crowd shifts their attention.

"CANAANITE!" they cheer.

The warrior is dark-skinned as well but Arab-looking, with a giant mop of curly black hair and a thick beard. He is wearing nothing but a short, patterned miniskirt, revealing a body strung with dense muscle. His weapon is a bronze sickle-sword that he spins hand over hand as he dances for the crowd. The two men see each other and begin to hurl insults in their native tongues. The lights turn back on, unveiling the dozens of giant drums still being played by a bunch of diaper-wearing Asians and the combatants square off.

The battle begins and when it is finished only one man remains alive. Two more rounds of hand to hand combat take place, each one more lurid and bloody than the last. The gladiators are fashioned from classic archetypical shapes, bare chested warriors who lived in a time before guns and three piece suits. They face each other with nothing but crude weapons and fight until either they or their opponent no longer breathes. It is edge of your seat carnage and I think my neanderthal roommates back in Fort Mckenzie would have appreciated it fully.

This is way better than Ultimate Fighter, guy!

After the last fight, the music stops and the lights dim.

That's all folks, time to go move this party elsewhere.

The guards usher me and the other three survivors back down the hallway to our prison cells. I am left back in my fortress of austerity feeling like a worn out condom. The evening's savagery and my own part in it have hollowed out my insides, making me numb, blearily traumatized. Food is brought, the same shitty gruel I have been eating for days, and so is the little handful of crystalline narcotics. I look at the drugs like I never have before, as something more than somebody else's poison or something to trade for more food. I see it with a prisoner's eye, a caged animal's eye. I grab a few of the crystals and roll them in my palm, feeling the thin hardness against my blood stained skin.

A loud squeak. The steel door at the end of our giant room swings open, and four guards, including the Bulldog enter. Behind them, bending forward so as not to hit his shorn skull on the door frame is the tattooed titan, Kraker. Still wearing his tuxedo and bowtie, he could be the world's biggest and scariest penguin. The five men approach and stop in front of my cell. Kraker looks me over with a discerning gaze.

Surprisingly there is no haughtiness in his expression like the others, no superiority, no arrogance or disgust at my appearance or living conditions. Only cold calculating analysis.

An animal sizing up another animal.

Emboldened by my victories in the arena I stand and meet his gaze unflinchingly. We stare at each other like two lone wolves who find each other in the wilderness.

I am not afraid of you.

And the giant knows it. But he is also not in the least bit afraid of me.

The Bulldog with his varicose face opens the door and spits a few words upon me.

"Someone would like to see you."

I can only guess as to whom.

Swan.

Chapter 12

I have been standing for an hour, knees bent, meridians open, arms at chest height, head up, shoulders relaxed, feeling the current of liberation pulling the organ of my skin up as the current of manifestation runs through my skull, my spine, into my legs and disperses into the ground.

Dr. Christine Lau, my physician, my diminutive Asian emancipator, is beside me doing the same. My focus however is not on her, actually her presence has become barely noticeable, I am in a place of internalized concentration. I am only aware of my body and the resonant energy running through it. I am loose but not relaxed, I am engaged but not tensed, my awareness has not transcended the experiential world but become saturated in it until the lines between myself and the air around me are barely recognizable. I am a cat watching its prey. I am *Sung*.

Since the screening of my homicidal rampage on the Bottle Topz crew, Dr. Lau has had me on a strict regimen. Every day we stand for hours, attempting to bring what Dr. Lau believes is my trapped consciousness down into the nether regions of my spiritual self.

"By becoming more aware and sensitive to your physical presence, we will direct more Pranic energy to your lower egos. This is where the memories of your childhood are stored and because of your prolonged stupor, they have atrophied and closed themselves off from the rest of your emotions. These chi gung poses will direct the Pranic flow downward and reopen them."

This is what Christine Lau conjures up in the middle of the night. In my humble opinion, I do not think standing for hours is going to make me remember shit, but it is putting some muscle back on to my macerated frame. And there *is* something happening to my mental state. Standing puts me into a trance, and when I come out, I am surging with power. I want to run or fight or *fuck*. But for now while I am in it, there is nothing, there is no me, there is no my, all things are impermanent.

A small voice calls from far in the distance.

"Breathe in..."

I do, and the multitude of suns in the sky and the planets that worship them fill my chest.

"Slowly breathe out..."

It is a woman's voice I am hearing, a liberator's voice, a warden's voice.

"Open your eyes," she says, and the spell is broken.

I am back in the hospital, in the upstairs rehabilitation room. Dr. Lau moves in front of me. Today her dress is far less formal, black capri pants, loose longsleeved shirt, black and white tai chi slippers. Her hair is loose and flowing down on to her shoulders, and her usually bespectacled face is void of glasses, making her appear years younger. She could be a college co-ed fresh from a yoga class.

Now that my train of thought has been interrupted, my shoulders and arms immediately begin to ache. We go through a few, flowing movements to finish off the exercise and let our bodies relax.

Dr. Lau is staring at me, her expression so indecipherable I doubt that she even really knows what is going on behind it. Beneath the thin fabric of her shirt, I can see the outline of a bra that cups her tiny breasts and in my imagination the burning cornea of her teardrop scar.

"Did you experience anything, John, any recollections, any pictures or visions?" She asks.

I shake my head. I saw no images, no signs, no symbols, no sudden emergence of repressed memories. Only in my dreams do I see such vividness and Christine chalks all that shit up as some past life regression from the astral plane due to sixth Chakra excessiveness, yadda yadda yadda. My real memories, she believes lay hidden somewhere in an invisible emotional vortex. We just need to crack that nut open.

"Well let's continue with the next exercise." She eventually says, apparently not finding any more inspiration.

The next exercise consists of holding my breath and flexing my perineum muscles, hopefully invoking some kind of response from the old Muladhara Chakra. This process is thoroughly tame compared to all that other weird stuff that Dr. Lau did to me while I was catatonic. I wonder if she thinks I don't remember any of it.

Oh yes, dear doctor I do, I remember it all you demented quack you.

"Inhale...And hold," she tells me, and I think back to when she was behind me, tugging away as Marcus the Giant Blob had my head in the drink.

"Exhale. Inhale and hold."

I pull in my breath and flex. In my mind's eye, it feels as if Christine's palm is there, pressing hard as her fingernails graze my balls.

"Exhale."

Now I am envisioning doing the same kind of shit to her. Banging a Tibetan singing bowl over her ass for two hours and blowing incense into her vagina while she lays helpless, drooling on a hospital bench.

"Inhale...And hold," she says, and I wonder.

Who the fuck she is to order me around anymore? I am not the same invalid I was when she found me. I am a man, I am more than a man, I am a wild fucking beast!

"Exhale."

The flexing has given rise to something more than repressed memories. I open my eyes and see Christine is already watching me, her hands grazing her zipper. We stare at each other, and I finally understand what lies behind that unreadable gaze.

Want.

I leap forward and surround Christine as if I were made of soft taffy, finding her every crevice. Our clothes are gone in seconds, and I am at her throat licking the sweat from her skin and pawing at her naked flesh. Soon I am face to face with the dangling teardrop that hangs between her breasts.

Heart surgery.

I think she says, but I can't be sure. I am lost in the scarred pendant's burnished sepia. It swims in front of me taunting and teasing me, declaring that it will never be mine but it has no idea who it is dealing with. It will be mine, it always has been mine and to prove my point I take it into my mouth and suck it smooth. Christine's emits a series of oohs and aahs and just when I am about to really get the party started; she pulls my face to meet hers and tells me to hold on.

I watch her sun-starved body as she climbs up on to the padded bench, the same padded bench where she nearly drowned me and screened the video of me killing five men, and lowers herself down into the prone position, face down with her arms at her sides. There she remains, and my momentum falters for a second, confused.

After a few heartbeats, she lifts her head and says unequivocally.

"Do whatever you want; just don't come in my hair."

And then she puts her face back into the pale blue vinyl cushion and remains as still as a corpse.

Chapter 13

The scene before me is nearly incomprehensible. I see a King upon his throne, naked concubines at his feet, marble pools swimming with voluptuous nymphs and Greek gods come to life. I see bound and ball gagged deviants engaged in every manner of depravity, I see woman with man, man with man, woman with animal. I see feces and blood, sperm and bile. I see an orgiastic saturnalia in mid climax, its seams about to burst.

I am in the throne room of the emperor himself Don Swan. The human tower they call Kraker is ahead of me leading me through a minefield of frenzied sexual bliss. We are on a sandstone walkway that divides the room into two crescent shaped pools, sunken into slabs of speckled granite and sprinkled with purple roses. Past the pools is a maze of smoke-filled rooms, some hidden behind silk curtains, others open for the entire world to see what indecencies are being committed within. The walls are a breathtaking display of ornate carvings, life sized sculptures cut into the stone ramparts depict what must be the entire kama sutra in explicitly vivid detail.

Further ahead, the walkway opens up into a sitting room, where a bevy of stunning women are entertaining the men that are illustrious enough to join Don Swan's outer coterie. As I approach, still clothed in filthy rags and blood stained skin, I see the faces of the men who control the world, oil barons, multinational bank CEO's, politicians, middle eastern royalty, even a movie star I recognize from a poster. Here they sit, smoking opium and flavoured tobacco, talking shop and getting wristie's from super models as I walk through their ranks stinking of sweat and blood and death. A few catch sight of me as I pass and give me hearty applause and drunken bravos.

"Lion killer!" one yells in stilted English.

I'm a celebrity!

With the miasma from the hookahs floating into my lungs and brain, I could almost believe it.

The march continues, my only beacon in this fucked up place being the hulking figure of Kraker ahead of me. We descend a few steps and have now reached the antechamber that holds the King and his entourage. Don Swan is sitting on a literal throne. It is a monstrous thing, black and hideous, made from what looks to be gnarled branches that have been burned and lacquered. It is big enough to hold three more people, the Asian ravishers I saw him with at the parkade.

In another life.

And the long-limbed African. All three of the concubines are naked, with the exception of a few precious jewels flung around their necks and sparkly treasures in their ears.

Swan, the Kaiser himself is still wearing his tuxedo, minus the bow tie. His eyes are so red they appear to be glowing, and his mouth is locked in a joker's smirk. Whatever drugs he's taken they have undoubtedly taken effect.

"John!" he says and in his voice I hear the excesses of a privileged life.

"John, John, John, John Doe!"

Kraker stops me a dozen arm lengths from Swan and stands between us, off to the side, his mountainous frame glowering down at me. There are no other guards that I can see, and I wonder at the confidence Swan has in this man.

If the Caesar has only one bodyguard, he must be a hell of one.

I stand before the tribunal set before me, not knowing what to expect but my exhaustion and the dragon's tail that swims through the air loosens my tongue.

"Mr. Swan," I say, trying to sound casual. As if killing lunatics and lions in a secret underground coliseum is something I do on a regular basis.

"John Doe! You know who I am, but I know nothing of you!"

The King eyes me with a carnivore's intensity. He has the aura of a man that has to be followed no matter what the cause and I am sure multitudes do, happily.

"John Doe! The man without a past, the man without a name even! My people searched your records, they didn't find much. But they did show me some compelling newspaper clippings. You were on Rig Nine when it burned down, were you not?"

"Yes, sir."

"Mmm hmm. You saved the lives of two of your crewmates?"

"Yes, sir."

"Where do you come from?"

"I don't know, sir."

"You don't know." He throws up his hands in mock exasperation and his harem giggles.

"You don't know. Nobody knows. Where did you learn to fight?"

"I don't know that either, sir."

"He doesn't know." Swan looks to his courtesans as they look at me, their naked bodies slithering between tendrils of smoke.

"Well, young man, you were tremendously entertaining tonight. My guests were highly pleased with your performance. No man has ever killed three lions in one battle, not even my champion, Kraker here –"

I look to the giant.

So you fought in the arena did you?

"-And then to kill a fellow Bestiarius afterwards, brilliant. That has never happened before."

I am left flummoxed by his praise.

"Thank you," I say dumbly, and my spirit scalds me from within.

You are being held prisoner illegally, this is unlawful, you are a free man!

But those arguments don't hold any weight here; the rules of the outside world don't apply in the domain of Swan.

"You are not a junkie are you, John?" he asks.

"No, I am not."

"But you are not without your demons are you?"

The eyes of the people around me feel like needles prodding my skin.

"No," I say. "I am not."

We all have demons, only some of us have the riches to build a macabre playpen for them.

"What do want in life, John?"

Swan's question catches me off guard. My intoxicated mind has become distracted by the scene happening beyond the throne room. Lying on a bed of cushions is a naked woman who must weigh over five hundred pounds. Her gelatinous form is folded over so many times, all the secrets of the Catholic Church could be hidden within her cracks and crannies. On top of her are four swarthy teenage boys, crawling and clambering, tending to her every sexual desire.

"Life, John, what do you want in life?" the King demands to know.

One of the Sherpa's heads disappears between the woman's unshaven thighs, and she throws her head back, crying in ecstasy.

"To survive, sir," I reply without thinking. "I want to survive."

The Swan stares at me, as if I just revealed some great cosmic truth.

"Yesssss..." he hisses. "We all want to survive; this is instinct, the instinct that is indigenous to us all. But once the needs of survival are met, all this superfluous nonsense steals our attention, but you, you have nothing, nothing but the need to survive. This is purity, the purity of purpose."

The Khan stares at me, and I feel my spirit twisting. I think back to my training, I should be bending my knees, sinking my presence down but something inside doesn't let me, some little piece of me wants to be uprooted, swept away into the heart of this man's madness and held there until I am shredded into nothing.

"I want this purpose to blossom, John, I want the purity of combat, the art of life and the glory of death to become your only thought, I want it to become the yoke that pulls you, the obsession that dominates you."

Swan's voice rises like a wave and his women rise with it. The Ebony goddess walks her long fingers into the waiting cradle of the ravisher beside her as the other Asian beauty sinks to the floor and takes a breast into her mouth. Behind them, the ivory-skinned blob recites crass poetry to the bony immigrants that are making frantic love to her armpits, and above us all, watching with the disinterest of a light house, stands the colossus Kraker.

"I have created a world." Swan continues, "Where man can hone his primeval abilities and put them to the test. You and all the other combatants who fight in the coliseum are not like normal men, you are warriors like *Les Neuf Preux,* destined to die in battle."

Swan's eyelids flutter in rapid succession making me think of hummingbird wings.

"Do you know of The Nine Valiants, Les Neuf Preux, John?"

I shake my head, and thin tracers erupt behind the people in front of me.

"The Nine Valiants." Swan says, pointing to an alcove where nine statues in medieval garb stand in sentinel formation holding their weapons in front of them.

"Three noble pagans, Hector, Julius Caesar, Alexander the Great. Three noble Christians, Godfrey of Bouillon, King Arthur and Charlemagne. And three noble Jews, King David, Joshua and Judas Maccabeus. They were the personification of chivalry and soldierly courage, known for their honour and prowess in battle. They were the epitome of what a warrior should be, the pedigree of Mars himself you might say. This is what I expect of the men who enter the hallowed grounds of the arena. This is what I expect of you."

The King's inflamed pupils have ground his irises into dust and they cast a black shadow upon my shoulders, cloaking me in his banner.

"From now on you are a combatant in my house and you will be treated as such. You will be fed, you will be clothed, and you will be trained. Your life in the outside world is over; to the people you knew you are nothing but a ghost, a fading memory. Your life is here now, in the arena, and the only way you will leave is in the glory of battle."

I look upon my master and my heart swells with a new drug, belonging.

"And we will give you a new name, something appropriate for the coliseum."

Swan's voice softens in contemplation.

"John, John, John...Hyrcanus...Do you know who John Hyrcanus was?"

I shake my head, slowly this time, not wanting my drugged vision to swirl again.

"John Hyrcanus was the nephew of Judas Maccabeus." Swan says, pointing to one of the sentinels cut into the wall.

"He was the high priest and leader of Judea, the predecessor to modern day Israel. He led an era of conquest that made Judea the most significant power in the region and was known as a just ruler and skilful warrior. This is whom you will model yourself after."

Beyond the throne of Swan, the obese woman squeals with delight as her four lovers climax upon her blubbery flesh in rapid succession. I stare at her enraptured face and wonder, not for the first time.

How the hell did I get myself into this?

Turning back to Swan and his writhing consorts, I feel my sensibilities crumble beneath their glitter and authority. All that I was, the freed mental patient, the obscure loner, the angry young man will need to be cast aside if I am going to endure this place.

If it's an animal they want, that is what they will get. One so fierce it will strike terror into their self-inflated hearts.

Swan looks upon me and sees no change except for maybe the confidence he believes he invokes. The Goliath however, Kraker twitches his nose as if he smells something in the air, premonition perhaps.

The days that follow are a waking man's nightmare. Swan's poetic words of glory and honour are soon buried beneath a hailstorm of violence. I have been moved into a barrack-like construction of stone cells, to live, eat, sleep and train with my so-called brothers, twenty five men whose sole purpose, it seems is to provoke and harass me. The house of Swan is made up of twelve separate *Ludi,* or training schools for combatants. Each *ludus* has between twenty and forty men, all hardened killers from every type of background, some are convicted criminals or prisoners of war, others are mercenaries who have given up their freedom to pay a debt, some are kidnapped steet-fighters. A select few, I have heard, were trained their whole lives to fight in the arena, they are slaves from democracy free paradises like Burma and North Korea. Wherever they came from, they are now in the domain of Swan and it is here we all remain.

And the only way you will leave is in the glory of battle.

The ludi and the men that train under them are not all owned by Swan. In fact he only owns one, which I am a part of, the rest are property of various degenerate billionaires who use the schools as extensions for their shrivelled dicks. Swan houses the ludi under his roof, to ensure secrecy I'm sure, can't have anybody finding out that the world's richest men own a bunch of slaves and make them fight to the death, how embarrassing, but the other plutocrats pay for their training, weapons, food.

Steroids, growth hormones, whatever, you name it we got it!

And I'm sure a little recompense to the Khan for building and maintaining the giant pen for us animals. And animals we are. The men I see around me are not like the well-spoken, violent but romantically noble, peculiarly hairless actors from the movies. The men I share roof with are insane, all of them. Some conceal it better than others but there is not one unshattered psyche in the whole sweaty mob. Killing people, taking life is not an action that can be executed and then forgotten. It fractures the mind, robs the soul of its divinity. It reverts a man to his primeval roots, making him a caveman. That is what we are here, cavemen, void of intelligent thought or word, we are nothing but our instincts.

Kill or be killed.

We are kept in check of course. There are multitudes of guards to stop us from butchering each other, as well as three *Doctores*, men who have survived the ravages of the arena and now teach us how to do the same. We are divided into groups and put under the tutelage of one Doctore according to our fighting style and size. Since I am the runt of the entire litter by a good thirty pounds, I am in the smallest group, who wear no armour and carry only a knife, cestuses or some other equivalent. The next group up use larger weapons such as long swords and axes and the third unit of combatants, living giants fed a daily diet of anabolic steroids, are allowed helmets, shields and armour.

It has been decided that I am to fight with two *sicas,* long curved daggers designed for close quarter slashing and stabbing. During sparring, I am permitted only blunted replicas but when I face the wooden man, a cross shaped figure, I am allowed to use the two real blades that Swan has given me. The training grounds are modelled after ancient roman ludi, sand floors, stone walls, a false sun that rises and falls just like the real one. I feel like I am on a movie set, one that I can never leave.

My Doctore is an anomaly, he has only a blackened stub for a tongue, cut off in battle they say and so he teaches us with low grunts and the end of his whip. Our training consists of a series of sequential movements called forms. Since not every man has the same weapon, some have to be adapted but in essence they are roughly the same. As a combatant progresses, he must learn longer and more complex forms, some as lengthy as three hundred moves. After the practice of forms, we move on to sparring, where we beat the shit out of one another for hours on end, memorizing the weaknesses of others and trying to correct our own.

Since I have arrived, I have bested every man with relative ease; even with all their training they are too big, too slow, too cumbersome. I am demon unchained, whatever gift I received as a child it has grown into a monstrous thing, hastened by the freedom this place grants. Here, I can sink down into the dirt and gnaw at the bones of savagery like an ogre and there is no one to tame me, no police to stop me, no hospitals to cure me. There are no prisons when you are imprisoned, and there is no fear when you consider yourself already dead.

My arrival and abrupt rise through the ranks have not gone unnoticed. The other combatants treat me as anathema, calling me *Rat* in their respective languages. The only person who does show me any interest, other than hatred, is our tongueless Doctore. Every day, he spends countless hours instructing me in better and more elaborate ways to kill a man. Today, he is showing how to defend against a *kama*, a weapon similar to a small farming scythe used in Asia to cut rice. My opponent is a Japanese brute named Benkei, a second tier combatant, temporarily demoted because he is the only one in the ludus capable of using a kama.

And because the rest of my troupe are tired of having their asses handed to them.

"Come...dirty *nezumi*," he says beneath the rumble of a thick accent.

We are squared off, weapons in hand, with the silent Doctore watching our every move. My practice *sicas* are before me tips up, the blunted blades ready to deflect advancement but the Japanese warrior doesn't attack. He waits patiently moving in circles, not giving any ground and not taking any either. His shaved head glistens with sweat but his eyes reveal no fatigue, he is a coil ready to spring, he is trained, he is *sung.*

The Doctore grows tired of the impasse and cracks his whip.

The crowd doesn't want to see two bitches dancing, fight!

We move simultaneously. Him moving right as I feint left. I turn and roll beneath his first swing with ease, his eyes unable to follow my blurred form. I arise behind him, my chest centimetres from his back and my blade at his throat. His breath freezes in his chest, he drops his weapons in forfeit and the fight is over in seconds. The Doctore grunts his disapproval and motions us to begin again.

This round take your time, the crowd wants a show not a prison shanking.

Even if I moderate my speed, as I have been doing for weeks now to keep my full potential a secret, I am still light years faster than any man in the ludus. The preternatural quickness that has been with me since my beginning has multiplied into something superhuman. Even the most trained and embattled champion has no chance against it.

Welcome to your destiny guy! This is what you were born to do!

Benkei moves back to position and is about to attack when the Doctore stops us and points. We both turn to see a crew of men entering the training ground. Leading the pack is the pimply bulldog, now known to me as Fallon, the head of security. Trailing him, are a couple of his pompous mutts and Kraker. The giant steps forward and the Doctores crack their whips for silence.

Kraker's speech is neither low nor high, refined nor gruff. He speaks with a voice so surprisingly average it sounds almost anticlimactic coming from such an unusual man. He could be a telemarketer calling at dinner time.

"In two days time there is to be a melee between houses. Three men from each house, thirty men in total, fighting as individuals to the death, until only one man remains."

There is a murmur among the combatants. Exhibitions are frequent during the three months between games but they are usually small affairs, only two or three men losing their lives in spectacles for Swan's more affluent colleagues.

"Also there will be a battle of champions between the House of Swan and House Najjar in honour of the Editors Son reaching adulthood. Flamma, come forward."

Flamma, our house champion swaggers through the crowd, swinging an immense belly wrapped in scars. He, like most of the third and second tier fighters forgo the vanity of chiseled bodybuilder abs and pad themselves in fat to protect their organs from spilling when they get slashed.

"You are to represent the noble House of Swan in the coming battle," Kraker says.

A clamour arises from the men as Flamma pounds his chest and bares his teeth.

"Ashoka...Benkei...Hyrcanus..." Kraker continues and it takes a moment for me to realize one of those names is mine. "Come forth."

The three of us approach, Benkei my training partner, Ashoka, a tall imperial-looking East Indian and myself, the hated *rat.* As I walk through the crowd, I am followed by odious looks and muttered curses.

"You three will be fighting in the melee and although you are brothers in this house, when you enter the arena you will be fighting as individuals and only one of you may make it out alive."

We give each other sideways glances, assessing our newly appointed enemies.

Time to die, little flowers, time to die.

Kraker's eyes rest on me.

"Fight and die well."

He and the guards turn and leave and we go back to our training with the false sun shining down above us.

***

Two days later, the fever of battle is upon me. Fear mixed with anticipation and the need to prove myself. To enter the coliseum and show the world the beast I have become, that is my one true desire now. Only in my dreams do I remember the man I was before this and even they have begun to fade under the shadow of my new identity.

Hyrcanus, the Lionkiller.

And soon to be the victor of a thirty man battle to the death.

The four of us are walking the long halls that run underneath Swan's kingdom. Benkei is ahead of me and has traded his *kama* scythe's for a curved katana blade and a shorter wakizashi. He is dressed up in white asian pyjamas and looks the quintessential samurai warrior.

Ashoka, the tall East Indian is beside him, prancing like a peacock, his hips thrusting forward with every step as if he were fucking the air in front of him. He is canopied in gold armour, breastplate, greaves, a malformed helmet that covers half his face. His weapons are a short dagger, a small round shield and a bizarre weapon called an *urumi,* which is a series of four thin, meter and a half long, flexible blades, reminiscent of bandsaw blades, stemming from a normal sword hilt. It is designed specifically for fighting multiple attackers and unless you are a master of *kalaripayattu*, you are more likely to decapitate yourself than injure anyone else.

And Ashoka is a master.

I have seen the Indian dispatch many opponents in training with ease, using his flexible sword.

Past him, leading our little tea party is the barrel-chested Flamma, the undefeated, our house champion, moving as a tank beneath his mounds of fat, muscle and copper armour. He is dressed as a roman gladiator called a *hoplomachus,* and wears leg wrappings, greaves, a brimmed helmet that covers his entire face, a small round shield, a gladius, a spear and a loincloth that he has never washed because apparently ball funk is good luck. He is big, strong and almost as arrogant as Ashoka.

And tonight he may meet his end.

He faces the champion of House Najjar, apparently a seven foot tall Kazakh who is also undefeated.

I am dressed in little more than a sarong, much like the Egyptian I saw fight in the last games. My hair is greased and pulled back in a long ponytail. The two sicas feel good in my hands, like extensions of my limbs and the sand beneath my bare feet welcomes my every step. My only burden is the feeling of surrealism that has crept into my head. The granite archways appear as a movie set, the men in front of me, actors in costume.

This is not real, none of this real.

And yet it is. Somehow it is. I am entering a place where I must fight for my life and two of the men in front of me must die if I am to leave.

As we reach the gate to the arena, the giant portcullis, the feeling fades and in its place comes only cold, calculating clarity. Beside the portcullis is a dugout that looks out onto the arena. Flamma removes his helmet and walks through the entrance way, taking a seat on the bench that runs along the wall. He fights after the melee. Ashoka, Benkei and I shuffle towards the lowered gate and Benkei gives me a reptilian stare.

Inside the arena I hear the house speaker introducing the various houses and the men that are representing them in the melee. Three men stand in front of every entrance way, dressed and armed in every conceivable fashion. They are a living timeline of warriors passed, from the Bronze Age to the Iron. We are the last to be called, the iron portcullis abruptly pulled up from its slumber as the words, *HOUSE SWAN,* reverberate though the coliseum grounds. My *brothers*, and I enter the arena with our weapons in hand and the fervency of murder in our hearts. We turn to our liege lord, the great and mighty Swan and bow our heads and drop to one knee in obeisance. He rises and calls to us.

"Fight and die with honour!"

As we rise back up, Benkei's voice slithers into my ear.

"Now you die, dirty *nezumi.*"

Ashoka hears him and gives me a cold-blooded grin in agreement.

I turn back around and see that the arena holds only the owners of the ten houses and the extra attendees for House Najjar's birthday party. The pitiful turnout makes my stomach flip in disgust at their extravagance. The house speaker calls us forward from his podium and my thoughts turn to the situation at hand. I look upon the twenty nine other men encircled before me and I wonder for a brief instant.

Could one of them be my equal?

They are trained killing machines, all of them.

But can they catch me?

That question will be answered in a matter of moments as the speaker yells out.

"Begin!"

***

In my dreams I am surrounded by a stampede of wild beasts. I am a ball of fear, searching for some respite from the terror of what sieges above me. I am a child, weak and afraid. I am unable to stand up to the circumstances that threaten to crush me on all sides.

But that has all changed.

Now I am a man and the fear that suffocates me in my sleep, electrifies my body and sets fire to my soul when I am awake. I am Michael, I am Raphael, I am Gabriel the Archangel. I am the threefold flame. I am carnage let loose.

I am Hyrcanus.

And all the stupid bastards that shit on my name will hear it from their own lips as they exhale their last breaths.

Die Motherfuckers Die.

The melee begins and soon the blood is flowing. The first one to attack me is Benkei, the Japanese sisterfucker. Most of the other houses have an unspoken agreement that they will not kill one of their own until it is absolutely necessary but the Japanese warrior's hatred for me supersedes this and his blade is the first to try to flay my skin. He comes at me with a ferocity so unexpected it catches me off guard, and I dodge his first slash by mere centimetres. By the time his second and third have come and gone I am fully aware who my enemy is and am ready to take the offensive. He lifts his curved sword above him with both hands on the hilt, sure that his next swing will find its home in my skull but a dagger is thrust into his ribs and then another. I am not where he expected me to be, in the matter of an eye-blink I manoeuvred to his left and punctured his lungs with my sicas. Now he is on his knees looking up at me, a petulant expression upon his face.

"...Dirrrty...*Rattt...*"

He drawls, the blood filling his lungs and rising up to his mouth, to spill between his teeth.

And those are the last words he speaks. I slit his throat and move on.

You were nothing Benkei, fucking nothing, and you dared to challenge a god!

I swivel, assessing the slaughter that fills the arena. The men have become a heaving, sweaty, bloodied mass. They are what I imagine an ulcerated stomach to look like as it consumes itself. Many have already fallen, patches of necrosis in the swirling mosaic of mortification and their bodies are soon pulverized as others dance to the death on top of them. With no one able to stop me, I race through their ranks becoming the demon of their shadows. I slash and I stab, cutting undefended tendons, slicing tender arteries. Many die without even knowing I am their killer. They fall as though a plague is upon them, their blood coating my body like the water of the holy, because this is my baptism, this is my rebirth, this is my sacrament in the church of Swan. And as the minutes pass and more warriors find their doom at the end of my daggers, the last few petals of my humanity wither and fall, perishing beneath the canopy of my new divinity.

The thirty who entered the arena soon became twenty and then ten and now five. Four men stand before me, their figures only vague outlines as the bloodlust clouds my vision turning everything into generalities. I see only enemies, large, small, near, far, none of it matters, they are adversaries and need to be extinguished. I run head long into their midst, leaping over the corpses that litter the ground. They have seen the butchery I am capable of and decided to unite as one against me.

Fools. You are insects under my boot, there could be a hundred of you and you would still fail.

I reach their perimeter and a compact Arabian is there to greet me with a giant scimitar in hand. He swings, misses and his face is in ribbons. I cut out his eyes as he screams for his god to ascend and protect him.

Allah! Allah! Allah!

He dies as another combatant approaches. He is fat and slow, his armour heavy and his weapons too large for close combat. My daggers strike out, finding and piercing the chinks in his chain mail, filleting his internal organs. He goes down like a rhinoceros with me on his back, shrieking.

Only two men now separate me from victory, a blacker than black African wielding a spear and an axe and the Indian peacock, Ashoka, his whip like urumi in his hand. The three of us are equidistant from each other, sidestepping in a triangular standoff. Ashoka and the African are both tall and muscular, the former's sinewy frame hidden beneath a cocoon of gold armour and the latter's protected only by his ebony skin. We rotate in a circle, they too cowardly to make the first move and I, content to bask in the final moments before triumph. In my peripheral I see the crowd in the stands, on their feet and mesmerized by the spectacle before them.

Mesmerized by me.

They came for a show and they received a firsthand glimpse of a god taken human form.

I am the threefold flame, I am the unstoppable Juggernaut.

I am Hyrcanus.

My gaze reaches the two men left in the arena and they see the truth of my words and what is left of their courage crumbles. I leap forward and the African thrusts his spear. Spinning, my sicas pointed outwards, I come upon him and peel the skin from his bones. Lost in the kill I fail to see the four strips of metal coming towards my head until it is almost too late. Ashoka's urumi resembles branches of lightning as it whips through the air and connects with the tender flesh of my shoulder. Exquisite pain erupts from the four deep incisions and a new found respect for life surfaces within me.

That's right, you are not a god, you're just a punk kid and you bleed just like everyone else.

I get to my feet and try to shake off the fear. Ashoka sees my hesitation and a malicious smile forms on his lips.

"You see the truth of it now Rat!" He calls. "Ashoka is the winner! Ashoka fears no man!"

He lifts his urumi and cracks it. The four flexible blades unwind and seek me out. They are faster than even I can move and their motion unpredictable, so I jump backwards, keeping enough distance between us that his weapon cannot reach me while I decide on a tactic.

Ashoka takes this time to taunt me with words of my cravenness.

"Come, come now, Rat! Can you only stab men in the back, Rat? Come face me Rat!"

The tall Indian looks up to the crowd as if to say.

I don't know what to do? He is such a coward!

He flutters his long peacock eyelashes and my dagger is moving out of my hand before I realize what I am doing. The curved sica spins end over end, ready to split Ashoka's pompous face in half, but before it can reach its destination the Indian dashes the dagger from the air with a flick of his urumi. The four blades scintillate like moonlight on a river, and my weapon is gone but the other sica is soon flying through the air and I not far behind it.

Ashoka moves as though he were dancing, the urumi

strikes once again, and my other sica, my last weapon is caught in its web and causes the Indian, not the least bit of damage. But as his blades hit mine and his attention is diverted to his purpose, a blurred form reaches the margins of his being. I slip beneath the net of his weapon and come upon him barehanded. We are so close I can smell the sour milk of his breath. I take my middle and ring finger and thrust it into the soft flesh of his throat; he lets out a soft gurgle as I release him from this life with a sharp pull. The tall peacock falls to the ground, his feathers plucked and the crowd cheers his passing. I look up into their howling faces, feeling both exuberant and numbed.

Hyrcanus, they cry, and for a brief moment I have forgotten what it is to be human.

***

Moments later I am back in the underground passageway, a medic attending to the cuts on my back as four guards stand nearby watching us. Flamma emerges from the dugout, his helmet and weapons in his arms. We stare at each other and surprisingly he nods his head in respect. The last of the bodies are swept from the arena and he dons his crested helmet with its purple plumes and struts upon the sands as the house speaker cries out his name and the bleachers shake with applause. He thrusts his spear to the sky and the audience yells out his name.

"FLAMMA! FLAMMA! FLAMMA!"

And what will they cry if he loses this battle? Will they mourn his passing? Like they did for the twenty nine others out there?

The cold mercury of fatalism glaciates my heart, pulling me from my delusions of godhead. Sad visions of the future play our before me, and I see a life wasted beneath the marionette's string. I see myself as Flamma, the mighty champion stripped of all humanity and higher purpose, destined only for death and victories soon forgotten.

I need to get out of this place, I need to run, I need to escape.

But there is nowhere to go, no asylum within these walls or outside of them. I have no family, no past; it's as if I was bred for this place, the man with no name, the gunslinger fading into the horizon. I look to the arena and the battle that is about to begin, but these things no longer ignite my heart, my bloodlust has been sated, and I feel only sadness.

Flamma's opponent is a seven-foot tall Kazakh dressed in greaves, arm guards and scale armour that turns him into a crimson serpent. His bare head is capped with flowing red hair, in his hands he carries a medieval hand and a halfer sword and a solid rectangular shield that bears his emblem, a giant sea serpent demolishing a wooden ship. His name is Royskillin, he is the champion of House Najjar, and he has never been defeated.

The two square off and begin to hack at each other immediately, because of their size and the weight of their weapons and armour they cannot afford to have a long drawn out fight. They need to kill quickly or else fall victim to exhaustion. Within the first few seconds, I can see they are evenly matched; Flamma does not have the reach of his adversary but his long spear makes up the difference, and the scarred gladiator is surprisingly quick for being so rotund.

The fight continues at a balanced pace until Flamma's spear is broken in half by a well placed stomp of the red serpent's boot. From there, he is at a severe disadvantage. Within a matter of minutes, he is separated from his shield, his helmet and his life. Royskillin's long sword swoops through the air and cleaves Flamma's head from his body. And the people, who not so long ago were celebrating the man's life, are now on their feet rejoicing his death.

Royskillin stabs his sword into the severed head and displays it to the crowd, toting it up and down as if it were a trophy. The bloodied arteries cling to the edge of his steel as he bows before his liege lord and the party of roisterers. They applaud his victory, and he swaggers to a spot, not ten feet in front of me, just below the viewing box of House Swan. There, he flings Flamma's ghoulish countenance to the ground and points the scarlet tip of his blade at someone above me in a suicidal show of temerity.

Words spew from his mouth, however there is only one I recognize; Kraker.

He is challenging Kraker to fight him!

I am as surprised as the rest of the people watching from the grandstands. I can only imagine the reactions of the people above me.

There's no chance he will do it! Would Swan allow such a thing?

I stand up for a closer look, prompting a curse from the little brown medic. The Kazakh spoke in his native tongue.

I have defeated your champion House Swan! Do you have nothing else to offer?

Murmurs cultivate within the crowd and soon they are chanting.

"Kraker! Kraker! Kraker!"

I cannot see what is happening above me, but from the crowd's reaction I assume a decision has been made. I press closer to the opening in the dugout, and suddenly two tuxedoed legs appear right before me. Kraker has jumped from the viewing box, a twelve foot drop and now stands upon the black sands of the arena, bow-tie and all. He takes a few long strides towards Royskillin, tossing off his shirt and tie, and as he gets closer to his opponent, his immensity has never been so apparent. The Kazakh stands seven feet tall, and Kraker towers over him by at least twelve inches. The two stare each other down as Kraker waits for someone to bring him his weapons.

The creak of the portcullis sets my teeth on edge as the guards open it and the acned bulldog Fallon crosses the threshold of the coliseum. In his hands are two monstrous double sided battle axes that appear to be so heavy even his steroid infused muscles have trouble holding them up. Kraker takes the weapons and turns to his Khan, Don Swan and bows in deference. The King's voice rings through the air, flowery words about honour and glory, champions of the past, heroes yet to come. As he speaks, Kraker's shrouded gaze finds me in the sunken bunker and pours ice upon my skin. His lips pull back into a smirk, revealing tiny baby teeth.

"Kraker. You remember that guy? I seen him twist off a lug nut with his bare hands!"

Swan finishes his speech and the tattooed titan turns to face his adversary. The signal to begin is given and the two giants square off. A deep residual silence seizes the air, no one daring to breathe lest they miss a moment of the confrontation. From my spot in the dugout, I watch the two men as a scientist would watch the dance of molecules in his microscope. Every step, every muscle twitch, every stance, every swing, every counter, every block, I study the combatants and memorize them because some day in the future it may be me they are facing.

Which one, depends on who survives this night.

After only a few seconds however I already know who will win. And with every swing of his sword, so does Royskillin. The Kazakh thrusts, dives, lunges, jabs, hacks and spears but Kraker's guard is impenetrable. The giant moves with a grace that belies his immense size. His form is perfect. The only mistakes he makes are on purpose to enthral the crowd. His battleaxes sweep in ferocious arcs, seemingly ripping the fabric of space apart and crushing Royskillin's will. He is unstoppable.

He is the Juggernaut.

Sadly the champion of House Najjar has realized this too late, and I wonder if he regrets his decision.

The loud clang of steel reverberates through the air as Royskillin's shield, the giant rectangle with the painted serpent, is knocked out of his hand, and he rolls to the sand, stunned. Kraker paces above him, waiting for him to gather his wits, and I take note.

Could this be a weakness? His sense of showmanship?

Royskillin, the red serpent, gets back to his feet, and I can see the desperation in his eyes. He knows the struggle is lost, but what else is there for him to do? He gathers his strength for one last charge, lifting his blade high and driving forward. He attacks with the determination of a champion, and I have to say he falls like a champion as well. Kraker blocks his advance with one axe and severs his hand from wrist with the other. Royskillin's sword with hand still attached falls to the ground as his other arm is removed at the shoulder. The red headed giant collapses to his knees, the pools of blood gathering at his sides matching his scale armour. A look of sublime acceptance stills his face. Then it comes, the executioner's blade. Kraker takes his head and raises it in salutation to the ravenous crowd. They cheer until their breaths give out and the colossus keeps his title of undefeated.

Chapter 14

Higgins woke up with a smile on his face. Beside him, hidden beneath the folds of a silk blanket were his two china dolls, Betty and Veronica, still sleeping softly, their naked bodies a tangled reminder of last night's delectations. His cheeks pulled back into a deep yawn as he looked over at the alarm clock beside his bed. Six thirty, just enough time to get cleaned up, drive back home and take Kade and Chastity to school.

What a perfect life!

He sat up and looked around the finely furnished bungalow that Don Swan had so graciously given him, contemplating if he had enough time for a quick shower fuck before he went home.

Nah, you better get moving old boy, you had enough fun last night. It's going to be a long day.

It was always a long day after an exhibition, especially an exhibition as eventful as last night's. A thirty man melee, won by that skinny vulture, Doe, *fucking unbelievable,* and then a fight between Royskillin and Kraker, what an evening. The giant's victory would have been enough to keep everyone's tongues wagging for months but combined with the bizarre outcome that preceded it, god it had to be one of the most memorable spectacles in the arena's history.

Where did that kid come from?

John Doe, or as he was now known Hyrcanus, had little to no back story. He had been working for Swancor since the beginning of last winter, how convenient was that? After being released from a halfway house in Calgary, where he had stayed briefly after serving a sentence for the killing of five men back when he was seventeen, before that nothing.

Shows up out of thin air, and kills five armed street thugs with his bare hands!

How was such a thing possible? When he was still just a kid!

Then there was the rig blowout.

"Unbelievable! He is a superhero! I would be dead if it wasn't for him!"

Doe's coworkers said he moved like a blur, like he was superhuman. Of course anyone reading the article would just take this as exaggeration but Higgins had seen the skinny vulture in action and he *did* move with superhuman speed. He had mowed down some of the world's deadliest men in seconds.

Where did he come from?

Higgins needed some answers and today he would get them. The forty three year old slid off of his pillow top bed and put on a robe. As he did so, Betty, the feistier of his two concubines rolled over, opened a torpid eye and looked him over through a film of sleep dust. A thin string of drool escaped her teenage lips, touched down on the caramel skin of her shoulder and slid into the black crevice of her armpit.

Hmmm, perhaps he did have time for an extra long shower after all.

As he drove Chastity and Kade to school, Higgins looked about the streets of his city and felt a little discomposed. Fort Mckenzie was a slushy, gritty, mess. Spring had sprung early and the town was not ready for it; instead of cool crisp air and bright fluffy snow, there was the tang of melting manure and piles of brown slop in the streets.

Fucking la nino or el nina.

The world was going to shit so might as well take what you can while you can.

Beside him in the passenger seat was Higgins little princess, Chastity. So perfect in her father's eyes that sometimes it was hard for him to even look at her.

"How was your work, Daddy?"

"Good Pumpkin, really good."

"Did you catch any bad guys?"

"Not last night."

"Are there no more bad guys to catch, Daddy?"

"Of course there are more bad guys to catch, right, Dad?" Kade said from the back. The eight year old had his father's looks but his mother's tongue, an appendage that was getting more unruly by the day it seemed.

Because of that trailer trash kid he keeps hanging out with.

Kade's best friend for the last couple years was a queer looking white boy from Arrow Park, one of the shittiest neighbourhoods in the city.

"Don't interrupt your sister, Son."

Kade gave Chastity a sneer through the side mirror.

"Sorry, Dad, but there is always going to be more bad guys right?"

The question actually made Higgins think for a minute.

"I guess there always has to be villains, if there is going to be heroes."

"Are you a hero, Daddy?" Chastity asked.

"I am a police officer, Pumpkin."

"Yeah he's a hero Chastity!" Kade exclaimed, as if the point was obvious.

"He's a superhero! Hey, Dad, Jake and I are making a comic book about this guy who eats the scabs from dead bodies and then he becomes invincible."

"Ewww, that's gross, Kade!"

Kade grinned at his sister, happy at her response.

"Don't try to scare your sister, Kade. Okay munchkins, here we go," Higgins said as he pulled into the school parking lot. He leaned over and kissed his daughter and gave Kade the pound.

"I'll be picking you guys up instead of Mom, okay?"

"Okay, Daddy, bye, love you!"

"Bye, Dad!"

Higgins stayed and watched as his two most precious possessions exited the car and headed towards Queen Victoria Elementary School. Kade's friend Jake stood waiting for them at the bike racks, holding a rolled up comic book, which he quickly unfurled for Kade to inspect.

Higgins glared at the kid with a disapproving eye. He was too poor, too white and too weird. His Father was MIA and his Mother, the few occasions that Higgins had spoken with her, had seemed to be a real oddball. Maggie her name was, a woman so bland he could walk past her a dozen times before recognizing her. She was a nurse at the hospital and the only thing, Higgins really remembered about the conversations they had is that she had told him she'd been to the Stuwix Indian Reserve on many occasions. This struck Higgins as incredibly bizarre; Stuwix was not a place that many people visited unless they were looking for drugs, guns or a fight.

Weird woman.

She definitely wasn't born here. Her syntax had traces of the immigrant and she had that off-putting look that those Hutterites from the colonies have, where they stare at you like fish from a bowl. And so did her son. Hmmm, hopefully Kade would move on from his friendship with the boy and find some more suitable companions.

***

Later in the day, when Higgins was suited up and back in asskicker mode, a sudden snowstorm overtook the skies above Fort Mckenzie and bombarded the city with icy sleet and fierce winds. The air became a swirling miasma, forcing people indoors as waves of hoar coated every exposed surface, extinguishing the morning's hope of an early spring.

"Holy crap, where did this come from?" Constable Drake said from the passenger seat of the police cruiser.

Higgin's eyed the impenetrable grey wall swirling above the streetlights and replied.

"It'll pass."

Drake raised his eyebrows in obvious disagreement as his scarred cauliflower ears became almost comically big.

"Not by the time we get to the reserve."

Higgins silently agreed but didn't want to stop his investigation just because of a little shitty weather.

"It'll be alright."

Drake shrugged his shoulders, he knew better than to argue with his superior when he was in a hunting mood.

"So what do we know about this kid?"

"Doesn't sound like there is that much to know. He grew up on the Stuwix, went to school in town, when he got his oil cheque he blew most of it and ended up down in Calgary,

148

there he got arrested for some petty stuff, breaking into cars mostly and selling coke."

"And he and this Doe?"

"Other than what that piece of shit RJ told us, I don't really know."

First thing that morning, Constables Higgins and Drake had paid a little visit to an old acquaintance, RJ, otherwise known as Raymond Jensen, meth dealer and loan shark extraordinaire, in an effort to get some information. They had shown him a picture of Doe and asked if he knew anything about him.

"Yeah I know that guy man. He came here with that fucking chug, Youngblood, they tried to rob me man. Stole my knife, he even punched my woman!"

Higgins glared at the punk with his fake gold chains and even faker I don't give a shit attitude. The only reason Higgins let the drug-dealer continue breathing was because RJ knew where almost every piece of junkie trash in Fort Mckenzie could be found.

"Shane Youngblood?" Higgins remembered the name from a newspaper clipping describing the rig blowout.

"Yeah. Mothafucka."

"Where's he at?"

"Last I heard, he moved to his parents place out at Stuwix. It was all boarded up but he and some of his chug buddies moved in there."

Higgins lips pulled back in a sneer.

"Enough with the fucking chugs, RJ."

He hated racial slurs of any kind.

"What's the address?"

"I don't know, it's a blue place all beat up."

Higgins grimaced, that could be a lot of places on the reserve.

"And?"

"It's just past main street on the right hand side. And he's driving a new F-250, all jacked up."

Once the two police officers reached the outer limits of the Stuwix Nation main town site, Shane Youngblood's house was actually an easy find, even through the fog of the pervading blizzard. It was a powder blue one-story, built from the same generic blueprint as every place on the reserve, with windows covered in plywood. A Dodge Caravan and a brand new lifted Ford F-250 were parked in the driveway, their metallic exteriors plastered with fresh ice.

"What's the play?" Drake asked, as he got out of the police cruiser.

Higgins flipped the collar of his jacket, trying to keep the freezing wind from reaching his bare neck.

"Just get in get out, we'll question the kid later."

Drake nodded and the two cops walked to the front of the house, went up the front steps and kicked the door in.

"Police Motherfuckers!" Drake yelled with an ear to ear grin on his face.

This was his favourite part of the job, scaring the living hell out of faint-hearted tweakers. He and Higgins entered the premises with their guns raised. The first thing they encountered was a poetically sad scene and a stench that seized the stomach. Three shocked and shivering shells of human beings were huddled together under a pile of blankets that were more stains than fabric. All around them were a profusion of disgusting adjuncts, mouldy food, refuse, piss pots.

"Hands up!" Drake barked.

Higgins inspected the three as they lifted their arms and recognized none of them as the man they were looking for.

"Shane Youngblood, where is he?"

One of the derelicts pointed through to the kitchen.

"Downstairs," it said and Higgins was surprised to hear a woman's voice beneath the square face and matted hair.

"Who else is here?" he demanded.

"No one," she said.

Higgins nodded to Drake.

Stay here and watch these fucks, I'll go find Youngblood.

He manoeuvred through the mounds of garbage and made his way into the kitchen. Sitting in the middle of the floor, where a table should be was a burning barrel with pieces of wood and plastic inside, still smouldering. The ceiling was a blackened smear and the air barely breathable.

Fucking Savages.

Once through, Higgins creeped down the basement stairs until he heard mumbling and a dry grinding sound. Going further, he saw the tenuous form of a man working beneath a fluorescent light. Shane Youngblood was pant and shirtless, slicked with sweat despite the cold, trying to shove a flat head screwdriver into a short log of wood.

"I know guy... I know guy... I know you're in there... I know you're fucking in there guy," he muttered; twisting the screwdriver deeper into one of the many holes he had already dug into the wood.

Higgins crept to the bottom of the stairs.

"Watcha doing, Shane?" he asked through grinning teeth.

Youngblood barely even looked up.

"I know it's in there, I know it's in there! I know it guy! I just have to get it!"

Youngblood hacked at the log with the utmost concentration, seemingly unconcerned about the police officer that just entered his basement.

"What's in there?" Higgins laughed.

Around the table, down on the floor were a half dozen other logs, chipped to pieces and stained with blood.

"It! It!" The tweaker hissed. "It's in there I know it's in there, I just have to get it out!"

Higgins could see the cracked and bloodied fingernails on Youngblood's hands. He had stabbed himself numerous times but didn't seem to have noticed.

"I need you to come with me, Shane; we need to have a little talk."

Shane nodded profusely.

"Yeah, yeah, no problem, no problem, no problem! I just have to get it out, first I have to get it out!"

Higgins eyes glittered in the shadows.

What a great find, a bonafide Junkie spinning like a top.

Even if the kid couldn't tell him anything about John Doe, he would make an excellent addition to the Swan household.

And the world will be a brighter, cleaner place.

Chapter 15

My love affair with Dr. Lau, with all of its sick, twisted, inappropriate but thoroughly enjoyable little bits and pieces seems to finally be coming to an end. My *lover* as I now think of Christine Lau, even though there is nothing lovely about what I do to her during our liaisons, has begun to pull away from me, her visits becoming less frequent, her manner more distant. Sometimes, when I lay alone at night, staring up at the empty ceiling I wonder.

Now that I am no longer a feeble-minded, drooling sack of shit, has she lost interest in me? Has she found some other homicidal maniac from the streets to play out her little rape fantasies?

Perhaps.

Or maybe, just like the dawn blooming into day and the dusk into night, all things are impermanent and must change, lest they become stagnant, and that is what an affair between an institutionalized mental patient and his nutcase doctor can never become; stagnant. We were meant to burn like a comet, blow like a tempest, seethe like an MDMA high, grinding our teeth against one another until the sun comes up and then...Disappear, never to lay eyes upon each other again.

But Christine Lau forgot the most crucial part of the fairy tale romance; that it needs to end at the climax. Once Prince Charming saves Snow White and bangs her brains out, the curtain goes down, and the credits start to roll. No one wants to see the grisly aftermath of her having ten kids and getting fat, while he goes out and finds some other comatose teenager to awaken with his gilded sabre.

That's me. I realize. *I am Snow White, brought back to life by the kiss of a Princess.*

And now my princess is abandoning me. I can see it in her beady little eyes as she sits down and takes out her papers. I can see the aloofness in her posture, the rigidity of her spine, the official manner in which she places the stack of folders upon her lap, the remoteness of her gaze.

The wedding ring on her finger.

The wedding ring on her finger?

How did I not notice it before? The giant diamond that spits cold laughter every time she moves her hand.

Because she's never worn it.

It seems Miss Christine Lau, MD FRCPC, Lying Bitch, is actually *Missus* Christine Lau MD FRCPC Lying Bitch.

Oh the webs we weave.

"John," she says, and I hear only more lies and deceits. "John, we need to talk. The hospital board has... "

She is folded together like an origami flower, every little piece neatly ironed and perfectly arranged. I look upon her coiffed flawlessness and can barely repress my need to pull her charade apart, make her mine, make her beg on her knees, make her squeal my name as I have so many times in the last month.

And who could stop me?

We are in a conference room, far from the ears of any do-gooder male nurses. But no, I am not a rapist, except when my doctor asks me to be.

"...And with my recommendation you are being released."

Released??

I must have misheard.

"What?"

"You are being released, John. It has been decided that you are of sound mind and no longer a danger to society. This afternoon you will be transferred to a halfway house. There you will be given the opportunity for education and the ability to join the workforce. You will also be given a government issued identity card and a social insurance number."

I suck on her words for a second. Release, freedom, liberation. What does any of that even mean? What do I have waiting for me in the outside world?

What do I have in here?

I look at Christine and she mistakes my despondency for accusation.

153

"I apologize for the suddenness, John, but your sentence is up and the..."

My sentence is up? Does she think I can't read a fucking calendar? I was seventeen when I was arrested; a minor. I could have been released last year if someone recommended it.

"You want to get rid of me," I say, not really caring but goading her anyways.

She straightens her glasses as her lips pucker into a cat's asshole.

"I cannot help you anymore John, we have accomplished a lot, just a few months ago you were completely catatonic, but I am afraid the memories from your childhood are lost forever and no matter what I do, I can't help you recover them."

"And...What about us?"

"All the *exercises* we did John, were solely for the treatment of your mental imbalance, and now that we have reached the limits of what we can cure, they no longer need to be performed."

They no longer need to be performed.

It seems the fairytale is truly over. Christine keeps talking, but I don't listen anymore, as far as I am concerned she has left the room. She is done with me, and I am done with her. My thoughts are now on the future, the world beyond these walls. There is a voice deep within my soul, telling me I am destined for something great. It reminds me of my intellectual death, my rebirth, my rehabilitation, and now it applauds my emancipation.

Something amazing awaits you Johnny boy, something extraordinary.

Christine finishes her speech and gathers her papers. She looks to me, and I to her and there is nothing there. We are like two swingers waking up from an orgy, only hours before we were entangled in the most intimate of human expressions and now we are strangers again, gathering our clothes and running for the door.

"Goodbye, John," she says, handing me a stained piece of cloth.

The head-kerchief.

I have not seen it since Christine showed it to me months back. I look up into her crimped little face.

Goodbye Christine, may the gods have mercy on your demented little soul.

Chapter 16

The girl is a petite dark-skinned minx. Her hair is long and wavy and the darkest of browns. Her eyes are thin almonds, her nipples round hazelnuts. Her lips are full and beautiful but the expressions they make are always barren and ugly. She gathers the rest of her clothes and waits for the guard to open the door and let her out of my cell. Soon she is gone and I am left with only the taste of her upon my tongue and lips.

She was given to me for a night, as a reward for my victory in the arena. A female slave, probably stolen from some backwater village and brought here to be used as a plaything for Swan's stable of gladiators. I'd like to say that when she arrived I did the honourable thing, like the guys in the movies and put a blanket around her, built her a fire, taught her English, whatever, kept my dick in my pants but I didn't. When she bared herself to me I reacted as if I were an animal, I pounced like a savage, because that is what I have been reduced to here. And she did not cry, she took and gave in kind, clawing my back and squeezing my throat in a choking grip because she too has been reduced or perhaps I should say elevated to a state of pure instinct.

With no memory of the past and no insight into the future, man regresses back to his most primeval of identities.

Primeval, yes that is what we are here, eating, sleeping, pissing, shitting, fighting and fucking. We are void of all the grandiose rhetoric and superfluous horseshit that suffocates the rest of the world. Extravagances such as love, family, friendship are unnecessary in this dire place. They are in fact dangerous, luxurious jewels that if you grasp too hard will cut you to ribbons. That girl will never love me, she will never love anything again, we are as snakes in the desert or badgers in the dirt. We survive. We accept our circumstance and adapt to it. And the life that preceded this one, the people, the faces from the past, the brothers and sisters we cared about? They must be forgotten, buried, dead. Period.

But some things are easier said than done. The old head-kerchief is in my hands as I think this. The stained slab of cloth, the mysterious little piece from my past, the only thing left to remind me of the life I once had and the questions still unanswered.

What are you? Where did you come from?

I ask the cloth but the questions could just as easily be directed at myself.

***

A week later I am in bed alone and already wishing for another visit from the minx however there is no chance of that happening now, not with the games taking place the following day.

The Great and Secret Show!

No combatant, no matter how favoured by the higher ups is allowed a woman before a match. Sucks the fire from the veins, they say, quashes the killer urge.

The Taoists believed this as well, so Christine Lao told me. They thought a man was born with only a certain amount of vital force in his body and when it ran out he died. This *Jing* was concentrated in certain places in the body, especially in a man's semen. If a cell of blood had one unit of Jing than a cell of bone marrow had a hundred and a man's sperm a thousand, the most in the body. So the Taoists learned all kinds of ways not to lose any sperm during their ancient bonefests. Some refrained all together and became monks but others mastered the art of dry firing, separating orgasm from ejaculation and taking that explosive sexual energy and pushing it up into their brains, hoping for enlightenment.

Dr. Lau tried a few times to teach me these techniques, strangling my cock just before magic time but this just ended in messy results. So instead, she asked me to deposit my spilt *Jing* into little plastic containers, which she would take away with her after our little liaison had finished. What she did with all that stuff I'll never know.

Sleep eventually comes and with it the buried past. I see Shane, the Youngblood, the consummate simpleton. We are on the rig floor, throwing tongs and racking pipe. He is singing Johnny Cash and his face is covered in blood.

It burns, burns, burns.

A fountain of drilling fluid springs up between us and I try to reach through it to grab him but I can't, the pressure is too strong. I scream his name, trying to push my way through the wall of black mud. Then the fire comes, an explosion as bright as the sun and I am awake again, back in the underground prison, laying on a thin mattress and covered with a scratchy wool blanket.

Forget him. I tell myself. *Forget it all, your life is here now.*

And today, perhaps my death as well, because today is the games.

***

There are five of us from House Swan fighting in tonight's battle. Two huge third tier brutes draped in heavy armour, two midsized second tier brutes carrying long weapons and me, the cursed rat. My victory in the melees made me a top pick in the first tier combatants however I am still not a favourite amongst my brothers. Where once they treated me with contempt, now they look upon me with superstition, staying clear of my presence and avoiding me if they can during training.

Tonight I am to fight a Tertiarius or a third man. First I am paired against another first tier fighter and the winner of that must fight against the winner of another first tier battle. The winner of that gets to live another day. Compared to fighting twenty nine other men at once, it should be a cake walk yet the nervousness of battle still spurs my heart.

The five of us reach the entrance to the arena and sit down. The body odour from the biped beside me, a sinister looking Syrian, nearly makes me wretch. He stares down at me as if I am to be his next rape victim, so I turn my attention to the coliseum floor and the pomp and gaudery taking place there.

Before the real matches begin, some of the poor demented Fort Mckenzie tweakers unlucky enough to get caught in Constable Higgins net are tossed into the arena to be

158

massacred by exotic animals. Those that survive, if there are any, get promoted to the rank of Bestiarius, the animal fighters and settle into the dungeon, where I used to live. From there they await their eventual death at the hands of a lion or tiger or perhaps if they survive long enough they can rise to become a combatant. But only two men have accomplished such a thing, myself and Kraker.

For tonight's extravaganza, two abnormally large and ferocious looking grizzly bears have been set loose in the coliseum. The animals are rabid aberrations, so aggressive their handlers use shock collars to keep them from attacking one another. As they sit, frothing at the mouth, the opposing portcullis to my left flies opens and four dishevelled men are pushed on to the sands. I look into their panic-stricken faces, remembering when I first had to prove myself in the arena, fighting the two Russians with Russ the mismatched cowboy at my side.

My gaze scans the frenzied faces, one by one, trying to stir up some empathy, but not quite managing it, until I see someone familiar. A sunken caricature of a human; crumpled and deranged.

No! No! No!

He is so familiar yet I can't place how I know him or from where.

It can't be! It can't be! It can't be!

At first I think of the tweakers I got arrested with. Russ, the Scarecrow, the Tinman, then it comes, horrible realization.

It's not him! It can't be him!

My heart collapses in my chest. My lungs stop breathing. It's Shane.

What the fuck is he doing here? What happened to him?

The Youngblood looks as if he lost twenty pounds and aged ten years. Meth scabs scar his face; his hair is a mangled rat's nest. He looks as hollow as a dead tree and as scared as any man could possibly be. He turns in circles, staring at the crowd until he sees them. Two bears galloping across the arena.

He is a dead man, there is nowhere to go.

The blood surges, synapses fire, there is no rationalization. All that I have buried, all the things I have tried to forget are now in front of me, about to die for a second time.

NO!

I can't let it happen. I jump through the dugout window before the guards even know what is happening. In less than a second I am on the arena floor, racing across the black desert, daggers in hand.

Chapter 17

Calgary Alberta straddles the border between the foothills of the Rockies and the sweeping barrenness of the western plains. It is where I presumably grew up, but I feel no kinship with the city or its people. It is a charmless place, saving all of its courtesies and attentions for tourists that come to get a glimpse of *real* cowboys, although most of the guys wearing ten gallon stetsons sell real estate and probably have never ridden a horse. It is a place in perpetual growth, a gluttonous chick fed by the regurgitated oil reserves in the north and everyone walks with a purposeful stick in their ass.

The inertia of commerce is at everyone's back, and I feel as if I have been thrown into a herd of buffalo and am running only because that is what everyone else is doing. In the span of only a couple months, the slow tedium of the hospital has become a distant memory. I am being molded by my environment, the sudden need for *things* has arisen, I want money, and lots of it, I want electronic thingamajiggys, I want cool clothes, nice sunglasses, a cell phone, more friends, a dope ass car, a cold coca-cola, bigger muscles, a bigger dick. Actually I don't want these things, I need them. But I am at the bottom of the totem pole, and it's a long way up.

First the cash, I need the cash.

The halfway house, known by us residents as the B-House, is a funky medley of caseworkers, facilitators, ex cons, ex mental patients and drug addicts. Most of us go about our little routines, trying not to show too much interest in each other, but there are exceptions. One just arrived yesterday, a jittery weasel of a kid, who has already earned a dozen warnings or so.

And today he is coming to work with me.

B-House is associated with a few work placement outfits that pick up guys and take them to job sites around the city. For the last two weeks, I have been working on a framing crew, building cookie cutter boxes in the wastelands of suburbia and I actually don't hate it. Summer is coming to an end, and the days are dry and warm. My soft, institutionalized hands have begun to callous over, and the unhealthy tallow of my skin has turned a robust copper.

Today we are putting on the roof. My job is to staple down sheets of plywood to the trusses and make sure the new guy doesn't fall to his death. There's barely a cloud in the sky, birds are chirping, and the thought of Christine Lau's stiff naked body and the cold cadaverous touch of her lips hasn't even entered my mind.

"Alright," I say to the kid. "Take the other stapler and follow behind me."

"Oh yeah guy, don't even worry, I've done this kind of shit before. I've been on tons of job sites man, swinging a hammer, putting up drywall, roofing, putting in windows, trim and finishing, I've been-"

"Alright," I interrupt. "Just follow behind me and make sure your staples hit the wood underneath."

The kid looks as if he is about to say more, so I turn away and start firing off the pneumatic stapler. We make it through three sheets of plywood before he has to go down and use the shitter. I continue working, listening to the thrum of traffic and the pedantic voice of our crew boss below. A breeze comes, and the dry smell of dirt, wood and durum fields comes with it. I look around, suddenly fearful that the claustrophobic openness of this world might fill me with dread, but it doesn't. I am alive, I am free, and I am no longer afraid.

When the kid comes back I can tell something is off, his pupils are huge, and his mouth is dancing an Irish jig. His jerky marionette-like movements make me so uneasy I put down my tool and watch him, readying myself in case something happens.

Sure enough, his foot catches on the air hose and he falls to his knees. Any normal person would just grab on to the two by four nailed to the roof so they wouldn't slip off, but whatever drugs this kid has taken have twisted his reasoning, and he begins to swing his arms and legs as if he were drowning. His air gun slips off the roof and stupidly he reaches for it. Momentum takes him and he is about to go over the edge, but I reach out and grab a handful of his greasy hair and yank him back to safety. He hits the plywood hard, and a squeak escapes from his lips.

"Holy Jesus fuck guy!" he says as I pull him further up, so we are above the safety block.

"Relax, Kid!"

"Holy fuck guy, I almost went over man, that was fucked, I almost went over –"

"What is your name?" I ask.

"Uhhhh...Shane guy, Shane Youngblood."

"Shane, go over to the ladder, get off this roof and don't come back up until you can walk properly."

The Youngblood looks up at me and gives me a doltish nod. A voice from down below, our foreman yells.

"What's happening up there? Who dropped this air gun?"

I am about to answer, but surprisingly the native kid calls out.

"I did, sorry, Boss."

"What the hell you doing up there? You could have killed somebody."

"Sorry, Boss."

"Yeah, yeah. Get down here and grab it then."

Shane leaves and I don't see him again that day. But the day after and the day after that he somehow always finds himself at my side. At first I just ignore his inane comments and retarded behaviour, keeping my head down and working, assuming that he will get the hint and eventually fuck off. But as days turn into weeks, the rodent-faced native kid somehow wears my hostility towards him down into something that resembles friendship. Between the gaps in his bullshit, I learn that he is just a screwed up orphan like myself, a piece of afterbirth that the universe has shit out and society has shit upon. He tells me of his life as an addict, a dope dealer and a petty thief. He tells me lies that even he believes, stories that were never true and will never be true but in his heart I see an honest heart, a good heart, a guy who would back me up no matter what. I see a loyal friend, which

163

can mean a lot when you don't have a person in the world. And besides, with him never shutting up, I have no time to think of *her*.

"Fuck, Johnnie, you gotta come check this shit out guy!" The Youngblood is sitting at the communal computer in the B-House common room, doing what he usually does, looking at porn.

"You know they're gonna kick you off that thing again," I tell him from across the room, where I am trying to enjoy a bowl of Kraft Dinner in silence. Through the window, I see the last breaths of autumn, a season far too brief in this part of the world.

"No dude, this is some weird ass shit that Larry was looking at."

Larry Knickerson is our head supervisor, the disgruntled but respectfully fair dictator of B-House.

"I looked up his search history and guess what he was googling guy? Guess?"

Outside the dying leaves curl up before me, the wind pushing them from the cradle of their homes and down to the waiting graves below. Soon the snow will come and smother them with a frigid embrace and all will be silent.

"Ass Fuck with Head in Toilet!" Shane yells. The kid has no sense of what an *inside* voice is.

"Hahaha, ass fuck with head in toilet, that's what he was looking up dude! What a fucking weirdo, guy! Who looks up that shit? I mean I seen some weird shit, you know like those two chicks eating each other's shit and fucking dogs and whatever, but I didn't look that stuff up guy, you know? Dudes just showed it to me, I wasn't spanking it to that stuff, that's sick, but Larry guy, this is what he jerks off to, guy. Ass fuck with head in toilet, hilarious, Hahaha."

As Shane ponders the depravity of our head supervisor, I contemplate the future and my impending release from B-House. My probation is coming to an end and soon I will have to find another job and another place to lay my bones. Shane's will soon be up as well; given that Larry Ass Fuck with Head in Toilet or anybody else at B-House doesn't catch him doing coke again and send him back to jail.

"What's the name of the town you were talking about up north?" I say to the Youngblood.

"Huh?" He swivels around to face me. "Uhhh, you mean Fort Mckenzie?"

"Yeah. You think you could get us some jobs up there?"

Shane's face lights up.

"Oh fuck yeah guy, I know everybody in that town. We could go make tons of cash, there's so much work man, I know a guy who works for Swancor, could probably hook us up."

"Swancor?"

"Yeah man Swancor. You never heard of it? It's like one of the biggest oil companies in the world guy, they got some huge operations going on up north."

"Oh yeah?"

"Yeah man, let's do it! A buddy of mine picked up the Desperada from the impound lot, and it's at his house guy. When we get out of this fucking place man that's what we'll do, cruise up fucking north guy."

The Youngblood gives me one of his signature smiles, a smile so ugly it could peel paint, yet so wide it reaches my own face.

Chapter 18

Higgins, proudly dressed in his Red Serge, with its gold buttons, leather riding boots and wide brimmed stetson, stood tall in the private viewing booth of his King, Don Swan. In front of him on all sides were the most wealthy and powerful people on the planet, the movers and shakers, the conquerors, the puppet masters, the clandestine overlords, the sheiks, the sovereigns, the pharaohs. Here, they sat and drank, and he was among them. Not only that, he was a glistening jewel in the crown of the man who oversaw them all, a trusted servant, a general, a baron.

Beside Higgins, a few feet to his left, was the man himself, Don Swan, looking dapper in a fresh tuxedo. Buzzing about him was an entourage of women, debutants, and esteemed guests, and as always, the giant Kraker. Whereas Swan looked imperial in his dinner jacket and black bow tie, Kraker appeared a gorilla in his.

I can't believe how far he has come.

It was years ago that Higgins first laid eyes on the tattooed goliath. He had been on a stakeout; four Hell's Angels had been butchered in an alley for no apparent reason, so he was keeping an eye on their clubhouse, trying to uncover some answers. As he was about to call it a night, Kraker arrived, dressed all in black. He kicked in the door of possibly the most dangerous place in Fort Mckenzie and proceeded to annihilate every one of the occupants, sending five men to hospital, paralysing one and outright killing two others.

Higgins knew better than to enter the premises and waited until the mayhem was over. When Kraker came back out, he pulled a gun on him. The two stood in complete silence for what seemed like minutes. Higgins thought the man was going to do something, run, rush him, something, but surprisingly he got to his knees and let himself be put into cuffs. Higgins, who was already a conscript in the Swan army, took his chained beast straight to the Castle to be detained. There, he found out that Kraker was an escaped convict from Alaska, a murderer who had assaulted a handful of prison guards in an unbelievable escape.

Why he let himself be so easily captured was a question that still irked Higgins. Why didn't he run? Or fight?

Later, when the man won his freedom and weaseled his way into Don Swan's favour, Higgins came to realize that Kraker was not just a brainless killer but a brilliant tactician who had secured his future and was now only second to the Khan himself in power.

Maybe he let himself be taken because he knew he could get out of it?

Either with his fists or his wits.

The reason behind the biker attacks remained a mystery, same as the murder in Alaska, they were just more threads in the cloak of secrecy that surrounded the tattooed giant. Higgins had never gotten answers and now he never would; Kraker outranked him. Swan had given him the wooden sword so to speak and with it, the ability to behead those that displeased him.

Superficially, none of that bothered Higgins, he pretended indifference. It was only in the depths of the night he plotted how to remove the giant. However, when the stars faded so did his schemes. Kraker was not one to be outplayed. No, it was better to let things unfold on their own. In time, Swan would see who the better man was, the more loyal retainer. Or maybe the oaf would just get himself killed. No one was invincible, contrary to what Kraker had demonstrated so far.

Maybe even tonight?

If anything, the last exhibition proved that the giant's ego was not immune to provocation.

***

The grizzly bears were like nothing Higgins had ever seen. Huge, rabid beasts, pumped full of hormones that doubled their already immense size, they frothed at the sight of the four tweakers. Shane Youngblood was one of those wasted junkies. The kid had given no insight into the enigma that was John Doe. Even after a good smashing, he revealed

167

nothing useful. The two met in a halfway house, they worked together, they were friends, he didn't know where he came from, he had no idea that he'd even been in a mental institution.

Fucking useless.

Higgins ears suddenly pricked as he caught pieces of a conversation nearby.

"So that ragged little man, what was his name? Hyrcanus? He won the melee? Unbelievable! Is he going to fight tonight? He is?"

Doe was going to fight tonight. Ha! The vulture was probably in the dugout below him right now.

I wonder if he'll recognize his old buddy? Haha!

Just then a pale figure came sprinting across the coliseum floor, carrying two daggers.

"Look it's him! It's Hyrcanus!"

Higgins looked, and the man was indeed John Hyrcanus. His long black hair whipped behind him as he raced towards the attacking bears, trying to intercept them before they made it to the floundering tweakers.

"Oh, is this part of the show, Don?" A woman near to the King asked.

Don Swan's polished exterior showed no signs ruffling, but Higgins felt the anger when their eyes met.

"Of course it is, Diane." he said to the twinkling woman. "Of course it is."

All eyes went back to the scene on the arena floor except Swan's. The King leaned back and whispered something into Kraker's ear.

Looks like you just fucked yourself Doe.

Higgins, like most, knew that the punishment for interfering in another man's fight was immediate death. Kraker would now radio Fallon and give him the kill order.

But why isn't he?

Instead of relaying his King's message, Kraker was actually arguing with him. Higgins tried to lean in and listen but the sounds of the people drowned their voices. He resumed watching until Kraker abruptly got up and left, apparently winning the dispute.

What was that about?

He gave Swan a questioning look, but the King sat forward and said nothing.

Down in the arena, Hyrcanus reached the two bears and was in the midst of prying their attentions away from the other men. A series of violent roars echoed through the stands as he drove his daggers into the flank of one of the beasts. From there, he came upon the other and slashed at its face. Soon both animals were drawn into the fray, and Hyrcanus danced through them as though he were a mongoose, exhausting a pair of cobras. His blades disappeared in a crimson haze and within minutes all that was left of the bears was a mound of twitching flesh.

Jesus, he is fast!

Standing upon the bodies, Hyrcanus seemed not to notice the people driven mad by his display. He stared out upon the black sands, searching for someone. And Higgins knew who.

Shane Youngblood.

As the two men approached one another, the arena grew silent. Hyrcanus dropped his daggers, embraced his friend and eventually Youngblood embraced him back. The people in the stands looked upon this sad little scene with confusion and slight embarrassment.

What the hell is this all about?

After a few moments, Don Swan rose from his throne.

"John Hyrcanus, you stand before us a victor!" he called, and the people began to clap.

"You have fought bravely, saving these men from a gruesome death. However; you have also broken one of the Arena's strictest rules. No man may interfere with another man's battle!"

The audience grew grim as Swan's words resounded through the underground coliseum.

"These men were to survive by their own strength, not yours!"

Higgins smirked.

How the fuck were they supposed to survive that? They would have needed machine guns to kill those things.

"And any man who defies the rules of the Arena must be punished accordingly!"

A low grumble billowed through the bleachers. A few voices even called out for pathos.

Don Swan raised his chin, daring anyone to openly defy his governance. When no one did he continued.

"However, because of your valour, I have decided to show you some leniency and allow you to die in battle... At the hands of a Champion!"

The portcullis below was raised and out walked Kraker; dressed for battle. Around his waist was a boiled leather loincloth. Engraved silver coiled his extremities, catching the light from above and holding it in a suffocating embrace. The tattoos around his eyes fluttered as if aflame. He was truly awe-inspiring, and Higgins had to admit, he was shaken by the man's appearance.

Jesus Christ.

Most men would shatter just having such a man look at them but Doe did not. In fact, he ushered his friend Youngblood back towards the arena wall and stepped to meet Kraker in the centre of the coliseum.

What a ballsy bastard!

The skinny vulture looked as though he were an infant beneath the shadow of Kraker. His curved sica daggers nothing but toys compared to Kraker's double edged battleaxes. Yet, still he came, settling into a low stance as he drew within striking distance of the colossus. In that infinite second before battle, Higgins had a bright comet of a thought.

This is it! This is how that giant son of a bitch dies!

After tonight, he would rise to new dizzying heights of prestige within the empire of Swan. With Kraker out of the way, there would be no one to impede his ambitions.

It all ends here!

The light, however, quickly turned to darkness as Kraker began his assault. The giant attacked with the vigour of twenty men and the ferocity of a demon. Doe was an amateur, a fluke, running like a frightened gazelle, not even attempting to fight back. He skipped side to side, sprinting in circles, barely staying ahead of the razor-sharp axe blades that were coming for his head.

Eventually the people in the stands began to boo his performance. They raised their fists and cursed, they spit in disgust. Kraker, Goliath incarnate swung furiously, coming within centimeters of a killing blow but always just missing.

It's a ruse! Has to be!

Higgins could feel it in his bones. Doe was tiring the monster out.

The fight continued for minutes until finally, in an act of desperation, Kraker threw away an axe. He took the other with both hands and began moving towards the far wall, where Shane Youngblood and the rest of the tweakers were still hiding. Seeing his intentions, Hyrcanus had to finally stand his ground.

Now we'll see what the fucker is made of!

John Hyrcanus feinted left, sidestepped right, rolled underneath the titan's blade as he charged and for the first time blood was spilt. Kraker's hamstring opened up into an angry red gash, and the crowd cried out in surprise. Hyrcanus jumped back to his original position, blocking Kraker's way. Kraker swung again and Hyrcanus disappeared. The giant bellowed as he was struck in the abdomen. Seconds after that, a red streak appeared on his lower back, just above his hip and then his forearm, then his bicep, his knee, his stomach, his cheek. Soon the colossus was draped in blood from head to toe.

My god, Doe is going to do it!

Kraker became so sluggish he could barely move. Every time he lifted his arm, by the time it came down he had suffered a dozen new wounds. Hyrcanus swirled around him like a tornado, gradually grinding him down to nothing. To everyone watching, it became painfully obvious that his previous cravenness had been nothing but a deception. Now he was a vampiric tempest, sucking the life from the failing champion. He ripped and he tore, until finally, Kraker, the undefeated titan of House Swan, dropped his weapon and fell to his knees.

And a spectral hush strangled the air.

Hyrcanus walked behind the kneeling Goliath, who on his knees was still taller than his executioner, and without a hint of magniloquence proceeded to slit the man's throat and kick him to the ground. Resembling a centuries old redwood, Kraker fell to the sands of the Arena and remained there, never to rise again.

Higgins, like the rest of the people watching, stood dumbstruck. John Doe had done the impossible. He had beaten the invincible. And now, the police constable's idle daydreams were a reality. He probably would have continued to stand there, slack-jawed and stupefied for minutes had not someone called his name.

"Higgins," Swan whispered and as Higgins turned, he saw something on the great man's face he never thought possible. Grief. Heart-wrenching, plaintive, murderous grief.

"Kill him."

Higgins stared into the King's spuming eyes.

"Kill him and his little fucking bum buddy now!"

He turned back to the arena and saw Doe moving back towards the ragged effigy that was Shane Youngblood. The two wrapped their arms around each other and Higgins looked back at Swan.

Yes.

He nodded.

Yes sir.

Chapter 19

The monster falls. His life's blood drains from him by the gallon. His herculean form twitches face down in the black sand until; finally, the death knell is struck. My heart is a galloping hoof. My pale skin awash in fresh red paint that steams above me in phantasmal wisps. The whorl of people in the stands bark like dogs, spinning and churning, spinning and churning, pulling me down into their corrupted whirlpool, drowning me in a charybdis of their most base desires.

HELL! HELL! HELL!

They cry.

Or maybe it is something different, I don't know, I don't care. As the adrenaline fades so does all hope.

What have I done? What am I doing?

Then I see it. The piece. The reason I broke my master's leash.

I see him.

Shane comes to me like a whipped dog, fearful and stunned. When I wrap my arms around him, he shakes as if I were a predator, not his protector. His arms do not rise until I grasp his face and make him look into my eyes.

It is me! It is me, old friend!

"Look! Look!"

And then he sees through the masks I have been forced to wear, the skeins of violence, and recognizes the man underneath. He lifts his arms and returns my hug, convulsing as the poison of fear leaves his body. The warmth of his tears thaws my frozen marrow, and soon there is nothing left, but the love I feel for this man. We stand for days in that embrace, not knowing what words need to be said; not knowing what horrors will find us next. We look upon each other and see the cruelty that destiny has dealt, the softness that has been chiseled away and the charred severity that remains. I look upon my only friend in the world, suddenly wishing for a different life and the bullet tears his face apart.

One second, Shane is in front of me, alive, breathing, afraid, relieved, confused, alive, alive! And the next he is gone.

The bullet hits him just above the ear and comes out the other side of his head in a vibrant explosion. Bone and gore erupt into the air and he falls limp in my arms, a hundred and forty pound paperweight. I pull him close, the muscles of my jaw unable to shut and stop the screams that are coming from within. I try to keep him up, but he has turned into a long cumbersome bag of sand, so my hands slip and slip.

Snap!

Something sharp and hard and hot hits my neck, and I am falling alongside the Youngblood. I hit the ground, still alive but unable to move. Another bullet has been fired and shattered my spine; I am paralysed from the neck down. Shane is in front of me, his face slack and rubbery. Slow blood pours from his wound on to the ground in syrupy spurts. All I can hear is thunder, the shifting of mountains.

Hell! Hell! Hell!

Shane stares at me, as if in accusation.

Why couldn't you stop this guy?

I am fast but not faster than a bullet motherfucker.

Hands wrap around my numb legs and pull me from my resting place. Shane and I are dragged from the hallowed grounds of the coliseum as the crowd surges.

Are they celebrating our deaths or protesting them?

I cannot tell. Guards rush by with the other two surviving tweakers. Up until then I had forgotten them. Feet shuffle. We are in the dark catacombs beneath the arena grandstands. Bright white pain spiderwebs across my skull as I am turned over to be scrutinized by my murderer.

Higgins round, brown face looms over top of me, his Bolshevik tongue slipping between the gap in his front teeth, tasting the air. His cheeks are flushed as though he just finished a fat steak or a tasty fuck. Instinct takes hold, and I hold my breath.

Don't move...Don't breathe...Don't blink.

Why I should pretend to be dead, doesn't really register. I

am dead, if not now than soon, I am paralysed, there is no way out of this mess. Nevertheless, I do my best doornail impression, and Higgins, in his stupid Dudley Do Right fucking uniform, bends down and whispers.

"Thanks, little buddy, thanks a lot."

I have no fucking clue what he is thankful for.

***

Hours later we are loaded into a vehicle, Shane, myself and a few more unlucky souls that happened to die that evening for the entertainment of Don Swan and his pals. I am thrown into a pile, with all the tenderness one would give to a corpse, by the rough hands of Fallon and his lackeys. Once finished, they jump into the front and soon we are moving.

The darkness hides the dead men from view, my nose however paints a graphic picture. I see exposed bones, dangling eyeballs, semi-sexual flaps of skin, vital fluids escaping, along with the freed souls of the damned. I try to move, roll, shake, push away the cadaver that lies upon me like a drunken lover, but there is nothing, my mind and body have disconnected, I remain still.

It is strange how quickly these things we deem permanent can be swept away. Just hours ago, I was a moving weapon, my body a vision of deadly grace and all it took was a little snip of thin nervous tissue to turn me into a vegetable.

Same with Shane.

Just hours ago, the Youngblood was a man, a piece of this world, my brother, and now he is a nameless hunk of meat, soon to be worm food.

There is no me, there is no my, all things are impermanent.

The van rocks and we rock with it. Minutes pass into what must be hours before we arrive at our destination. Fallon opens the van door, and a cold spring wind enters to caress the skin of my forehead and ears and my cheeks, the only parts of my body I can feel anymore. I see a world of stars set like diamonds in a mantle as I am lifted from the van, along with the rest of the corpses. Grey moonlight drips from the faces of the dead and alive alike; turning us all into ghastly shades.

As I am carried, I see that we are in an industrial junkyard. Massive hunks of disjointed metal are strewn everywhere, pieces of drilling pipe, crushed seacans, mangled derricks. The smell of sulphur and other toxic hydrocarbons tickle my nose, giving me a solid answer as to where we are.

The oilsands.

The open mining pits of Swancor's northern Alberta's operations stretch for thousands of kilometres. Once all the black gold has been squeezed, all that is left is scorched earth and the noxious tailings ponds. This is where we are.

This is where they are going to leave us.

I think back to the conversation I had with Shane as we flew over the oilsands on our way back from rig nine.

"Looks like a great place to bury a body," he had said.

The irony from that offhand statement is almost as sickening as the sight of the corpse being carried beside me.

We reach a cargo door that is sunk in the ground, just inches above a small black tailings pool. Fallon reaches down, unlocks the door and rolls it back, revealing one the most macabre scenarios I could ever imagine. Piled on top of one another, in a hidden cistern, are a heap of bodies in various stages of decay. The smell that arises is so vile; it takes every ounce of my willpower to keep my guts from retching.

"Fuck sakes!" the lackey to my left calls out.

"Yeah, let's get 'em in there and get the fuck out of here." Another one says.

The sound of splashing water and the dull thud of meat on meat fills my ears. My handler walks up to the nightmare in the ground, and for the briefest of seconds, I see a handful of faces from my past.

Russ the mismatched cowboy, Misty, Tinman, the Cowardly Lion.

They are all here. They are all dead. Four bodies buried in sludge, never to be seen again, never to be remembered.

Russ has had his head split open, in what I recognize as an axe wound. He must have been used by one of the other houses as a practice dummy.

Sorry cowboy, looks like you'll be riding that methamphetamine pony up in heaven now.

The meth scabs on his face have turned into horrible black growths, thick crystalline lesions that cover his chin and neck. Surprisingly, they have a concentric design and do resemble a flower or perhaps a Hindu mandala. Black Orchids.

Looks like the kid was right.

A wide chunk of human hamburger lands in the cistern and then it is my turn. My handler gives me the old heave ho and I am flopping through the air, soon to land right on top of Russ, my cheekbone smacking down hard directly on top of his. I imagine we must look like a couple of young darlings, faces pressed tight, staring starry eyed into the distance. But instead of a setting sun or a sublime landscape in front of us, I see only Shane, my old compadre, being thrown into the black pit after me. He splashes down into a pool of muck and my broken heart pieces itself back together and beats at the cage of my ribs.

Get up, John! Get the fuck up! Kill these motherfuckers!

But I can't. I'm sorry Shane, I can't. I can't even bring myself to speak, to beg for my own life. I should be announcing myself to these bastards and pleading for them to take me to a hospital. Maybe I could live a decent life as a quadriplegic, get a small apartment, Canada's got a great healthcare system, they would probably give me a live in nurse to feed and bathe me. Maybe it would be Maggie, and she could tell me what she knows about me. Maybe in time I would get some feeling back in my arms, be able to take care of myself. Maybe someday, I could even walk, maybe fight, rejoin the house of Swan.

Maybe, maybe, maybe...

They killed you buddy boy. You broke the rules and this is where you will stay. They didn't load up Kraker's gutted corpse and ship him to some hidden oilsand's graveyard. He's probably getting stuffed right now, so he can be mounted on a wall beside Don fucking Swan's headboard. No, better to stay quiet, wait it out, pray to those gods that don't exist.

Red power, white, whatever, can you please get me out of this?

The last of the bodies is thrown into the pit. Fallon is above us, his face a boiling stew. His eyes find me and remain there in what must be his most studious of expressions.

"It's crazy." One of his lackeys says. "I can't believe this guy took down Kraker."

Fallon doesn't look away. He stares at me in silence.

"Nobody's invincible," he says finally and reaches down to close the door.

The screech of metal on metal rattles my teeth as the blackness becomes absolute and I am left alone with only my shattered thoughts and the stench of the dead to keep me company.

Chapter 20

"Come back, John. Come back to me."

A crackle. A hissing in the distance.

The Static!

"Ignore it, John."

"Why should I listen to you? Deceiver! Undoer!"

"Reconnect, John, reach down."

"I can't! I can't! I can only feel my face!"

Festering flesh, a necrotic moonscape.

Hisssssss.

Bone against bone.

"Do not fall victim to distraction."

Ripples in the silence, an uprising.

"It's coming!"

"Don't let it, John! Stand your ground!"

"I can't. It's too huge!"

A moving wall, a crumbling parapet.

"Don't run, John! Ground down, let it go through you!"

The Static approaches, preparing to snuff me out.

Snap. Crackle. Pop.

I am ready for deliverance, but she is not.

"Open your eyes, John! Open your eyes!"

"Why?!"

There is only darkness, inside and out.

"Do it, John. Do it for me."

I am, as always, her puppet, even in this place.

My eyes open and there is nothing. Nothing but the end.

"Look closer."

Thunder in my ears, corruption in my nose, despair in my heart.

"Look, John. Look!"

"I... See it."

A glistening jewel.

"Good, John! Good!"

Beneath me, it stirs, a child's delusion, seed of the chimera.

Dr. Lau spreads her legs.

"Come closer," she whispers.

I do and her petals unfold. She smells of perfume, so potent, it makes my head spin.

"Do it, John."

I feel a demon's pressure against my skull. The static?

"No baby, the static is gone, gone forever, now take a bite."

I have only an instant. She is smothering me with her thighs. Behind me, the wave has reached its crest.

Decide Boy! Decide!

I do, pressing my nose into her ovaries. She cries out. I glide my tongue across her labia and sink my teeth in. Her essence turns hard in my mouth. Diamonds grind to dust between molar and fang.

Her screams become my own, ecstasy into agony.

I am reborn.

***

The lesion is in my teeth, its crystalline edges desperately trying to hold on to the flesh of Russ's chin. I pull back, peeling it from its resting place, and swallow it down. The moments that follow are filled with revulsion, disgust, loathing. The bodies beneath me call out in gargled horror movie voices.

Cannibal! Cannibal!

But the black orchid is gone. I have done nothing I tell them. And maybe I have. The lines between reality and illusion have evaporated. One minute I am in the hospital, under the thumb of Christine Lau, the next, chewing on a dead man's face.

But did I? Or was I just imagining?

Maybe I am still in the hospital, tied to a bed with brown leather straps, gazing blankly at a painted concrete ceiling. Maybe I am still insane, maybe I was never cured...Maybe none of this ever happened. The rigs, Shane, Maggie, Don Swan, Kraker, the arena, did I make all that up? It seems impossible, but so does an underground coliseum filled with a thousand billionaires watching men kill each other.

The static.

Did the static ever leave?

I tune my ears, trying to hear its somniferous crackle. I open my eyes and try to pierce the shades of blackness, looking for its dull luminance. Is that it? There in the depths. Is that a cool stupefying mist upon my face or is it Russ the Mismatched Cowboy's weepy skin.

I look further, listen harder. There is something, a fiery red dot coming towards me in an ever widening circle. It breaches the centre of my brow and purges my insides. Soon I am enveloped, the thousand tongues of god lash at my skin telling me to.

AWAKEN!

The pain is unbearable. It feels as if my blood has turned to molten rock, erupting from a spot deep within my stomach.

The Black Orchid! It's working!

The vast nothingness that was my body has been found and reattached to my brain. The strings of my nervous system hum like the threads of a harp; turning crude flesh into something transcendental. Black orchids erupt from my pale human flesh and spread their obsidian petals, turning my body into a landscape of blossoms and blooms, a geometric masterpiece. Soon I am covered, head to toe, the vast web of new tissue finishing its metamorphosis by entering my pupils and making my vision super-human. The darkness ignites in front of me, and I can see every gory detail of the sepulchre.

The intimacy of Russ's face pressed against my own fills with me with sudden revulsion as his magnified countenance appears with crystal clarity. I press away, using my new found strength, and my arms go right through his flesh as if it were wet tissue paper. I roll on to my side and come face to face with the missing patch of his chin.

The piece you ate.

Disgusted even further I pull up and out of his corpse and thrust my body towards the ceiling. The rolling aluminum door explodes outward as I launch through it, flying over twelve feet into the air. Landing in the muck, I take a second to marvel at the transformation that has occurred. My arms and legs and torso look to be made of bleached leather wrapped in thick bands of black silica. My ears pulse with a thousand far away sounds as my nose filters every possible aroma within a twenty mile radius. My heart has been replaced with what must be a flock of angry hummingbirds, and if I don't move soon, I think my brain will hemorrhage.

The metal door of the cistern folds like paper in my hands as I peel it back and reach down for Shane. Careful not to crush him in my mutant grasp, I pull him out of the pit and lay him down on a dry patch of moonlit dirt. With my new vision, he seems to glow with an eerie green iridescence, and for the briefest of seconds my mind tells me he is alive, about to open his eyes and greet me with a smile.

Holy fuck guy! Was I just dead?

Yeah you still are buddy. His eyes never open; I toss him on my shoulder. The least I can do is get him out of...

The hammering in my chest increases. Cold fire thrums through my veins. A feral scream escapes my lips and I am running. The black orchid has taken control, I need to move, howl, shake the world to its foundations. The pieces of junk unlucky enough to be in my warpath are soon pulled from their resting places and tossed into the atmosphere. Tangled steel jungle gyms, massive lengths of pipe, broken down pieces of machinery, a huge Caterpillar mining truck. Hunks of metal weighing thousands of pounds go flying as I barrel across the oilsands graveyard.

Past the wreckage is a wasteland of scorched earth. I sprint across it at a breakneck speed. An hour passes, maybe two, the moon has disappeared, and a cheerless spring morning is making its ominous arrival. Somehow I have turned myself around, I am going north or maybe east now, fuck I don't know, my brain feels as if it is going to explode.

Eventually, I come to the edge of the oilsands. The Boreal, my old sanctuary, unfolds in green and brown waves. I leap over a twenty foot high pile of bulldozed trees and soil, overburden they call it, and crash through the timbers like a meteor.

Hours pass and the milky white sun above turns the few remaining snow piles to slush. I run as if in a dream, the sentinels to my left and right, becoming vacillating towers, the ground below, a vast keyed instrument that sings with every step. The weight on my shoulder, whatever it is, I forget now, has begun to recite old cowboy poetry. I am coming to a place of pure exhaustion. The effects of the black orchid have reached a burning pinnacle but still I am running and thrashing through the bush.

Run, run, run.

I continue west. My nose tells me there is a building approaching. The distinctly human aromas of tobacco, bacon, cheese, fresh bread, old dust make a golden path in the air. A second later, the silhouette of a wooden cabin appears through the timbers. There is something so familiar about the place but my mind doesn't have the energy to figure out what.

As I reach the small clearing that surrounds the home, the last ember of the black orchid goes out and I collapse violently to the ground. Shane's dead body falls with me and his limbs fold beneath him at grotesque angles. I look up and see that my alien vision has receded, the world around me has become blunted and undefined. The black affliction on my skin no longer exists; I am a scant, pale young man once again.

A door opens. Someone approaches. I look up, but the figure is a blur. My eyes wander drunkenly and find a talisman suspended in the sky. As my head drops, a white condor hovers over me and smothers my eyes with its wings.

Chapter 21

I awaken to pure, unadulterated agony. A heroin withdrawal times a thousand. My bones shake and itch, my lungs burn, my tongue aches, my teeth chatter, my stomach is a star gone supernova. My body screams with every movement and I can't stop moving.

At least you are alive.

Ha. Death would be a delight compared to this.

A particularly torturous wave overtakes me and I cry out, smashing my face against the bars of the cell. The hooks dig deep and I hold my breath. It feels as if my insides are being scooped out with a rusty spoon. After a few horrendous moments I open my eyes and look through a rose tinted lens of blood.

Where the hell am I?

My hands are wrapped in a death grip around a couple vertical bars attached to a locked sliding door made of grey wood. Below my shoeless feet is bare dirt covered in hay. A horse stall in an old barn. The air is mouldy and full of dust. A cast iron stove in the corner crackles, the yellow and orange flames giving off the only light in the building.

I know this place.

I look to the left and see a stainless steel table, barely visible through the dimness.

That's where I dropped the wolf. This is Henry Yellowbird's place.

As soon as I think of the old medicine man's name, he enters the barn and another wave of pain overtakes me. I drop to the ground, grunting curses.

"John," he says, jogging over.

A muffled groan is my only reply.

He unlocks the door and grabs the blanket I have discarded from the floor and wraps it around me. I toss it off in a rage.

"What is that made of, fucking sandpaper?!!"

He throws it back on and shoves a dried root into my mouth.

"Chew this," he says, and I immediately try to spit out whatever it is he's given me.

He covers my mouth and the root unleashes a potent spice so sapid it makes my eyes water and my nose run. I try to pull his hand away but the old man is unbelievably strong. He holds me for a few more seconds, staring silently with his smoke-filled gaze and surprisingly I begin to feel a little better. The incisive stabbing pains slow to a dull throb and I actually begin to enjoy the taste of the medicine. Henry lets me go and after a moment he nods, telling me to spit out the manducated pieces.

"Better?" he asks.

"Better," I reply, but secretly I know the worst has yet to come.

A hopeless yearning has infected my heart. Fields of shimmering black flowers dance behind my eyes, tantalizing my senses, begging me to go back to that rotting tomb and eat every piece of scabby skin that I can get my hands on.

"How did you find me?" I ask.

"You found me."

Right. The white condor.

"Where's Shane?" Visions of his twisted body scurry across my mind.

"He's here. In the house. We'll be preparing his body soon for the departure ceremony."

Departure ceremony? You're a little late buddy, he's long gone.

I look to the key at his belt.

"You locked me up."

He slowly nods, and I know that when he leaves he'll be locking me up again. This is probably a good idea, I'm already trying to remember my way back to the industrial wasteland and Russ's drug filled corpse.

More. More. More. I need more!

If it wasn't such an absurdly disgusting request, I would be asking Henry to go for me right now. My teeth begin to chatter even though I am boiling. The medicine man gives me a look of concern so genuine; I have to avert my gaze. I look up the rafters but there I see dozens of black orchids exploding like fireworks, so I squeeze my face shut.

Enough, enough, enough, enough.

But the agony continues.

Henry stays with me, singing low melancholy melodies, tending to the fire, giving me water, but mostly he just sits, watching and waiting for me to get better. When he leaves, he shuts the gate and locks it. I drift somewhere between restless sleep and harrowing wakefulness. Sometimes I am screaming, picking at the locked door until my nails are bloody, sometimes I am shivering in silence, as timid as a little bird, frightened and tragically weak. The faces of the dead race through my mind until they become redundant. Night becomes day and day night; I am an illusion to myself, swinging wistfully as the seas of perception rage below.

***

I see the boy Jake, Maggie's son, peering at me. His eyes are questioning, his mouth stretched in pedantic concern.

"Do you remember me?" I ask and he nods.

The light from the fire throws flecks of red and orange into his pupils and for a moment I see a reflection of myself. Not me now, but as a child, the same age as Jake and there is a strong resemblance between us.

"You were right," I tell him. "About the black orchids. I ate one."

He becomes an exclamation point and a question mark, all wrapped up into one.

"What happened?"

"I was shot, a guy shot me in the back, paralysed me. I couldn't move anything but my face and then they buried me in a grave with a bunch of dead druggies."

"Was it like I said?" he asks. "Were they all fighting each other like in *Fight Club??*"

I shake my head and a thousand tiny butterflies wake from their slumber and flutter around the edges of my ears. I swallow hard, waiting for the cacophony to stop and then I continue.

"Not quit. But there was fighting, like in Gladiator you

remember that movie? There were swords and lions and bears and guys dressed in armour. I was a gladiator. I beat the champion and they didn't like that so they got rid of me."

Jake listens enthralled.

"And when they buried me, I ate one of the drug scabs, just like you said and it brought me back to life."

His jaw drops.

"Did it give you superpowers?"

I nod.

"I could run like you wouldn't believe and nothing could hurt me, I could punch through metal."

"Then what happened?"

"Then the magic wore out and it became poison."

"Is that why Henry is helping you?"

I nod.

"And that guy, he was your friend?"

"Shane," I say "His name was Shane."

"Did they kill him too?"

Yes they did those fucking bastards.

"Yes. Yes they did."

The screech of hinges interrupts us.

"Jake," a woman calls out. "Jake where are you?"

"I am here, Mom."

Maggie.

For a brief second I am infected all over again and my senses are on fire. As she walks towards us, her heels hit the dirt floor, reverberating like hammer strokes on a coffin.

"I told you not to come down here," she says.

Jake looks at her as if that is the most ridiculous thing he has ever heard.

"Go and see Henry. C'mon get going."

Jake gets up to go and I realize that this is no longer a dream. I rise from my place on the floor, trembling on legs made of jelly and watch as he passes his Mom and leaves the barn. Maggie comes close and the shadows paint her a distant charcoal. Her clothes are thick and warm, her skin so white the freckles on her face almost glow. She looks at me and suddenly I am ashamed of my debilitated state, my unwashed face, my matted hair, my bare chest.

"You were talking in your sleep," she says and in her voice, I hear a world forgotten.

"You were talking in Hutterisch."

Hutterisch... Hutterisch... Hutterite German.

"Do you still speak it?" she asks.

"I..."

Repressed memories, past lives, chakra imbalance.

"I don't know," I say.

"Do you remember me?" she says.

"I...I don't know."

"Do you remember where you grew up?"

I shake my head and the butterflies return. Ears fill with applause.

"I don't remember anything," I say.

"You grew up on a Bruderhofe, a Hutterite colony."

A Hutterite Colony?

I think back to what I know of Hutterites, and there is not much. They are the queerly dressed little pods that sell eggs and vegetables at the farmers markets. They drive around in huge white vans, because there are always thirty of them and the men have potato farmer beards where they shave only their moustaches. The women dress like washer women from the sixteen hundreds. They are deeply religious, antisocial, weird and...

I was one of them?

"We both did." Maggie continues, "We lived far south near a place called Pakowki Lake. We were part of the Kriegerleut, a branch of Hutterites not many people know of. Do you remember any of that?"

I try, clambering for something in the dusty recesses of my brain.

"I remember an old man," I tell her. "And some kind of riding arena."

Maggie's eyes begin to pool and the fire from the stove dances upon the reflection.

"What else?" she asks.

"There are animals, horrible animals and a small girl."

"Do you remember why you were there?"

I shake my head.

"You were being trained. Your whole life you were being trained."

"What do you mean?"

She sucks back her tears and lets out a long slow breath. I wait for her, trying to be patient.

"We have to start from the beginning," she whispers, then more loudly. "From the beginning."

"We were Kriegerleut, anabaptists, we didn't get baptized as children but as adults if we chose to. We believed in non-violence, like all Hutterites, and the Mennonites and the Amish and our ancestors were persecuted for many years in Europe. The leader of the Hutterites was a man named Jakob Hutter and he was burned alive in the fifteen hundreds for being a heretic. After Jakob Hutter was killed, a missionary, Hans Kral was arrested and tortured. He was stretched on the rack and put in a tower dungeon that was so humid, his clothes rotted off. After two years on his way to be executed he escaped and became the new leader the Hutterites living in Moravia."

She stops to see if I am still following. I nod, even though I have no idea where Moravia is, or what any of this has to do with me or her or our past.

"When Hans Kral became leader of the Brethren he secretly started a breeding program. Publicly he told his people to follow the path of non-violence but after the death of Hutter and all the horrible things that had been done to him; he had gone a little mad. He believed that God had shown him the way to stop the Kriegerleut from ever being persecuted again; he believed that for every generation there would be a child born, a protector of the faith. This person would be able to fight off the attacks from outsiders and because God had chosen him, the Brethren would be justified in breaking the code of non-violence, so he chose two people, a boy, Jakob Amon and a girl named Magdalena, and when they reached puberty they were married and had a child, a boy named Jakob, after Hutter and his Father. The boy was taken from his parents and trained by Kral. You see, when he was imprisoned, he watched from his tower the men training below for war."

"When the boy reached manhood at the age of thirteen he was married and they too had a boy, who they named Jakob. He was trained as well, first by Hans Kral and then his Father. And so it went on, for hundreds of years, as the Brethren were chased across Europe by one group or another. These Kriegers or warriors defended the faith, protecting the Kriegerleut, while many other branches of the Hutterites were killed and converted. By the time the eighteen hundreds came around there had been a revival in the Anabaptist communities and many moved to North America to escape persecution, now from the Russians. Our ancestors immigrated to South Dakota but moved to Alberta during the First World War. They built a colony near Pakowki Lake, like I told you and it was there that you and I were born."

She stops for a moment to catch her breath, but I am too puzzled to let her rest for long.

"And this Krieger, this warrior?" I say.

"The last *trained* Krieger was you," she replies. "You were a defender of the faith; you were the offspring of Jakob Amon, chosen by Hans Kral. The first born son of the first born son. Can you not remember any of this?"

Her exasperation quickly turns to grief and more tears fall. I try to placate her with my eyes but I have nothing to give, I don't know what she is talking about. The memories are not there.

"I'm sorry, I'm sorry. It's just been so long," she says. "I've been alone for so long and now that I have found you...You don't remember me."

"Then tell me."

"You were my *husband*," she cries.

"But..." I begin. "We must have been children."

"We were, we were twelve. That's how it worked; the Krieger had to born when the parents were their healthiest, that's what the Leut believed. Your Father was thirteen when he had you and his Father was fourteen when he had him. The *high elder* of the Bruderhofe was your great, great, great Grandfather."

The old man in the barn.

190

"I...I don't understand, what happened? How...? This doesn't make any sense."

"Your whole life you were trained to fight. Every day you and the other Kriegers, your Father, Grandfather, Great Grandfather, you all went to this barn they built way out in nowhere."

I envision a group of shirtless bearded men wearing suspenders and boxy little hats, beating the shit out of each other and I almost begin to laugh.

"Then they all died."

"What? What do you mean?"

"They all died, everyone. My parents, my sisters and brothers, your family. A hundred and ten people, all of them dead, within a couple months."

"Why?"

"Nobody knew, the high elder wouldn't let any outside doctors in to see what was happening. Everyone just got sick. At first it was like they all were going crazy, they were talking nonsense and walking with these jerky movements. Nobody could remember anything, I would ask my Mother a simple question and she wouldn't be able to answer me. It was terrible. And it just got worse. Pretty soon everyone on the colony was having seizures and suffering from severe dementia. And a couple months after it first started, people began to die and the only people still healthy were Elder Jakob and you and I. And he did nothing to stop it. It was in the hands of God, he said."

Maggie's voice vacillates with emotion and the pain of my drug withdrawal suddenly seems selfish and insignificant.

"Later I found out it was variant Creutzfeldt–Jakob disease. The human version of Mad cow disease. I don't know how it happened, one of the cows must have got infected and then we ate it. That must have been how it started."

"What about us?" I ask her and she just shakes her head.

"I don't know, I don't know why it didn't affect us... I don't know, it just didn't. I remember... There were so many bodies, our entire bruderhofe. And we were the only ones left to take care of them and clean them and then... Bury them."

My mind reels at the idea of it. Two thirteen year old children and a man in his sixties digging graves for a hundred and ten of their family members.

"By the time everyone was gone, Elder Jakob had gone insane. He blamed you for not protecting the colony. You were supposed to be the Krieger and you let everyone die."

"But wasn't he a Krieger as well?" I ask, confused.

"Yes, but, he was old, you were young, it didn't matter, he had totally lost his mind. He would take you to the training barn everyday and do all sorts of terrible things. He made you run through the horses as they stampeded in circles."

The hallway of hooves.

"He said he had to make you faster, quicker. Then he started catching coyotes and making you fight them with your bare hands."

The whorl of teeth.

"It was horrible. I thought he was going to kill you. And when you were gone one day I had Jake."

"You were pregnant?"

Flick! On goes the light.

"Yes. I was pregnant the whole time everyone was sick."

The images just get worse, now I envision Maggie as a plump, soon to be teenage mother, handling a shovel and wrapping fresh corpses.

"It was just before my fourteenth birthday. You were in the training barn; I wasn't allowed to see you so I had him in the house by myself."

"Jesus Christ."

"It was so scary, but, it was magical as well. He was perfect, so healthy and alive, when there was only death everywhere else. And after a few days I went to see you. You had been in the barn for almost a week and I didn't know what was happening, so I took Jake and we snuck in and you were so beat up, worse than I had ever seen you before. You were in the middle of the arena covered in blood and dirt and there were dead animals all around you. At first I was so scared, you, you looked like a monster but then you looked up at me and when you saw what I was holding you started to smile. But then..."

She looks at me, her face cracked and purged of joy.

"...*He* came, and, he said that he was going to start training Jake that day, and you were never worthy to be a Krieger. He said that he was going to take him and excommunicate us, but when he came for Jake, you went mad, you ran at him and the two of you started fighting, you were rolling on the ground and he threw you into the wood stove. Then the barn caught fire but neither one of you cared; you just kept fighting. I tried to get away but he grabbed my Tiechl, and threw Jake to the ground and..."

Two fingers curled, wrist flat and hand as tense as iron. Thrust the hand forward, just to the side of the Adam's apple.

"And then you killed him. You killed him to protect us. And when it was over we tried to get out, but the fire had spread, so we ran to the other entrance. We were almost free and a beam, a fucking beam, fell from the rafters..."

Her face finishes the sentence.

And that's when I lost you.

"I pulled you the rest of the way out. The barn was almost gone by the time you woke up. You, you, didn't know who I was, you, you..."

Her constitution crumbles.

"You couldn't remember anything, you were like a child, just staring at me, and the blood on your hands, with these big scared eyes. And when the fire trucks were almost there, I didn't know what to do, I thought they would tell the police and you would get arrested for murder. So I screamed at you. 'Run! Run!'

Laufen! Laufen!

"I screamed and I screamed, but you didn't understand so I started to slap you. Finally you left, running through the field... And I never saw you again, until that day on the street."

"You recognized me?"

She nods.

"And you recognized me. I could tell. I just. I didn't know what to do. I'm sorry I drove away."

"It's okay."

"And we were supposed to meet, and you didn't show. It was like I lost my chance. Like, I lost you all over again."

I watch her from between the bars of my cell.

"I'm sorry," I say, but she knows the words are unnecessary.

"And now..."

She lets out a harsh cough of a laugh.

"You show back up and Shane is dead, and Henry says that you were possessed or something, I don't know, I don't know, it's just so..."

I finish her sentence for her.

"Fucked up."

"Yeah." She chuckles, wiping the remaining tears from her cheek.

"Yeah, it's all just so fucked up."

We stand in silence for a minute, drinking in the moment. There should be a thousand questions racing through my head but surprisingly there isn't, it all makes sense, the quickness, my ability to fight, it all came from a childhood spent in a barn somewhere being disciplined, groomed for violence. And my lineage was that of hardened warriors, an unbroken line of Fathers and Sons, protectors of the faith.

And now there is no faith.

So what does that make me?

Of this entire group of people that I was supposed to protect, only two now remain, a wife I don't remember and a son I don't know.

"How did you get here? To Fort Mckenzie I mean?" I ask.

She lifts her chin and the dark tombstones beneath her eyes lighten.

"After the fire, the police came. They took Jake and me, put us in social services. At first they said they were going to try to find us a home in another colony but as the investigation went on and they found all the bodies and it became clear what had happened, things changed."

"What do you mean?"

"At the time, there was already this big scare about Mad cow disease. An infected cow had been found in Red Deer and a bunch of countries closed their borders to Canadian

194

beef and America was next on the list. That was from just one cow. And now they had a hundred people dead. There had never been a human death from Mad cow disease in Canada before and because of what it would mean if anyone found out, they just buried the story."

"What? How? That seems..."

Impossible?

"It was actually pretty easy because we were such a closed community. Regular Hutterites are anti-social but we were in the extreme. High Elder Jakob didn't let any of the men get photographed for driver's licenses, we didn't have birth certificates, women never left the colony, babies were always born there, it was like we didn't exist, so all they had to do was put us back in our graves."

"And you?"

"We were the only ones they told about the disease; the news reported it as some kind of cult suicide thing, like Jonestown. And to make sure I didn't tell anyone, they said they would take Jake from me forever. I promised, and they gave me a new identity, new social insurance number, birth certificate, everything. They set us up in Edmonton, in a group home, where we lived until I was eighteen and then we came here. I didn't really know why at the time, I just wanted to get away from the home. But when I saw you, I knew, I knew why I had come here."

"And the High Elder? Did they ask about him, how he was killed or how the fire was started?"

"No. Once they found the other bodies, that was all they cared about."

She begins to tremble and I wonder if I should be reaching out to her, consoling her, telling it's all over now and everything is going to be okay. Is that my role here? The long lost love, the new found Father?

Because that is not me.

I am a monster.

However, when I look up, I see that Maggie doesn't want, nor need my comfort. She is weather beaten, resilient, tough. All she expects of me is to listen.

"Jake is my...Son," I say.

"He is," and her voice reveals nothing but the fact. There is no accusation, no allotment of responsibility or guilt.

"What happened to you Jakob?" she asks suddenly.

I look at her quizzically.

Jakob. Your real name is Jakob.

"I'm sorry, I mean, John, where did you go? Where have you been? What happened with Shane?"

My gaze hardens.

"I didn't kill him."

She balks slightly.

"I didn't... I didn't say that you did. I just want to know, what happened?"

What happened? Fuck, what a question.

I look up at the rafters, the cold emptiness.

"They killed him."

"Who?"

Three faces, three grinning faces.

"It doesn't matter."

"What do you mean?"

"It doesn't matter because they are all dead men."

Chapter 22

Maggie and I talk for a bit longer. She has told me her story and now she wants to know mine.

What is there to say?

I am a murderer, a trained killer. I have slaughtered people; I have eaten the flesh of the dead.

And plan to do it again.

There is truly nothing to say.

I cannot tell her the things I have done, the things I plan to do. They are monstrous. Some might say necessary, even justified, yet still monstrous. Man has a folded heart, and I choose not to show Maggie the horrors buried within.

Maybe after?

Maybe after all this is over, we can try to resurrect a relationship? A friendship? I'll be able to unburden all of the darkness.

I don't think so.

Can you fall down the rabbit hole and come back out unscathed? Unchanged? I look upon myself and can no longer distinguish my true identity from the monster reflected in other people's eyes.

She tries to be patient. Giving me time. But when the night grows cold and my silence uncomfortable, she makes her farewell and leaves me to revel in my sickness. I spend the night in a shivering, sweating heap.

By the time the noon sun rises, the worst of the withdrawal is over. The proverbial hump has been crossed, and Henry unlocks the door to my cell and lets me run free with the wind in my hair. Actually I shuffle about as fast as his old half-blind collie and I probably smell even worse. He lets me into his house, where I take a shower, and afterwards he makes me a sandwich. As he separates the cold, fatty strips of bacon, I can't help but think of Shane's bloodless corpse in the next room.

"Can I see him?" I ask, but he shakes his head.

"Not now, his body is being purified."

I'm guessing this entails some sort of arcane ritual, perhaps a mummification process, maybe the burning of some mystical plants and the anointment of liniments and herbs. The idea being that my old amigo will be squeaky clean before they put him on the pyre and light him up.

I push the vision from my mind as the bacon begins to sizzle.

"Thank you for the clothes," I tell Henry.

He has given me a worn but clean pair of jeans, cowboy boots, a flannel shirt and an old brown work jacket. The clothes I came in wearing, the little egyptian skirt, were discarded but to my surprise the tattered bonnet was still tucked inside.

Maggie's head-kerchief.

The Tiechl, as she called it, is bunched up in my pocket right now, its mysteries unriddled. After my Grandfather pulled the bonnet from Maggie's head, I must have taken it from him as we fought. All those long years, I kept that thin piece of fabric with me and never knew where it came from, where I came from, and now that I know, it really doesn't seem to matter.

There is no me, there is no my, all things are impermanent.

I am a soldier now, a byproduct of the war machine, and after Shane's funeral tonight I will have to find a weapon big enough to fill the hand that reaches for it.

Black Orchid.

It is the only answer.

"You know," Henry says, putting a plate full of delicious smelling food down in front of me. "I've seen that look in a lot of men's eyes."

I pick up a cornered piece of sandwich and wolf it down in one bite.

"When the whole mess started out here with the oil, I was working for a farrier, shoeing horses. He was a good man, honest, worked me hard but paid me right. My Grandfather was the chief of the tribe then, and this man, Anakausuen was a good, good friend of his, like brothers. Anakausuen's woman that walked beside him was Talutah, Blood-Red she was called. She was born a young angry soul and was unhappy with her station. She mistreated Anakausuen, but he bore her anger in silence and never spoke ill of her, even when the rest of us did."

Henry gives me a slow, reflective smile.

"When the oil companies came, we began to get money every month. At first it was only a little, twenty dollars a month and then fifty, by the end, every member of the band, was getting hundreds of dollars. It was too much, everyone became sick with money, we were like pigs eating as much as we could. The alcohol came, and the drugs came, and people started to die from this sickness."

The medicine-man's wrinkled face unfolds like a wool blanket, giving me a brief glimmer of the young man that once dwelt within.

"It was a sad time, but it was what Power had set out for us, the red and the white, they spread their wings around us, and we should have been still when they moved. Anakausuen was one of the few men who didn't change when the money came. He worked as the rest of us sat around and drank away our minds. He worked, but his woman was not the same as him, she took his money as well as her own, and spent it faster than it came. And so she asked him to give her a child, so they would get more money, but he told her no. They had two sons and both died when they were young, and Anakausuen said he would not lay with her until she was fit to be a Mother again. So to get back at him she began sleeping with another man, and it was not long before Anakausuen found out."

Flakes of dead skin fall from Henry's lips as he chuckles to himself and I wonder.

What was my Father like?

Was he a wise man? A kind man, an honest man? All I know of him is someone else's memory of him, a reflection of a reflection.

"And one day, I went to see him. I had boughten a brand new Ford F-100, and I wanted Anakausuen to see it, even though I knew he would not approve, I wanted him to see it

199

anyway, so I drove out to his house. He lived on the far side of town, in a wood cabin that he and his Father had built." Henry says, giving me a little wink and rolling his eyes around the room we are in.

Was it this cabin? Were you driving that old F-100 that's parked in the driveway now?

"I went into his house, and it was empty, so I went down to his barn, where he still shoed horses and there he was, with a shotgun across his lap. The woman that walks beside him, Talutah was dead on the ground in front of him."

The corners of Henry' lips curl up into a capricious grin and my mind sings.

I know this madness... I know this madness.

"I said, Anakausuen, what have you done? And he looked up at me, with such coldness, it was like I never knew him at all, and he put the gun to his chest."

Henry chuckles at this as if he were remembering the punchline from an old Archie comic, not the horrific end of a murder-suicide.

"He had the same look that you have now," the old man says to me, still chuckling. "He had that same look."

He reaches over with ancient hands and slowly pours me a cup of steaming tea. The crumbs on my plate grow stale, and the dead body in the next room lays in eternal quietus. Outside, spring tries to justify its presence to a world not ready for it. Flakes of white snow fall as the immature leaves and buds on the forest floor sulk in displeasure.

"I'm not planning on killing myself," I state, and Henry raises an eyebrow as if to say.

Oh no?

Billows of steam mix with the smoke from the old man's eyes as he cools his tea.

"After that day, I changed," he says, sipping. "I quit all of my vices because you see, when the Red Power is in control we must slow down, we must be peaceful and reflective when the world is fast and aggressive. The Red Power pulls us down, into the earth and it is the White that pulls us up towards the heavens, it is the movement of both, the balance between them that makes us whole, and if we do not respect that balance, it is we who get torn apart."

"You don't believe that the men who did this to Shane should be punished?"

"Punishment is just a word. Easily adopted to the cause of any who care to use it."

I reflect on his words.

"What about justice, blood for blood?"

"Is that your ideology speaking or your instinct? Do you want to kill for justice or do you just want to kill?"

The man looks, and I realize I am an open book to him.

"I...Both."

Henry turns his teacup.

"I cannot tell you what to do or not to, John."

"But you think I should stay? For Maggie? For Jake?"

"Your decisions are your own. I realized a long time ago that there are a great many things beyond my control. I only know what I can feel, what I can see and smell and hear, what my ancestors have taught me. I know that when a man runs downhill, he eventually loses control."

***

Shane's funeral envelopes my senses, it's as if a minacious circus has sprouted up from the ground and enchanted me with baleful wonderment. Pear shaped women with braided hair and cheerless faces tend to the body, which has been laid upon a wooden pyre as feathered old men covered in beads pound small round drums and chant 'Ah-hey anah...Ah-hey anah...Ah hey anah'. Torches have been lit, stories have been told in a tongue unknown to me, and the mercurial clouds above have protected us from the prying eyes of the night sky.

Every face I meet is a cauldron of mistrust and anger, swirling like quicksilver. These people hate me, they loathe my presence, they think it was because of me that one of their own is dead; they think I am to blame and if it weren't for the presence of Maggie and Henry, I'm sure my time here would be short.

"Where's Jake?" I say to Maggie.

She is wearing dark clothes, blanched skin and a sad expression. Her face is bare of makeup and her hair pulled tight. I try to look at her with the eyes of a former lover, but the notion seems ridiculous, so I just let it fall to the flattened earth.

"At a friends," she replies and again her voice reveals nothing. No protectiveness, no anxiety, It's as if she knows I won't be here long enough to really affect her or her son's life.

And the cat's in the cradle and the silver spoon...

The pounding of the drums matches the beating of my heart. Torch-light courts the darkness as tall pines and spruces casually watch the romance. In the far depths of the shadows, behind the dark-sides of the people around me, I see a fitful, tremulous aura rising.

...Ah-hey anah...Ah-hey anah...

Henry is in front of Shane waving a braid of smouldering sweetgrass and rubbing its smoke into his folds. When he is finished, people begin to line up and pay their respects. I look at the wistful faces as they pray to the spirits, trying to see if their sadness is truly for Shane or if they are just grief-stricken in general.

You are all here now that he is dead, where were you when he lived?

It's funny what the human ego will wrap a banner around and try to claim as its own.

He was my friend, I knew him better than you, we had a deeper more meaningful relationship than you did, my pain is more authentic than yours.

In the end, everything is always about us.

As the last of the mourners steps away, Henry comes and tells me to go say goodbye to Shane.

He's already long gone. I want to say. *He left the instant that bullet left the gun, man.*

But I nod and shuffle forward to the rhythm of the drums and look down upon the Youngblood's shrouded form. The pyre beneath him is made up of fragrant cedar and spruce logs, and I have a sudden urge to throw a match and run from this place in a mad frenzy.

But I don't, I just stand like a gargoyle and watch my dead friend. Only his feet and hands are uncovered, so I reach forward and take his hand in mine. I try to think back and remember a prayer or something, but for someone who grew up in such a religious place, it's remarkable how little of God's presence seems to reach me. As I stand waiting for some divine inspiration, I feel something hard and gritty on the inside of the Youngblood's palm. Nonchalantly turning it over, I see something grotesquely familiar.

In the centre of Shane's hand is the perfect mandala of a black orchid, the fat elliptics of its petals suddenly calling out to me with a siren's lullaby.

...Ah-hey anah...Ah-hey anah...Ah-hey anah...

Without moving my eyes, I scan the characters in my peripheral; no one has noticed the beauteous bounty before me. I try to pull myself from the moment, imagining how Shane could have grown such a huge lesion on his palm. When he was smoking he must have been holding his exhales in his hands like many tweakers do, so that the meth crystals will accumulate there.

...Ah-hey anah...Ah-hey anah...Ah-hey anah...

I was going to go back to the oilsands graveyard to find my secret weapon, but this will save me the trip.

...Ah-hey anah...Ah-hey anah...Ah-hey anah...

The orchid feels like slick rock candy as it slips underneath my fingernails. Shane's cold fermented flesh has all the tenacity of phyllo pastry and soon the lesion is in my hand and swiftly tucked away in my pocket. A nightmarish wound remains, so I turn the hand back over and place it on the pyre.

Sickened by its sight and my own actions I soundlessly recite.

I have to do this my friend, to avenge you, to kill the ones who did this to you.

But the pledge sounds false even in silence. What does a corpse care of vengeance and justice?

The voices around me rise in coronach.

Cannibal! Cannibal!

I swiftly spin a circle, suddenly terrified at being discovered.

...Ah-hey anah...Ah-hey anah...Ah-hey anah...

What does that mean? What are they accusing me of?

A hundred magpies emerge from the black eggs of their pupils and fly towards me, cawing shrilly. I stumble drunkenly from the pyre, tripping through a wall of pulsing voodoo drums, and making my way into the forest. The terrible funeral scene fades into the background and soon I can breathe again. It is too dark for hallucinations, and the incessant drumming has returned to a soothing cadence.

I stare at the trees around me, drinking in their presence and neutrality. There are footsteps behind me, but before I can turn to see whose they are, two long white figures slip through a clearing thirty feet ahead. Two broad, thick chested wolves with bright red discs for eyes.

Isis... Osiris...

The ghost-like creatures weave through the timbers with ephemeral grace, disappearing and reappearing with every step. As the footsteps behind me stop, so do the wolves, turning to face me. The wisdom of a thousand lifetimes ripples across the air.

Isis and Osiris, who forsook their only son.

The person behind steps on a branch and as it cracks the two effigies dissolve.

"You're leaving," Maggie says.

I turn to face her and see that Shane's pyre has been lit. Henry is walking backwards from the glowing cumulus as the rest of the people gather in a semi-circle. Twisted flames burst through the cracks with porcine insatiability, and soon Shane's body is lost in a castle of reds and yellows.

Holy Fuck, on to heaven guy!

"I am," I say to Maggie.

"Will you come back?"

I don't answer. I reach into my pocket and pull out her head-kerchief.

"Oh my god, is that my...?" She says as I give it to her.

She rubs her thumbs against the Tiechl's stained fabric.

"Did you have this the whole time?"

I nod.

From the beginning.

She looks up at me, but her face is obscured by the blaze.

She is a shade absent colour or dimension and the fire has grown into a phoenix, looming over her like a guardian spirit. Rippling crimson sheaths unfold becoming angel wings as a golden beak appears above her head.

Shane...

My hand tightens around the orchid in my pocket. I give Maggie one final look and then I am gone, running east through the forest.

The Red Power has spoken.

Chapter 23

Never had Higgins felt such a fear. It was an agonizingly ambiguous feeling that permeated his whole body and the reality beyond. It was what he imagined having cancer must be like, elusive yet palpable at the same time.

Who could have done this?

And things were going so god damn well. After Kraker's demise at the hands of that wunderkind Hyrcanus or Doe, whatever you wanted to call him, Higgins' fortunes multiplied exponentially. Surprisingly, Swan's grief had not lifted but turned into a debilitating fugue and so he handed over the reins of Kraker's operation to Higgins with nothing more than a perfunctory wave of the hand. The keys to the castle, they were in *his* hands now, and there were going to be some serious life changes. He told his wife to start looking for a plot where she could build her dream home, something in that awkwardly named new development, Mountain Pleasures. He took his pick from a new crop of consorts and moved into a different wing of the Castle. He started looking at Costa Rica and beautiful beach front bungalows with banana trees and warm winters and high walls to keep out the locals. He looked upon a future so bright it hurt his eyes.

And then this shit had to happen!

Constable Drake stood nearby, so did the acne-ridden head of security Fallon. Both were silent, their usual stolidity tempered by the sight before them.

"So who's missing?" he asked Fallon, who was in charge of disposing of the bodies from the Arena and was the first one on the scene after the incident had been reported.

"The combatant Hycanus and his tweaker pal," he responded with not so subtle accusation.

The two you shot, that's who's missing.

"Nobody else?" Drake asked.

Fallon shook his head.

Higgins bent down and picked at a piece of torn steel. The

depressed bunker had been ripped open from the inside, which was concerning to the say the least, but even more of a worry was the sight around the grave site. Around the three men, on all sides was complete carnage. Whatever came out of that hole was strong enough to knock around an eight thousand pound rig mast, rip open three inch thick steel and flip over a Caterpillar 797 mining truck.

Some kind of monster.

A corpse from within had lost the connecting tissue around its mouth and stared up at him with a look of comedic shock. On the man's chin was a piece of missing flesh, probably rotted off. There were two huge depressions in his chest, as if something heavy had stepped on him.

Or pushed down.

Higgins cellphone began to ring. Standing up he answered it, and heard his wife on the other end of the line.

"Hey baby."

There were streaks of mud splattered upon the bunker door.

"Hey, baby."

Settling back down on to his haunches, he could make out half a muddy hand-print.

"You busy?"

Reached in and pulled out the bodies.

"What's that?"

"I said are you busy?"

Higgins turned, assessing the wreckage.

No tire marks, no signs of a vehicle, where did they go?

"Uhh, yeah, baby, I'm kind of just in the middle of something."

To his left, Higgins saw what looked to be human footprints.

Bare, shoeless.

"I'm sorry sweetie; I just wanted to see what time you were going to be getting home tomorrow morning?"

He followed the footprints in a circle.

Smashed this, smashed that.

"Uhh I'm not too sure; it's probably going to be a long night."

With Drake and Fallon in tow, Higgins followed the tracks north and then west.

"Well I have a yoga class at ten thirty; can you be back around a quarter after?"

Whoever did this, carried them out here.

Beyond the burial site and the encompassing garbage, there was only the dystopian wasteland of the oilsands.

"Umm, yeah I can do that."

"Perfect, thanks babe; also Jake is spending the night."

Higgins walked a bit further, losing the tracks. After ten feet, he found one again.

"Sorry what?"

He jogged another ten feet and saw a print for the opposite foot.

What the fuck?

"I said, Kade's friend Jake is staying the night."

Another ten feet and another footprint. It was as if, whoever had taken the bodies, could bound like a fricking gazelle.

"Can you hear me? You are breaking up."

"Yeah I can hear you."

The pattern continued as the three men walked until they reached a long banana shaped tailings pond.

"Okay baby, I'll see you tomorrow and play safe."

"I will, babe."

Click.

Higgins guessed that if he walked to the other side of the giant noxious pool, there would be more footprints, impossibly far apart.

"What's north of here?" He asked Fallon.

"Nothing. Just out of operations mining pits for miles and then some reclamation sites."

"And west?"

"More of the same, until the Stuwix."

The Reserve.

Shane Youngblood's home.

Higgins looked out on to the horizon as the sun sank beneath it and felt cold prognostic fingers reach into his stomach and take hold.

***

That night was the funeral games for Kraker. The *munus* was to be attended by the owners of every house and all their gladiators.

Each and every combatant. Over three hundred fighting men plus more trainees.

After what he had seen that afternoon, the idea of it made Higgins insides turn. Something was terribly off; his every bone ached with foreboding.

Why was Swan making such a big deal over Kraker's death?

The man was truly inconsolable. When Higgins told him of the happenings at the burial site, it barely registered.

Just fill it in. Bury it all. He'd said.

Of course, that's already been arranged but what about the missing bodies? The fact that the door was torn open from the inside?

Higgins hadn't told that part of the story because intellectually it didn't make any sense, but he knew what he'd seen.

He's escaped...He's coming...

Higgins shook his head, trying to clear away the cobwebs. He finished putting on his Mountie regalia, looked himself over in the mirror and for the first time in his life thought it to be a ridiculous costume.

I need to be preparing, not consoling a weepy old woman.

Never had he imagined that he would think such a thing of his King, his Khan, his Caesar but the Swan's recent activity had shown a weakness in the man, where Higgins thought there could be none.

It's as if his lover died.

No.

It was unimaginable.

Swan and Kraker?

Higgins quickly scanned over the last few years of his life. Kraker's prompt rise in the ranks of the empire, his unquestionable loyalty, Swan's reaction to his death.

Fuck sakes.

Higgins gave his head another shake. This was no time to

209

be analyzing things he shouldn't be, he had a job to do. Tonight was going to be one of the most spectacular nights in the Arena and he had to stay focused.

He left his apartment and made his way to one of the main entertaining rooms, known as the Atrium. The room was a vibrant jungle, full of exotic trees and ferns, brightly coloured flowers and volcanic rock gardens. Streams and fountains were everywhere, birds sung from the treetops, naked women and men strutted through dense foliage. It was truly a modern Eden, designed to arouse the senses, Higgins, however, always felt the place to be too stuffy and claustrophobic.

He found Swan and his entourage, walking along a pathway hemmed in by tall acacia trees and dangling vines. The King was dressed as always for such occasions in a sleek tuxedo and bow tie. The concoction that he was so fond of, a mixture of cocaine and some herb from south America, had obviously taken affect, his eyes were such a manic red, his irises appeared to be floating on pools of blood.

"Higgins. Join us," he said.

Higgins fell in behind his master and three consorts. Swan moved with a languorous suavity, plucking flowers as he went and bringing them to his nose.

"What is your denomination, Robert?"

"I am Christian, sir."

"I was a Christian as well, Anglican?"

"I am Anglican, sir."

"You are. Well, well, how similar we are. Do you remember the Apostle's Creed?"

"Yes, sir."

"He descended to the dead, on the third day he rose again; he ascended into heaven, and is seated at the right hand of the Father. He will come again to judge the living and the dead."

Swan stopped and looked Higgins in the eye. The police man saw a face so utterly ravaged with anguish, he became embarrassed and turned away.

"I forget most of what the church taught me, but that line has always stayed with me. Do you believe in the resurrection, Robert?"

210

Higgins thought of the open grave site and the two missing bodies.

"Yes, sir."

"I never truly did, it sounded too ludicrous to me, even as a child. But now I wonder?"

They reached the steps leading up and out of the Atrium.

"I wonder if a man was strong enough, if he was truly touched by divinity, could he rise from the dead?"

He looked to Higgins and Higgins saw what he was really asking.

Could it happen? Could my champion return to me?

"I don't know, sir."

***

The coliseum was saturated a false twilight. A thousand torches burned as the gladiators filed in from the twelve equidistant entrances and gathered into small armies in front of their house owners, looking solemn. In the stands stood a faceless sea of white and black, mourners who weren't truly in mourning. Of all the people there, only one man was truly distraught by the death of Kraker, and there he stood at their apex, and it was for him, and him alone this spectacle had been constructed.

Swan's bloodshot eyes were on the extraordinarily ornate coffin that was placed on a slanted base at the centre of the arena. Inside the coffin was the reposed form of Kraker, his hands folded on top of his black single breasted suit. Higgins thought that even in death the man looked menacing, with his bald head and swirling tattoos. Attached to the sides of the casket were the giant's battle axes, prominent amidst the rest of the decorations.

As Swan rose to address the crowd, a thick pimply figure slunk in behind Higgins and whispered.

"We have a problem."

Higgins turned to face Fallon.

"What is it?"

"There's been a security breach."

The two men discreetly left the viewing booth and went to the nearest security station. There on a wall of screens, Higgins saw his greatest, unspoken fears come to life.

Fallon's voice was an exposed nerve in his ear.

"He's already broken through the outer perimeter."

Higgins saw a giant hole smashed through one of the guard towers and six men laying on the ground in pieces.

"Where's he now?" Higgins mouth was so dry; the words came out as a choke.

The guard sitting at the controls switched the centre screen to a camera sitting above the main entrance to the castle. Fifteen men were there, dressed in black and holding automatic rifles. Suddenly a figure approached from the driveway and smashed into them with supernatural speed.

It's him, it's fucking Hyrcanus!

There was a brief spray of bullets from all sides as the men tried to fight the creature off, but their resistance was short lived. John Doe, wrapped in some sort of glistening black webbing tore through the guards as if they were paper cut-outs instead of flesh and blood. Limbs flew, and entrails were ripped from their proper places and Higgins tasted bile in his throat.

Jesus Christ...

"The attacker has entered the building," the control guard said mechanically.

"Alert all personnel to his position," Fallon ordered, pulling a sidearm from his holster.

*It's too late...*Higgins thought and with the slightest of whispers.

"He will come again to judge the living and the dead."

Chapter 24

She is a pale, thin wisp of a girl. Her usually auburn hair is a dark chestnut, beneath the penumbra of my head and the hanging lantern on the wall. She trembles as I touch her, as I pull myself on top of her. Guilt enters my heart, and I try to exorcise it.

This is your duty. This is what God expects of you.

I enter her, just as my elders instructed and her face alights. She reaches up and grabs the back of my neck. I feel hard, smooth calluses from years of kneading dough, milking cows, scrubbing floors. I try to be gentle, but I don't know what gentle is, this is my first time at doing this and maybe my last.

Once a Krieger has fulfilled his duty and fathered a son, he must refrain from marital relations for the rest of his life.

There is a hanging sheet that divides the room in two. On the other side of it, are five women, including my Mother and hers, watching us, making sure that everything unfolds accordingly. If I were to be too rough or make some kind of mistake during the consecration, they would descend upon us like a gaggle of geese, and I can think of no worse nightmare at this most intimate of moments.

Thankfully the culmination passes without incidence and I am left shivering, my body awash in a sensation I have never experienced nor could I have ever imagined existed before. Her pinched face resembles a flower as it opens up and I am stunned by the ardour in my heart. She pulls me down, so I am resting on top of her, and I feel as if I have left this world and am floating amongst the angels in Heaven.

"Jakob," she whispers. "Husband."

"Magdalena. My wife."

***

Jakob!...Jakob wake up!

"*John!... John wake up!*"

Maggie's voice reaches me through a fog.

"John, oh my god, please wake up!"

"...Magdalena..."

"I am here; I am here, Jesus, Jesus, what's happened to you?"

I open my eyes and see that I am in tatters. My shirt is gone, and my bare chest and arms look as if they have been distressed by chains. My muscles have withered, and my skin wrinkled. My pants are still on but barely, the threads riddled with bullet holes.

The sun has barely risen, but I know where I am. Shane's funeral pyre, now just a blackened smear sits to my left. Maggie is above me, looking stunned and horrified, Henry is behind her, he too, has a look of intensity upon his face.

Fuck I must look bad, if that old goat is staring at me like that.

"John... John!"

Maggie gives me a shake, but my eyes are falling and she can't stop them.

***

Wondrous, electric, maddening, primeval energy courses through my veins. I am on fire, the black orchid, a pipeline of fury that devours my soul. My vision is of a long tunnel, future events are no longer a mystery but destinations in the approaching distance. I see a wall, and it is destroyed, hunks of concrete go flying and a cloud of buzzing insects arrive to harry me from all directions. I see the source; long composite hives held by men wearing kevlar vests. The bullets bounce off my mutated skin, causing a galling din that reverberates through my newly improved ears.

I am hell! I am hell! I am hell!

The men are shredded by glistening black talons. Their blood coats my skin and their bones crackle beneath my feet. Through the tunnel, I see a forest of bent trees, warped to the point of phantasmagoria. Beyond that, sits a building so immense and caparisoned, it could only be christened a castle. I am at its steps in what seems a heartbeat, and more men and angry weapons are upon me. A thousand star-bursts erupt from their muzzles as they try putting me down, but there is no stopping the orchid's vehemence. I strike out, revolving like a helicopter blade. Fifteen men, fifteen twitching corpses, eviscerated.

Moving on...

Into the building, a magnificent foyer with a man made waterfall at its centre. I lift my nose, concentrate my hearing.

To the right.

I am running, flying really, on wings of retribution. The tunnel tightens, the hallway around me becomes a cannon barrel and I the ignited projectile. More men arrive, trying to hinder my progression.

I cut them down.

More men, the same as the others, dressed in flak jackets and abrupt terror.

They too are ripped to pieces.

I dig deeper into the honeycomb of Swan, eventually making my way into the vast catacombs of its underbelly. People pass by, smudged silhouettes, some innocent some not. Little rabbits running from the fox in their warren. A king's ransom in buried treasures, misappropriated fortunes, undreamt of scenarios, unbelievable secrets surround my peripheral, but I cannot stop and investigate these glories, no I must move on.

Before the magic runs out...

The black orchid has turned my flesh into something harder than steel. Walls become doors, defenders into pulp. Like a virus, I scourge the organism that is Swan until I reach its beating heart and crash through its iron ventricles. Before me is an audience in shock, an army of warriors dumbstruck. I see the coffin and the deceased giant inside.

What perfect fucking timing.

Past the casket, looking down from his skybox stands the great man, Don Fucking Swan, his face slack with stoned alarm. Beside him are his two remaining mutts, the pustulated bulldog Fallon and my cowardly executioner.

Higgins.

I turn before the people in front of me, letting them behold the horror.

I am the archangel! I am the threefold flame! I am your apocalypse!

The audience doesn't know what to think. Is this part of the show? Some strange new element to the grand spectacle? To prove to them I am no movie prop, I point to the man at their pinnacle and declare my intentions.

"Swan! Come and face me!"

My voice is not my own but a twisted replica, cut into a dozen threads and re-woven into a satanic harmony. The crowd turns to their leader and his chest swells, finding that imperial superciliousness once again.

"A million dollars!" He yells, looking down at the legions gathered on the arena floor.

"A million dollars and freedom, to the man who kills this...*Thing.*"

It's as if everyone inhales at once. The combatants turn towards me and their initial awe dissipates, the prize dissolving their instincts. They gather their weapons in unison, a jaw-grinding shift of iron and steel. I look to the King, standing upon his tower, as if to say.

Gods, what a mistake you have made.

The wave crashes and I let it. Hundreds of simian bodies pile on top of me in a heap of stink and sweat. Those close enough, try to stick me with weapons, but their blades bend and shatter as they reach my flesh. Soon we are so tightly packed no one can move, suffocated voices cry out, piddly little mouse voices that cause my belly to rumble in laughter.

Misfortune spreads her thighs, unleashing torrents of ill tides, for those grown weak.

The rumble turns to tectonic shifting and soon I am rising, burning through the masses. The gladiators fly back in all directions as I burst through them. Those still standing try to form a counter-attack, but this is short lived. They die. Then the men beside them die. I am the axe that clears the forest, the scythe that reaps the harvest. My obsidian fists break through skin, organ, bone, and soon there is nothing left of the army set upon me except a butchered field of steaming carcasses. A massacre site, slaughter redefined.

The people in the stands begin to panic. Former acquaintances, friends and lovers trample one another, trying to reach the exits before I turn my savagery upon them. But it is not them I am here for.

I am here for them!

Higgins and Swan are still in the skybox, staring down at the murder site traumatized. When they see me approaching, Higgins pulls Swan away as Fallon and a handful of his clones train their automatic weapons upon me and open fire. The bullets hit my chest with enough force to momentarily stall my progression.

I am getting weaker, the orchid is wearing off!

Realizing that time is running out, I dart back and forth, dancing around the falling artillery until I reach one of the marble pedestals that the viewing box sits upon. There, safe from the gunfire, I rest for the shortest of moments and then leap upwards, clambering on to the pillar and making my way into the skybox, where Fallon awaits me.

He has traded his carbine for a handgun and fires off a series of rounds as his minions surround me. There's still enough juice in my veins to take them down with relative ease. I am face to face with my former jailor. Surprisingly and to his esteem, he does not run but continues to fire his little hand cannon until I take it from him and tear out his throat. I lift my nose, over the fresh perfume of blood; I smell them, trying to make an escape.

Swan, Higgins.

I am galloping, sniffing out their trail like a bloodhound. The halls twist and turn for days, as if I were in a Stanley Kubrick film but then I see them, Swan, his patrician feathers all in a ruffle and Higgins, wearing his stupid Dudley fucking Do Right outfit.

Oh Canada, our home and native land...

They see me and Higgins orders his men to stay; as he and Swan turn a corner and continue fleeing. The sight of the two cowards reignites my fury, and I besiege the poor sinless guards with such violence the corridor soon resembles an abattoir. The chase continues into a room I recognize. The throne room where, it seems as if decades ago, I spoke with Don Swan for the first time. The cold emotionless faces of Les neuf preuxs, the nine Valiants gaze down upon the antechamber where he renamed me Hyrcanus, just as they did that day. Only now the crescent pools are missing their frolicking nymphs, and the backrooms are vacant drunken deviants.

Following my nose and the echoing footsteps, I go past Swan's absurd monarch's chair and reach another hallway, this one slathered with salacious tapestries. At its end, I see two men, the objects of my reprisal.

Hello Gents!

Past them is a giant steel door with a combination lock.

Going somewhere little flowers? Little sister-fucking flowers?

Higgins takes out his gun and starts firing. Beside him, Swan is fiddling with the combination.

Time to die!

The bullets bounce of my chest, giving them a moment's respite. Swan unlocks the door and begins pulling.

Almost there.

Five more feet. Higgins and I make eye contact.

I might not get to Swan, but I am sure as shit getting you!

Swan is through the door, Higgins nearly within my grasp. I reach forward, talons in search of blood.

Oooof!

A body hits my chest.

Don Swan collides with my mutant form. I grab him by the neck, surprised.

Higgins!

The craven has thrown his master to the lion. And now he's through the vault door and has it almost closed. I throw Swan to the ground. The door shuts before I can reach it. I smash with all my strength. The steel bends but does not break.

FUCKKK!!!

Constable Higgins, Shane's murderer, has escaped me.

I turn round to the rumpled man on the floor, balled up in the foetus position. Don Swan, the Khan, the great Emperor, has been reduced to nothing but a squalling child.

"Please...Please..." he cries and I think back to the arena, and the way he always raised his nose when the victims of his little games were pulled away, their legs smeared with their own shit.

Don't worry old man, I won't turn away, I am here to savour every moment.

Then the real screaming begins.

***

"John...John, please wake up!"

Blechhh...

A horrible vapour is in my nose, forcing me from my slumber.

"John," this time a man's voice, a resonant baritone.

Hands are beneath my head.

"I have... To go back...It's not finished..."

"What do you mean? Maggie says.

"Higgins..."

Maggie looks to Henry, her face gone white.

"What do you mean, John?"

"Higgins..." I am shaking, the palsy has begun. "...He got away..."

"Robert Higgins? Do you mean Robert Higgins???"

"The cop...He did this...He killed Shane..."

"Oh my god," she says. "Jake."

Chapter 25

Higgins was in his Mustang, going south on highway 63 at nearly two hundred kilometres an hour. He was in the centre of the road, hands clutched in a death grip.

Slow down...Breathe...

He told himself, but he couldn't, what if that *thing* was behind him, chasing him. He checked his rear-view mirror for the hundredth time.

There!

But it was just another tree or rock or working of his imagination. The sun was rising, and he was nearing town.

Slow the fuck down!

He forced himself to relax his foot off the pedal and made his way into his own lane as a semi-truck passed by. Fort Mckenzie lay just ahead, basking in the glow of bright blue spring morning. As he crossed into the city limits, he marvelled at how *normal* everything looked. The streetlamps, the stop signs, the storefronts, just as he had left them. It was as if the madness he just experienced had all been a dream, some alternate universe where he left Don Swan...

Jesus, did he really do that?

...To die at the hands of a man who was already dead.

Still in shock, he unconsciously took the necessary twists and turns that brought him home. He pulled into his driveway, opened the garage door, parked beside his wife's Mercedes and sat there with the engine running.

What...What to do?

He turned off the engine and tried to force himself inside but found that he couldn't. He was frozen, unable to think, unable to act. The freakish form of John Doe flashed across his mind, tearing apart flesh.

Jesus.

Higgins sat in silence, reliving every moment of the massacre, letting his thoughts be saturated by the things that would not leave. At first he tried to rationalize what he was seeing, Doe was just wearing a costume, or some kind of body armour, or maybe it wasn't John Doe at all but there was no denying what had happened, what he had seen.

John Doe had come back from the dead and become some kind of supernatural creature, hellbent on destruction. Somehow the acceptance of that made him feel better, he had seen what he had seen and no matter how crazy or unbelievable it was, it was true, and he couldn't just sit around and wait for the resurrected demon to come and find him. He had to escape, run, get Belinda, get the kids and get the fuck out of dodge. That was the only answer, jump in the car and start driving, to the states or Mexico, anywhere, just away from here.

What about the castle?

Jesus. How could he leave all that? The future he had just secured, the money, he would have to forfeit it all. But the castle was an open bank, a treasure chest just sitting there. Higgins knew where to find enough riches within those blood-soaked walls to keep his family fed for a dozen lifetimes. Could he risk it? What if Doe was still there?

As he sat in his car, weighing his options; Kade his eight year old son and Jake, Kade's little friend came into the garage, wearing t-shirts and sweatpants. Higgins rolled down the window as they approached, still lost in his own thoughts.

"Hey, Dad!" The boy was in high spirits for such and early hour. "Check this out."

He came up to the door and held up a roll of papers.

"Kade...I'm kind of..."

The boy unrolled the papers, revealing a homemade comic book strip.

"Jake and I made this last night."

The boys were so enthused they didn't care to ask why Higgins was sitting in his car in the garage or why he was dressed in his Red Serge or why there were flecks of dried blood on his tunic.

"We are gonna call it Black Orchid," Jake chimed, oblivious to Higgins disdain of him.

"Even though there already is a Black Orchid superhero,

she's a girl and ours is a guy and he can do way cooler stuff anyways."

"Yeah Dad, he can punch through walls and run really fast and he's bullet proof, and he has like super hearing and night vision. And he came back from being dead!"

Higgins felt a lead weight drop into his stomach.

He will come again to judge the living and the dead.

Higgins scanned over the drawings and saw a child's rendition of a man lying on a pile of corpses. He pulled it from his Son's hands a little too brusquely and began flipping through the pages.

What the hell is going on?

There was a character with black eyes and long black hair, getting shot in the back, rising from the dead, attacking a bunch of armed men.

He looked at the two little boys with superstitious dread.

"Yeah." Jake grinned. "And he's real."

"What did you say?"

"I said...He's real."

"What do you mean? Who is he?"

Jake faltered a little under Higgins manic gaze.

"He's my friend, John."

John!

"Where is he???"

The boys took a step back, suddenly alarmed.

Higgins softened his voice.

"I'm just curious about your comic book boys, is he from another planet or something? How did he get these super powers?"

Kade looked to Jake.

"No, he's from here, right, Jake?"

Jake nodded.

"Jake saw him on the Indian Reserve at his friend Henry's barn. He was really sick, and Henry was helping him."

"Henry Yellowbird?"

Stuwix, the footsteps at the gravesite lead towards the Stuwix!

Jake nodded again, looking uncomfortable.

"What was he sick from? How did he get his powers?"

"The scabs, they give him his super powers but afterwards they make him really sick," Kade answered.

"What scabs, boy?"

"The scabs from the dead bodies, the bums have scabs from their drugs, and when they die they turn black and if you eat them, you get superpowers and they look like flowers, that's why we called the comic Black Orchid."

Meth scabs, the tweakers in the pit!

Higgins thought back to the dead body with the missing patch of skin.

They would have thrown Doe's body right on top of the pile.

"The gravesite...What do you mean sick, for how long???"

The boy Jake took another tiny step back and said nothing. Higgins threw him an angry look, but the boy remained silent.

Fucking idiot.

Higgins eyes glazed as his brain tried to make sense of what he'd just heard. Scabs, meth scabs had brought John Doe back from the dead and turned him into that monster. And now he would be suffering from some kind of sickness.

He'll be weak, now's your chance! Find him and kill him!

What if...?

If what? What you just heard was all coincidence? Not fucking likely! Get to the reserve, kill him before he eats another one of those things and...

...Wait. The bodies were still there, Higgins himself had ordered the bunker to be filled in but Fallon, the man he'd told to do it was dead.

An idea rose within Higgins mind.

"Go inside, Kade," he said, handing back the boys comic strip.

Kade jumped back, startled as his Father's mustang roared to life.

"But..." the boy said, confused. "Where are you going?"

Higgins ghoulish face turned to Jake as he answered.

"I'm going to dig up some answers."

Chapter 26

"Hello! Oh. Hello, Belinda, this is Maggie, hhhow are you? Good, good, is Jake there? Can I speak with him?"

Silence, anxious silence. My left eye opens the slightest amount, and a wave of hellfire enters my skull.

God make it stop, make it stop, make it stop, make it stop!

The withdrawals have come to scour me clean.

"Jake! Jake, are you alright, is everything okay? Good, I want you to go somewhere where no one can hear you okay? Just do it."

Jake's tiny metallic voice, a million miles away. Henry's calloused hands on my broken ones, massaging, pulling out the poison.

It's too late old man, there is nothing left, all I am is poison.

"Is Robert there? Okay, I am...When was he there? Weird, what do you mean? What did you tell him?"

I have to get my senses back, get grounded, get past the pain.

Buck up, buttercup!

I try to open my eyes again, but the sunbeams have turned to spears. I wiggle my tongue around, like a lizard, searching for some moisture.

"What did you say about John? Tell me word for word, this is very important, Jake."

Henry's hands leave; he stands up beside Maggie, their backs turned towards me.

...Johnnnnnnnnny Boyyyyyyyy...

A succulent lullaby springs up from Shane's blackened pyre.

"You told him about Henry's??" she asks the phone.

I am overcome with dizziness. Lights start to flash behind my eyes, speckled formations.

Is this what dying feels like?

Maggie and Henry are still facing away; tender fingers turn to hooks.

...Here, Johnny Boy, over here...

"Okay, okay, no it's okay sunshine, it's okay, I know. Where did he go? Did he say he was coming here?"

Higgins is coming here, get you fucking ass up John!

I roll over and begin to crawl. Shane's smeared ashes are just ahead, black dunes, a chiseled desert.

The wasted remains of man's avarice.

"What did he say? He was going to dig up some answers...? Okay sweetie, I don't want you to say anything to Belinda or Kade about what we just talked about, alright?"

To my right and to my left are the twin spirits, pillars of white against the decimated wilderness.

Isis, Osiris.

The Orchid whispers into my ear and the words ignite the wolves' skin, turning their fur into a comet's tail. Dig up the answers...dig up the answers...

...Ah-hey anah...Ah-hey anah...Ah-hey anah...

"You just stay put; I am coming to get you."

...Dig up the answers...Dig up the answers...

I, the wolves, roam the charred landscape. There are steel giants for trees, inflamed lymph nodes for lakes, the air reeks of sulphur and sadness.

...Dig up the answers...

Henry and Maggie are talking, they haven't noticed my movement.

...Ah-hey anah...

Amidst the blackness, I see it, glistening like a star.

...That's it, Johnny Boy, almost there...

A black orchid perfectly unblemished floating in my old cohort's remains.

...Dig...Dig...Dig...

Higgins. Higgins. Higgins.

The gravesite, he's going to the gravesite.

We are there, the wolves and I.

Reaching out, raking, finding the iridescent dahlia.

...Yesssss, Johnny Boyyyyy...

I put the glistening slug to my mouth and swallow it

225

down. The effect is immediate. Eyes open, I am on my feet, long black lashes sprout from my skin, pulling the very last bits of me, my essence, my *Jing* from my organs to cover me in a monstrous exoskeleton. Henry and Maggie jump back, aghast at the metamorphosis happening before them.

I am bellowing.

The ashes of my humanity are put to rest as the transformation is completed.

John...John are you in there?

...Dig...Dig...Dig...

Maggie is a ship on the horizon, fading into memory. Henry takes her by the shoulders.

Magdalena. I am sorry, but it was the only way.

I am running.

Goodbye.

Chapter 27

Constable Robert Higgins stood above the pit, staring down at the pile of bodies.

This is your doing; you had a hand in this.

A mountain of decay, the smell so gut retching he could barely stand to go near it.

You have to, get in there.

The decimated face of one of the victims was visible in the fading sunlight. A patch of skin missing from his chin.

Pat...Pat...Pat...

Thick storm clouds were swirling overhead; it was beginning to rain, the first rain of the season, the start of a new beginning.

Get in there.

Higgins didn't know if he could. It was too grotesque, too disturbed, too *sinful.*

Hypocrite, fucking hypocrite! Get in there, find one of those things and eat it.

Scanning the crypt he saw one of the so-called black orchids. Beneath a tangle of limbs was a woman, her bare chest scarred with the dark ossified lesions. Misty, her name had been Misty. She had been a tough catch, a necessary catch since she'd witnessed another tweakers kidnapping.

Enough, get in there, then find Doe and kill him. Finish this nightmare.

Raindrops pelted the resinous pools around the bodies, causing tiny ripples. Higgins put a brown leather boot on a hanging piece of steel and pushed down, moving it out of his way. Bending down, he took a deep breath and hopped into the pit, landing on the back of a combatant, submerging the body. Lightning sparked overhead, illuminating the faces of the dead, giving them a brief semblance of life and Higgins breath caught in his chest.

Get on with it!

Dark once again, he lifted a sodden foot and stepped on to

the pile. Desperately wishing he'd kept his gloves on; he rolled the chinless man off of Misty and stared down at the flower-shaped scabs on her chest.

Do it!

The crust-like lesion reminded Higgins of rock candy as he peeled it from Misty's skin and held it up to the withering morning light.

Do it!

Thunder rolled, and as the world shook, Higgins was mesmerized by the orchid's spell.

Do it!

More thunder...Wait no...

What is that?

An impact, metal being pushed aside.

Doe!

The orchid slipped into Higgins mouth.

***

We can smell his blood, his hair, his breath. We can hear his beating heart, his boots in the muck, the movement of his throat as he swallows. We who are I, we who have become one, we sense another taking form within our midst.

Too late, John, you're too late!

But there is no John Doe anymore, no more Hyrcanus, no more Jakob, first born son of the first born son of the first born son, there is only the drug, the parasite and its dying host.

...Suck...Me...Dry...

We arrive at the junkyard, smashing through a heap of flattened metal. The entrance is impressive, rubble and debris spinning through the air, slamming into massive pieces of broken down machinery but the *Other.* When he arrives it is truly spectacular. A black and red demon ascending from the pits of hell, taking slow methodical steps, his face wrapped in bands of volcanic glass, his mouth pulled back into a maniacal grin that defies reason and physics. The falling rain becomes a symphony of strings, celebrating his every movement, the thunder its percussive accompaniment. We stand in veneration, the orchid and I, awed by his presence as he stands in awe of ours.

Higgins, his name was Higgins.

It doesn't matter anymore, none of it matters anymore, the past, the future, our reasons for being here.

There is no me... There is no my...

All that matters is movement, progression, integration, separation.

...All things are impermanent...

All that matters is that he dies as we die.

He dies as we die.

***

The two demigods collide. Pulling and punching, kicking and screaming, biting and clawing. Throwing one another into the sprawling jungle of industrial waste. Smashing each other with hunks of heavy steel, stabbing with spears of iron, choking with strands of braided cable. They tear at each other's flesh with talons instead of hands, ripping violent holes that drip turbid fluid instead of blood. Neither gains advantage, as one falls and the other rises, the tide suddenly reverses and that which was superior, quickly becomes deficient.

For a lifetime, they turn, forming and reforming, fluctuating like a revolving tesseract. No life stirs, except for the falling raindrops and the eddying clouds. No sounds can be heard over the clangour of metal as the nemeses battle. War is waged, and when it is finished there is no victor, only two men left defeated, lying side by side, their lives draining from them, into corrupted soil.

God I can see it...

Two wolves, their hides still a winter white, approach as the day lapses into dusk.

In the churning of the storm, amidst a backdrop of sheet lightning and echoing thunder he found them, all of them, years worth of memories, slipping down from the heavens like little pearls of water.

They sink their long fangs into the dead men's necks.

His Mother.

His Father.

His family, his childhood, it all came back to him as he exhaled his last breath.

The sun sets on an oilsands graveyard as two wolves carry two men back into the forest.

And *she* was there.

Maggie.

Her face as a child, glowering at him, her eyes as she got older, intrigued by his words, her mouth smiling as he kissed her for the first time.

Their child in her arms.

It was upon this picture he died, releasing his mind to the somniferous crackle of the rain.

The static, the static has risen.

CPSIA information can be obtained at www.ICGtesting.com
Printed in the USA
LVOW06s1028301113

363243LV00004B/16/P

9 781909 224650